Could this love nonsense really be worth the trouble?

To Adele Wilson the answer is clear: of course not! She has seen her two sisters dragged through scandal and heartbreak (not to mention every ballroom in London) to find the husbands of their dreams. That's why she said yes to the first British lord who requested her hand. And why *shouldn't* she marry him? He is kind, honest, and not sentimental in the least. Unlike his wilder, taller, more mysterious cousin Damien Renshaw, Baron Alcester. Ignoring Damien altogether would be easy if he were the sort of man intent on seducing his cousin's betrothed. But he is clearly trying to resist her, and his suddenly proper behavior only makes him more tempting to the usually well-behaved Adele.

Indeed, Damien appears to be bringing out another side of Adele, a heady, passionate, exhilarating side. It seems that fate is contriving to teach her—against her best intentions—exactly what this love nonsense is all about . . .

Special Markets Department, HarperCollins Publishers, Inc.
10 East 53rd Street, New York, N.Y. 10022-5299.
Telephone: (212) 207-7528. Fax: (212) 207-7222.

Avon Books by
Julianne MacLean

MY OWN PRIVATE HERO
AN AFFAIR MOST WICKED
TO MARRY THE DUKE

*If You've Enjoyed This Book,
Be Sure to Read These Other*
AVON ROMANTIC TREASURES

DUKE OF SIN *by Adele Ashworth*
HIS EVERY KISS *by Laura Lee Guhrke*
A SCANDAL TO REMEMBER *by Linda Needham*
SO IN LOVE: BOOK FIVE OF
THE HIGHLAND LORDS *by Karen Ranney*
A WANTED MAN *by Susan Kay Law*

Coming Soon

SIN AND SENSIBILITY *by Suzanne Enoch*

Julianne MacLean

My Own Private Hero

An Avon Romantic Treasure

AVON BOOKS

An Imprint of HarperCollinsPublishers

This is a work of fiction. Names, characters, places, and incidents are products of the author's imagination or are used fictitiously and are not to be construed as real. Any resemblance to actual events, locales, organizations, or persons, living or dead, is entirely coincidental.

AVON BOOKS
An Imprint of HarperCollins*Publishers*
195 Broadway
New York, NY, 10007

Copyright © 2004 by Julianne MacLean
ISBN: 0-06-059728-3
www.avonromance.com

First Avon Books paperback printing: December 2004

Avon Trademark Reg. U.S. Pat. Off. and in Other Countries, Marca Registrada, Hecho en U.S.A.
HarperCollins® is a registered trademark of HarperCollins Publishers Inc.

Printed in the U.S.A.

10 9 8 7 6 5 4 3

*This one is for Stephen,
for being the great love of my life
and the stuff heroes are made of.*

Many thanks to Kelly Harms, Paige Wheeler, and Nancy Berland. You are all a pleasure to work with. Thanks, Mom and Dad, for teaching me at a very early age what it's all about. Thank you, Cathy Donaldson for many years of adventures, Lorraine Vassalo for your assistance on Sleeping With the Playboy, Paula Altenburg for stepping forward to offer help the day before Christmas Eve, and the Romance Writers of Atlantic Canada, especially the supportive, ambitious ladies of the goals loop. And thank you, Michelle—my cousin, my friend—for the uncountable hours of conversation, laughter, and joy you've given me. Finally, thank you, Laura, for being my wonderful, darling girl.

I like the Americans very well, but there are two things I wish they would keep to themselves—their girls and their tinned lobster.

Lady Dorothy Nevill
England, 1888

Prologue

May 1884

Inside the lavish interior of the *SS Fortune*, steaming smoothly across the deep, dark Atlantic at night, Adele Wilson stood in her first-class stateroom and gazed uncertainly at her reflection in the mirror.

A heavy lump formed in her belly. Why? Everything was as it should be. Her mother was in the adjoining cabin to her left, her sister Clara to her right. Adele had just eaten a delicious supper at the captain's elaborate table, and was about to undress for bed and read a most thought-provoking novel before turning down the lamp and going to sleep.

She removed a pearl and diamond drop earring and watched it sparkle in her hand. She closed her fist around it, then looked up at her reflection again.

She felt oddly disconnected from the floor, as if she were in someone else's body. A stranger was staring back at her—an elegant, sophisticated heiress who wore a jewel-trimmed Worth gown from Paris made of the finest silk money could buy, and around her neck, an antique, pearl and diamond choker to match the earrings.

She turned away from the mirror, looking all around. Suddenly, even the room seemed wrong. *Wrong.* There was no other word for it. Carved mahogany panels covered the walls, the ceiling was painted gold with extravagant ornamentation around a dazzling crystal chandelier. The sheets on her fluffy bed boasted the ship's monogram, and all the fixtures, from the doorknobs to the lamps, right down to the nails in the bulkhead, were polished brass, pompously gleaming.

Sometimes it seemed as if she were living someone else's life. She had not been born with this wealth. She didn't even know how to feel comfortable with it. At the moment, she felt as if she shouldn't touch anything.

Adele sighed. What she wouldn't give to be riding bareback through the woods at this moment, as she used to do when she was younger, before they'd moved to the city and ventured into high society. Oh, to smell the damp earth and the leaves on the ground, and the green moss around the lake . . .

She inhaled deeply, longingly, wanting to re-member, but smelled only the expensive per-fume she wore. Feeling absurdly deprived, she exhaled.

It's nerves, she decided, crossing to her bed and removing the other earring and setting both of them on the night table. Tomorrow she would meet her future husband, Lord Osulton. An English viscount. The newspapermen would probably be there to greet the ship and take her picture. No wonder she was nervous tonight.

She would get through it, however.

Adele removed the combs from her honey-colored hair and shook out her long, curly locks, so they fell loosely onto her shoulders. That was better.

The door to the adjoining stateroom opened, and Adele's sister Clara peered inside. Clara had married the handsome Marquess of Raw-don the year before and had left her London home a month ago with her new baby daughter, Anne, to visit her family in New York. "You're still awake?"

Adele faced her sister. "Yes, come in."

Clara, still in her glittering evening gown, her mahogany hair swept up in a flattering bun, en-tered the room and sat down on the chintz sofa. "You barely touched your supper. Are you all right?"

"I'm fine." But Adele knew she couldn't fool Clara, who always strove to see beneath the sur-face of things.

"Are you certain, Adele? You're not having second thoughts, are you? Because it's not too late to change your mind."

"I'm not having second thoughts."

"It would be perfectly normal if you were. You barely know the man. You've met him so few times, usually at dull assemblies with Mother breathing down your neck. You've danced with him only once, which is essentially the only time you've been alone with him. And what was that, three or four minutes?"

Adele sat down next to Clara. "I'm just a little nervous, that's all. But I know in my heart that this is right. I'm sure of it. He's a good man."

"But you haven't had a chance to know for sure if there's any true connection between you. Some form of heat. Maybe you should think about enjoying the London Season just once before you marry. Imagine who you might meet. A dashing white knight, maybe."

Adele shook her head. "I'm not like you, Clara. You and Sophia were the adventurous ones, while I've always been sensible. Isn't that what Mother and Father said every time you and Sophia got into trouble?"

Clara smirked. "I can hear Father now." She put a finger under her nose like a mustache. "Why can't you two girls be more like your younger sister? Thank God we can always depend on Adele to behave herself—sensible, reliable Adele."

Adele smiled and rolled her eyes. "The fact remains, I don't wish to suffer through an entire

London Season being speculated about, and being forced to wear diamonds every night and flirt in crowded drawing rooms. The thought of it, quite frankly, makes me ill. I'd much rather be in the country—outdoors with the fresh air, which is exactly where my future husband is at this moment."

"You might enjoy the excitement of a Season," Clara said, sounding a little frustrated.

Adele shook her head again. "No, I would not. I am content with my decision to marry Lord Osulton. He is an agreeable gentleman and a very good match for me. From what I understand, he doesn't enjoy the city, either. He prefers his country house."

"But aren't you afraid you might someday wonder what extraordinary adventures you'd missed?"

Adele squeezed her sister's hand. "I don't seek adventure, Clara. In fact, I loathe the idea of it. I prefer a carefully laid out plan, free of the unexpected. Besides that, I believe that sometimes, the best marriages are *sensibly* arranged. Love comes later, when it has time to grow and become something more substantial, based on admiration and respect rather than *heat*, as you call it. Heat, my dear sister, is unpredictable and often burns."

"Heat is wonderful, Adele."

"Is it? Funny, I do recall when it was not so wonderful last year, when you thought your husband was going to leave you. You were miserable. I don't want to be miserable like that. I prefer a sense of calm without any of those difficult emotional ups and downs."

"But Seger did devote himself to me," Clara said, "and we are very happy now. What we have today was worth every minute of misery, no matter how excruciating it was at the time. Some things are worth fighting for, no matter how unpleasant the task. Are you sure you don't wish to postpone the wedding, and suffer through just one Season? You might discover the greatest romance of your life."

Adele sighed and stood up. She crossed to the wardrobe and began to unbutton her bodice.

"You would think," Clara continued, "being bookish, you might have read something about love."

"I've read plenty about love," Adele said with her back to her sister, "and I could never relate to those simpering, lovesick heroines stuck in towers, who fall for white knights. There are no towers or white knights in real life, Clara. There are only realistic men, and I am quite content to have found a most agreeable one for myself. Besides, it makes me happy to please Mother and Father. You should have seen Mother's face when I told her I had accepted Lord Osulton's proposal. I'd never seen her so proud."

"You cannot live your life to please others, Adele. You must think of yourself and your future. After the wedding, Mother and Father will return to New York, and you will be left in England on your own—no longer a dutiful daughter, but a married woman. You will be responsible for your own happiness and be free to choose what you want to do with your life. You should marry whomever you wish to marry."

"I wish to marry Lord Osulton. *Harold*," she added, deciding she should probably start referring to him by his first name now that they were officially engaged.

Clara smiled lovingly at Adele. "I daresay, you will do as you wish, won't you?"

"As long as it is the *right* thing to do. I have chosen my path, and I have made a commitment. I will not veer from it."

Clara raised a delicate, arched eyebrow, stood up, and walked to the door. "I suppose there's no arguing with you. You always were determined to do the right thing, even when Sophia and I tried to convince you to do otherwise. You missed some fun, you know."

Adele tipped her head at her sister. "I also missed a great number of hours standing in the corner."

Clara shrugged. "Adventure has a price."

"And you and Sophia were always willing to pay it."

Adele's maid entered and began preparing the bed.

Clara opened the door to her own stateroom. "We'll be docking overnight to pick up some extra passengers, then it won't be long before we reach Liverpool. We'll be there by morning. It sounds to me like you're sure."

"I am."

"Then I'm satisfied. I must go and check on little Anne. I'll see you in the morning." She walked out and closed the door behind her.

Adele smiled at her maid, and reached for her nightgown.

London's Savoy Theatre
Shortly after four A.M. the same night

It was a well-known fact among certain circles in London that Frances Fairbanks— celebrated actress and hailed by some as one of the most beautiful women alive—enjoyed lying about naked. Especially on the soft, bearskin rug on the floor of her dressing room, when the room smelled of sex and wine and French perfume, and she was gazing upon a lover.

Or rather, one lover in particular. Damien Renshaw, Baron Alcester.

He was by far the most fascinating man she'd ever met—tall and darkly handsome with broad, muscled shoulders and facial features that could have been sculpted by an artist. He was rugged and wild and unpredictable, and what's more, he was the most ingenious, instinctive of lovers. He knew just how to move to give her the most intense sexual experiences she'd ever known.

Yet there was immense tenderness in his lovemaking.

Frances stretched out like a cat and rolled over onto her stomach, resting her elbows on the fur. Swinging her bare feet back and forth behind her, she watched Damien sit down on the deeply buttoned settee by the door and pull on a boot.

He glanced up at her briefly with dark eyes that usually promised pleasure and seduction, but at the moment revealed only impatience.

He was in a hurry to leave, Frances realized suddenly with a frown, which was extremely out of character for him. Because Damien Renshaw—the irresistible black lion—never hurried *anything* in the bedroom.

Frances stopped swinging her feet. "You left your shirt on when you made love to me tonight."

She had to work hard to sound confident. It was not something she was accustomed to—working hard at it, that is. She was always absolutely sure of herself where her lovers were concerned. *They* were the ones who did the scrambling.

She swallowed uncomfortably and made a conscious effort to swing her legs again. "You're not angry about the bracelet, are you?"

Pulling on his other boot, Damien didn't look up. "Of course not. As you said, you fell in love with it."

Indeed she had. So much so, she'd purchased it herself and had the bill sent to Damien.

She sat up on her heels and spoke with pouty lips, hoping to kindle his flirtatious nature. "It was only a small bracelet. I didn't think it would matter in the larger scheme of things."

He rose to his feet, tall and beautiful as a Greek god in the flickering shadows of the candlelight. He searched the shambles of the room for his waistcoat. He spotted it in a heap on the floor—on top of some purple feathers and Frances's colorful costume from her performance that evening.

He picked up the waistcoat, slipped it on, then reached down to cradle Frances's chin in his hand. He grinned, his eyes sparkling instantly with the allure that reassured Frances that she was still the envy of every hot-blooded woman in London.

His voice was husky and sensual when he spoke, but at the same time commanding. "Next time, try to resist the urge. You know my situation."

She did, of course, know. *Everyone* knew. Lord Alcester was in debt up to his ears, and had been forced to lease out his London house to a German family, and take up residence with his eccentric cousin.

It didn't bother Frances, however. She didn't want Damien for his money. There were others who served that purpose. Damien's talents lay elsewhere.

He dropped his hand to his side and pulled on his overcoat. "My apologies for leaving my shirt on."

"You're not yourself these days, Damien. I hope it's not me."

"It's not you." He kissed Frances good-bye, leaving her ever so slightly distressed by this unexplained change in him.

* * * *

It was still dark when Adele woke to the sound of a thump in her cabin. She remembered they were stopping briefly on the west coast of England to pick up a few new passengers. She rolled onto her back, wondering how long they'd be docked.

She stared up at the ceiling in the darkness and thought about the conversation she'd had earlier with her sister. Clara had suggested that Adele should be reckless for once in her life. It was not a new conversation. They'd had it countless times before as children and as young women. Clara and Adele's oldest sister, Sophia, had often tried to lure Adele into their mischief.

Adele rested the back of her hand on her forehead and recalled a summer afternoon when they were girls, just after they'd moved to New York. Clara had gathered them together in the attic of their new house and said, "If we want to grow up, we must have an adventure. And everyone knows that an adventure must always start with running away from home."

Sophia's eyes had lit up, while Adele had been horrified. She had refused, of course, and argued the point of such foolish horseplay, and threatened to tell their parents.

Clara told Adele that if she breathed a word, they'd string her up by her heels, so Adele promised to keep it secret. Which she did. For about an hour. Then she told her father, who promptly marched out onto Fifth Avenue and brought the girls home and put them to bed with no supper. Adele, conversely, had been given an extra slice of blackberry pie.

Clara and Sophia didn't speak to her for about a week after that, but then they forgave her—as they always did—and told her they supposed it was her job to keep them out of trouble, because she was the sensible one.

Yet even now as women, Clara was still trying to talk Adele into misbehaving. Adele smiled and supposed it would never change. She'd be an old lady with a cane and spectacles, and Clara would try to convince her to dance in the rain. Adele smiled again and shook her head.

Just then, she heard another thump, almost as if there were a monster under her bed. Her heart leaped with panic, but she quenched the sensation because she'd stopped believing in monsters under beds many years ago.

Nevertheless, she tossed the covers aside to check. Her toes had just touched the floor when a man rose up in front of her. Adele gazed at the dark figure in terror. She sucked in a breath to cry out, but before she had a chance, a cloth soaked in a strong-smelling chemical covered her mouth.

Heart now blazing with terror, she struggled and tried to scream, but couldn't make her voice work. Then she felt weak and dizzy, and lost all sensation in her body before she gave up the fight and remembered nothing more.

BOOK ONE

The Adventure

Chapter 1

Somewhere in Northern England

Three days. It had been three long days, and now it was beginning to rain.

Adele rose from the hay-filled tick that served as her bed, and walked across the creaky plank floor to the window. All she could see in every direction were endless, rolling hills of grass and rock beneath an angry gray sky, swirling with the oncoming threat of a storm. Hard raindrops began to pelt against the glass.

It was barren and lonely, this part of the world, wherever it was. She hadn't seen one person. Not even a lone goat or sheep. There were no trees, and the wind never ceased. It pummeled the stone cottage on top of this sadly forsaken hill, rattled the windowpanes, and whistled eerily down the chimney. The door to the stable knocked and banged constantly. All day long. That, combined with the musty, damp smell of this room, was enough to make a person go insane.

Adele made a fist and squeezed it. She had been steered off course into fierce, treacherous waters, and she wanted her calm life back.

If she still had a life to go to. She wasn't even sure Harold—or any man, for that matter—would want her after this, because she had no idea what her kidnapper had done to her. All she knew was that he had undressed her at some point, because when she had woken up, she was wearing someone else's shabby, homespun dress. Beneath it, she wore petticoats and a shift with ivory stockings, but no corset and no shoes. She had no idea what had happened to her nightgown, nor did she know why he had undressed her. To be less conspicuous, perhaps, in getting her here? She hoped that was the reason.

Adele breathed deeply, determined to keep a cool head. She could not panic or lose control. It would do no good. She had tried everything to escape this room in the past few days. She had pounded and shook the door, she had shouted for help, used all her strength at the window, but her efforts had been futile. All she could do now was wait for something to happen—something she could act upon. Or for someone to find her. Surely her mother was searching, and the police were investigating.

Just then, the front door of the cottage opened downstairs and heavy footsteps entered the house. Adele heard them pound across the hard floor. The door slammed shut. Her heart quickened. Perhaps this would be an opportunity.

She walked to the center of the room and stood still, listening. There was more than one person. There were voices.

This wasn't the usual routine. There had only ever been one person here to bring her food and water. What was happening?

Suddenly, commotion erupted downstairs. Frenzied footsteps. A piece of furniture fell over. Or was kicked over. Was someone here to rescue her? Harold? But Harold would never face a kidnapper on his own. Or would he?

Her father? Oh, if only it could be him! But no, he was home in America. He wasn't due to come until the wedding day. Perhaps it was a constable. Or a neighbor who had discovered what was happening and had come to her rescue.

The footsteps pounded up the stairs and paused just outside her door. Every particle of her being froze with fear and dread. What was about to happen? Was someone here to hurt her? Ravish her? Murder her?

Her eyes searched for a weapon, but there was nothing. Nothing but a chair. She picked it up. It was heavy, but she would swing it if she had to.

The lock on the door clicked from the other side, then the door swung open. Two men walked in. One held a pistol to the other's head, and smoldered with highly controlled fury.

Large and solid through the chest and arms, he wore a heavy, black greatcoat that matched his black hair. Adele feared him instantly.

Was he her captor? She'd never seen the man in daylight. He had stayed hidden from her view. Was her captor one of these men? The dangerous-looking one with the pistol?

"Your name!" he barked.

"Adele Wilson." It didn't occur to her to ask why he wanted to know. Or to ask anything at all. All she could do was answer his question, because he expected an answer.

At that instant, the man he held hostage—a short, stocky fellow with rotting teeth and thinning hair—whirled around and grabbed at the pistol, lunged forward, and took hold of Adele around the waist. He pressed the cold, steel barrel to her temple. She dropped the chair, as fear shot through her. She'd never faced a gun before.

"Now the ransom!" His unsteady voice revealed his desperation.

For the first time, Adele looked fixedly at the other man—the dark, wild one—and understood that *he* was her rescuer.

He held his hands up in front of him, in a gesture that commanded both her and her captor to stay calm. His eyes held a strong warning that told them they had no choice but to comply.

She guessed he was in his late twenties. His dark, intense eyes and windblown black hair gave him the look of the devil, or something worse. Masculine to the core, rough around the edges, and fiercely commanding in an inherently primitive way, he was as rugged as the rocky hills surrounding this house. He looked as if he'd been traveling for three days straight and hadn't taken the time to shave or bathe or even sleep, because he'd been hell-bent on reaching this house. Reaching Adele.

Who was he? What were *his* intentions?

Her body quivered with fear and uncertainty.

"Harm her and you're dead." He took a slow step forward.

By the quality of his speech and his accent, Adele gathered he was well-bred. It surprised her. He didn't have the look of a polite English gentleman—at least not the type she had imagined from her small life in New York. This man was pure, unleashed aggression.

"Or you can take the money now, and *run*," he continued. "I recommend the latter choice."

Adele felt the other man's grip tighten around her waist. She sucked in a breath.

"You won't let me leave," he said shakily.

Her rescuer stepped out of the way of the door. "I will let you leave when you let the woman go. If you don't, I guarantee my patience will not hang about."

Adele felt her captor take in a deep, steadying breath.

He was terrified.

It was no wonder.

He pressed the pistol harder against her head. "I don't believe you."

Icy, paralyzing fear twisted around Adele's heart. This man wasn't going to simply walk away and leave them behind. Why should he take the risk that they might follow, when *he* held the gun and could simply kill them both and escape?

By the dark, calculating look in her rescuer's eyes, Adele sensed he was thinking the same thing.

Before he could devise and ponder a plan of action, Adele's self-preserving instincts took over. She couldn't just let this man shoot her. She had to do something. She dropped to the floor and sank her teeth into her captor's thigh. He screamed out in pain.

Her rescuer dashed forward yelling, and carried the other man with him to the wall, where they smacked into it, hard. They wrestled for a few seconds, both grunting as they tried to gain control of the pistol, while Adele scrambled backward across the floor.

She thought about running, but instead, a fighting instinct she hadn't known she possessed overtook her fears. She darted at the pair of them and leaped onto the shorter man's back.

Taking the pistol with him, he swung around and crushed Adele against the wall. The air sailed out of her lungs as she fell off his burly form, landing on her knees. He backed away and aimed the pistol straight at her heart.

Her pulse quickened as she stared into the barrel. She held her hands up to block the bullet—knowing it was a futile gesture—and shut her eyes. Rain pummeled the roof over her head, and wind shook the rafters.

"Damn you!" Her rescuer tackled the man just as he fired. The noise was deafening, the pain shocking. Adele sank from her knees to the floor, grabbing hold of her thigh and curling forward.

The two men rolled around until her rescuer swung the handle of the gun and roughly struck his foe on the head. The other man's body went still, while an ominous rumble of thunder boomed in the distance.

Clutching her throbbing leg, Adele stared numbly at the two of them.

Her rescuer looked up. "You're shot."

"Yes," she rasped.

He crawled toward her. Without so much as a second's hesitation, he tossed up her dress to uncover her leg from top to bottom.

Adele leaned back on her hands, trying not to show her sudden ridiculous sense of modesty in these circumstances. She had been shot. He—whoever he was—needed to see the wound.

She looked down at it. Her ivory stocking was stained red just above her knee, on the inside of her thigh. The whole area burned like nothing she'd ever experienced before. It was as if someone were branding her with a red-hot poker.

Clenching her teeth against the throbbing pain, she watched her rescuer's face briefly while he examined her leg. He had such a striking face—the kind that draws one's attention, clutches it in a tight grip, and doesn't let go.

He wrapped his large hand gently around her

calf and moved her legs apart to get a closer look. Her muscles stiffened. She had to fight the urge to squeeze her legs together. This was far too intimate.

"I must remove your stocking," he said, "to get a better look. May I have your permission?"

"Of course."

Her reply came instinctively, but after she'd said it and had time to think about it, she felt her modesty return. He was a man, after all—a handsome and frightening man—and he was going to remove her stocking.

She swept the petty notion aside, for it was not the time to be worrying about decorum. Meanwhile, her senses began to buzz like bright, snapping, electric currents. Adele closed her eyes and tried to focus on overcoming the pain.

The man's hands were gentle as he rolled down her stocking. He barely touched her skin; his movements were swift—as light as silk. He eased the stocking down to her ankle with great care, as if he were handling something very precious. Adele held her breath the entire time.

"This looks painful," he said.

It was. Her whole leg throbbed, and the pounding sensation reverberated all the way up to her shoulders.

Adele opened her eyes and watched his face again. His dark brows drew together with concern as he inspected the gash. He slid a hand over her bare thigh as he touched all around the wound.

She wanted to gasp in pain as well as shock, but she resisted. He leaned down. Closer.

A man's face had never been so close to her inner thigh before. Her naked inner thigh. She could feel his warm breath on her skin. A thousand winged creatures flapped violently in her stomach, sending her heart racing.

"It's just a graze, thank God, but you're still bleeding." He sat back on his heels. "We'll bandage it, and you'll live." He stood up and glanced around the room.

Looking up at him, so tall and serious above her, Adele had to fight the sense of embarrassment and intimidation that made her almost afraid to speak. She had never, *never* let a man who was not a doctor touch her so intimately before. "May I ask who you are? How you found me?"

He considered her question for a moment, then crouched down to meet her gaze at eye level. "I apologize, Miss Wilson. I should have identified myself."

Suddenly, he seemed to transform into a proper gentleman. At least his words were gentlemanly. His appearance was quite another matter altogether. He was unshaven, wild, and rough. His black wool coat looked shabby, dusty, and weathered, as if he'd rolled down a hill in it. There was intensity in everything about him, and it left her breathless and panicky.

Adele was nowhere near ready to relax. Especially when she gazed into his dark, gleaming eyes.

"I'm Baron Alcester," he said. "Damien Renshaw is my family name. I'm Harold's cousin."

Harold's cousin. Good God, she knew of him. Her sister Sophia had met him before, and had said that he was the complete opposite of Harold. He was irresponsible with money, and his mother had been a scandalous adulteress. He was following in his mother's footsteps, it was said, and led a careless life with a string of mistresses of questionable repute. The current one was a famous and beautiful actress.

"The ship's master at arms informed Harold of your kidnapping," Lord Alcester said, "as there was a ransom note addressed to him. Harold informed me, then the master at arms was released of his duty, and it was deemed that I should take care of things."

Deemed? By whom?

"I assured Harold I would bring you home quietly," Lord Alcester said. "We will travel under assumed names and meet your mother and sister in two days in a small village between here and Osulton Manor. She will then escort you the rest of the way, as if nothing had ever happened."

Adele was in shock. She was to travel alone with this man?

Still fighting the excruciating pain in her thigh, she struggled to collect her thoughts and understand the situation. "No one knows about my kidnapping?"

"Besides the ship's officer, who has agreed to keep quiet, no one except your family and

Harold's mother and sister. I suggested he not even tell them, but by the time he contacted me, he had already informed them. They have since been advised to keep it secret."

"To avoid a scandal."

"Yes."

Adele glanced uneasily up at her rescuer—a rake of the highest order—then at the unconscious man on the floor beside them, who had done God-knew-what to her while she was unconscious. She swallowed over a sickening lump in her throat.

Lord Alcester followed her gaze, then strode to her kidnapper. The uneven planks of the old floor creaked and groaned under his heavy footfalls. He was a large, muscular man. She would not want to be in the unfortunate position of being taken for his enemy.

Kneeling down, he pressed two fingers to the man's neck. For a long moment, he sat there—motionless and quiet. The wind from the storm outside moaned like a beast inside the stone chimney. The draft lifted the clinging cobwebs around the hearth.

When at last Lord Alcester spoke, his voice was low and subdued. "He's dead."

Adele swallowed hard, watching Lord Alcester's shoulders rise and fall with a deep intake of breath. He pinched the bridge of his nose as if a severe headache had suddenly taken root.

"Are you all right?" she asked, feeling strange asking such a question. She couldn't imagine him ever not being completely in control.

As soon as he met her gaze, his color returned, and he stood. "Yes."

She found herself trying to read his thoughts, but couldn't.

"I need to wrap your wound," he said. Then he was gone before she had a chance to say a word.

A minute later he returned with a small cloth in a bowl of water, and a bottle of whiskey. He shrugged out of his long black coat. "There's nothing downstairs to use for bandages. My shirt will do."

Adele sat forward to protest—partly because she couldn't fathom the idea of this man walking around shirtless—but the movement caused a stabbing sensation in her leg, like a knife gouging into her wound.

Lord Alcester knelt beside her. "Sit still. You'll worsen the bleeding."

His voice seemed strained and impatient. Was he annoyed with her?

"I'm sorry," she replied apprehensively. "I wanted to tell you we could use my petticoat for bandages. It has a bullet hole in it anyway."

He considered it for a moment, and nodded.

Adele swallowed. "If you would be so kind as to avert your eyes while I remove it?"

He paused. "Do you need assistance?"

Assistance? Her pulse drummed at the suggestion. She thought of his mistress, the actress, and wondered how many times *she* had accepted his so-called assistance.

Adele was astonished by the sudden depraved direction of her thoughts. It was exhaustion, surely. She'd hardly slept in three days. *Think clearly, Adele. Clearly. He is merely offering to help, in order to spare you pain.* "I can manage, thank you," she replied.

He left the room without a word, but remained just outside the door while she struggled to reach up under her skirts and free the ribbons at her waist. With more than a little discomfort, she slid the garment down over her hips.

"You can come in now." She held the petticoat out to him.

He took it and began to tear it into strips. "You might want to take a few swigs of that whiskey."

She eyed it uneasily. "No, thank you." She wanted to keep her wits about her in the coming hours, for she didn't know what those hours would bring.

He continued to rip and tear the petticoat, looking around the bare room with assessing eyes. "You spent three days in here?"

"Yes."

He met her gaze. "After I clean and bandage your wound, we'll move you somewhere more comfortable."

"Thank you."

The sound of fabric ripping filled a long, drawn out silence between them. Adele felt a great need to add conversation to that silence, for she needed to distract herself from her anxiety.

"I don't even know what it looks like downstairs," she said. "I was unconscious when I arrived, and sick when I woke up."

Lord Alcester stopped ripping. "Sick and unconscious?"

"Yes. I was drugged on the ship. He kept me drugged until I woke up here."

He continued to stare down at her. "Were you *hurt* in any way?"

She understood his meaning. He was wondering if she had been violated. She was wondering that herself, with more than a little concern. She knew nothing about such things regarding the female body.

"I'm not certain," she replied. "I didn't feel . . ." How could she put it? "I didn't feel *pain* anywhere. Except for a headache. But I suppose a lady couldn't be sure. Or could she?"

Good God, what kind of question was that?

His face revealed no hint of awkwardness. He bent down and dipped the cloth into the bowl of water and gently squeezed it out. He lifted his gaze to meet hers. It seemed, by the look in his eyes, that he understood the level of her anxiety. He subsequently responded with calm composure.

"It depends," he said softly. "Pardon my candor, but did you notice any blood when you woke up?"

She swallowed. "No, but couldn't he have . . ." *Lord, this was awkward.* "Couldn't he have cleaned it up?"

She'd certainly never had a conversation like this before.

"I suppose, if he were an exceedingly neat

person." Lord Alcester smiled, and Adele knew he was trying to ease her worries.

Continuing to rinse the cloth in the bowl, he said, "My suspicion is that you are probably fine, Miss Wilson. I believe you would know if something was wrong. But if you wish to be certain, a physician can examine you."

"He would be able to tell?"

"Yes."

"Would he be able to tell if I was—" She stopped. She couldn't go on.

"If you were what, Miss Wilson?"

"If I was . . . if I was with child?"

The idea was unsettling, to say the very least, but she had to ask.

"Not yet, I don't think, but let's deal with one thing at a time, shall we? It may not even be an issue."

Grateful that Lord Alcester was direct and honest with her about this awkward topic, she considered what she knew about the English aristocratic code. A woman was expected to be a virgin upon marriage to ensure any child born of the union was indeed the true heir to the gentleman's title. Perhaps Harold was worried. Perhaps Lord Alcester was worried, too. He was a member of that family, after all.

"I would like to be examined officially," she said, remembering that she was to become an aristocratic lady herself. It would be her code, too.

Lord Alcester held the cloth above her wound and squeezed water over it. "The Osulton family physician is a very good man," he said. "I'd trust him with my life. He'll be discreet, if you can wait until you reach the manor. You're not unduly worried?" His scrutinizing eyes lifted to look into hers. He often seemed to be assessing things.

"I am, but I can wait."

He nodded, appearing satisfied, then turned his attention back to the task of cleaning her wound. The droplets of water tickled her skin. A few times, her leg jerked upward from the intensity of the dribbling sensation—the odd combination of pain and tickling. She wished she could keep her leg still, but she couldn't. It began to tremble.

"Try to relax," he whispered, glancing up at her again. "Breathe deep and slow."

She did as he suggested, keeping her eyes on his the entire time. The rage and fury had faded from his expression. Now there was something lazily seductive, almost hypnotic, in his look. All the knots in her muscles began to untie themselves, while she stared at him.

"That's better," he said.

Slowly, the blood washed away, along with the tension in her neck and shoulders. Her breathing slowed. He had quite a way with his hands, his eyes, and his voice.

Lord Alcester leaned down to look more closely at the gash, then he reached for the bottle of whiskey. "This is going to hurt, but it must be done."

"I understand."

"Squeeze my arm if you have to."

She didn't want to.

He paused to give her time to prepare herself, then poured the amber liquid over the gash. He might as well have poured liquid fire on her. Adele clenched her teeth together to keep from crying out.

As soon as he tipped the bottle upright, she leaned forward and squeezed her thigh just above the wound. "God in heaven!" she ground out.

"My apologies, Miss Wilson."

He set the bottle down and reached for the bandages he'd fashioned from her petticoat. "I'm going to wrap the wound tightly to keep pressure upon it and reduce the bleeding."

Adele nodded in agreement. He tried to press a bandage to the gash, but couldn't reach it, as she had in the meantime unconsciously pressed her legs together at the knees. She was clenching her teeth together, too.

He cupped her other knee in his hand and gently pushed her legs apart, again keeping his eyes on hers the entire time. "It's important to do this properly," he said. "Relax if you can."

She struggled to still her racing heart—for no man had ever pushed her legs apart before—and forced herself to surrender to the gentle pressure of his hand. Slowly, he spread her legs wider, into a V on the floor, while she quickly and discreetly tucked the fabric of her skirt down to cover her more private area. She hoped he didn't notice her doing it.

"Perhaps you could bend your knee slightly," he said.

Adele did as he asked. He reached for more bandages and wrapped them around her thigh. His movements were swift and efficient. Before she knew it, he was tying the last one tight and sitting back.

"There." He stood up and offered his hand down to her. "We're finished. You can breathe now."

She hadn't even realized she was holding her breath until he'd said it.

He helped her rise to her feet. As soon as she tried to take a step, pain flooded through her leg. She felt suddenly dizzy and nauseated. "My word."

"Let me help you." He wrapped his arm around her waist. "Hook your arm over my shoulder and lean into me. That's it."

She began to limp beside him, and felt the thick, firm muscles of his shoulder and the solid, steady support of his body as a whole. He did not waver or lose his balance.

"It will be difficult to walk for a few days," he said.

"How will we ever get me out of here? For one thing, I don't have shoes. And it'll be torture to ride."

"No shoes?" He paused. "I'll go and come back with a coach and driver, and I'll bring you shoes. It will take only a few hours. We're not far from the nearest village."

She didn't like the thought of being alone

here again—alone with a dead man—but she would do her best to endure it, because it couldn't be helped.

They reached the door and hobbled together out into the hall. Adele glanced over her shoulder at her kidnapper still lying on the floor, and hoped she would not have to look at him again.

They reached the top of the steep stairs. Adele stopped and looked down. "This is going to be a challenge."

He turned to her and held his arms open. "Please, allow me."

Good God, he meant to carry her. Her heart did a little nervous flip at the thought of it.

Before waiting for her reply, he scooped her up like a doll in strong, able arms, and descended the narrow stairs effortlessly. When he reached the bottom, he carried her into the kitchen, where a faded upholstered chair faced the fireplace. Other than that, the room was unfurnished. There was only a small pile of kindling, some cooking utensils, and provisions to prepare a few meager suppers. The house had obviously been abandoned some time ago, and opened up again by her kidnapper.

Lord Alcester set her down gently in the dusty chair. Lightning flashed. Thunder rumbled almost immediately afterward as darkness began to descend.

"Excuse me, Miss Wilson," he said, "while I take my horse to the stable before it gets much darker."

"Of course." Yet she didn't want him to go.

She had been trapped here alone for three days, helpless and locked in a room; she had just been shot; she didn't know where in the world she was, whether it was Scotland or Ireland or France for that matter. She was an ocean away from her home, and he was all she had.

He raised his coat collar up around his neck and picked up the hat that lay on the floor. He must have torn it off quickly when he'd first arrived. She remembered the violent commotion she'd heard when the two men had entered, and could only imagine what had occurred between them.

Lord Alcester settled the hat on his head and turned to face her. His eyes glimmered with assurance. "The worst is over now."

It was exactly what she had needed to hear. Had he known? He seemed very intuitive.

He opened the door and let in a powerful gust of wind carrying a pattering of cold, hard rain. The gale swept into the cottage and whirled like a tempest, but he shut it out quickly when he slammed the door behind him.

Adele sat alone in the silent stone cottage, staring at the door and trying to come to terms with her situation. She couldn't believe she had been kidnapped and shot. Bookish Adele Wilson, who avoided adventure at all costs . . .

Her sisters were sure to be shocked when she told them her tale about being trapped in a proverbial tower and rescued by a "white knight." It was embarrassing, actually, to think of him that way. She had always called those romantic fairy tales silly and unrealistic, and she'd always said she would have preferred to see those heroines rescue themselves.

Well, she couldn't exactly call Lord Alcester a white knight anyway. He was more of a black knight, with his striking, ebony features. She remembered how intense and angry he had appeared when he'd first entered her room. Her knees had turned to jelly.

Then he'd killed a man. *For her.*

A cold shiver moved through her as she replayed that horrific moment in her mind, when she'd gazed into that dark barrel of death. She had been impossibly lucky. If her kidnapper had fired a fraction of a second sooner . . .

For the first time since that terrifying moment, she was able to fully contemplate it, and felt the fear shiver through her again. She labored to smother it, and turned her mind toward a silent prayer of thanks. How grateful she was to be alive.

And how grateful she was to Damien Renshaw—her future cousin. True, his reputation made her uncomfortable, and she would never get over the embarrassing fact that he had seen her naked thigh. But Lord Alcester was bold and brave and he had come to her rescue, galloping across England to what seemed like the ends of the earth. He had been her champion, when despite her own efforts, she had been unable to rescue herself.

She inhaled deeply and felt a rush of something she couldn't understand move through her—a tingling sensation. Adele glanced at the door and considered the night ahead, trapped in this isolated cottage with him, and suddenly found herself wishing with a disturbing sense of dread that in his place, the one to come to her rescue had been Harold.

Chapter 2

Osulton Manor

"**H**arold should not have sent him, Mama. It was a bad decision."

Eustacia Scott, Lady Osulton, lifted her impatient gaze from her embroidery and glared at her daughter across the blue drawing room. "Contrary to what you might think, Violet, your brother is not a stupid man. He trusts his cousin."

"I hardly know why, considering Damien's reputation with women."

"You *do* know why. They are best friends, and they share a bond that goes back many years. Damien is very protective of Harold, he always has been, and Harold knows it. He knows

37

Damien would not betray that loyalty."

Violet shook her head at her mother. "That may be true, but this American girl—Miss Wilson . . . Can *she* be trusted? Damien is a very attractive man, and you know what they say about those Americans."

"No, I do not know what they say."

"Oh, Mama, don't be so provincial."

"I am not being provincial. I simply do not listen to gossip or idle generalizations."

Violet harrumphed. "The Americans are passionate, Mama. How do you think they won at Yorktown? They were feral and wild, overtaken by a blazing fire in their veins—not unlike Damien can be sometimes. When they want something, they are unwavering and they spare nothing. They are like stubborn, unstoppable rams."

Lady Osulton began to stitch faster. "From my understanding, what Miss Wilson wants is *Harold*."

"She wants a title. And Damien has one, too. Plus good looks."

"A lesser title."

Violet raised a severely arched eyebrow. "I don't think it matters to these Americans. One is as good as another."

Lady Osulton laid down her embroidery and gazed across the room in shock. "Surely that can't be true."

"Oh yes, it is. Most of them don't even *know* that an earl outranks a baron, or a marquess, an earl. I heard it from the Countess of Lansdowne, and she herself is an American, though no one seems to remember that. She changes her voice, you know, and copies our accents."

Lady Osulton lifted her embroidery again, though she had not fully recovered from the inconceivable notion that *anyone* could think one title was as good as another, American or not. She couldn't hide the tremor of incredulity in her voice.

"The Countess of Lansdowne doesn't concern me. All that matters is that Harold has chosen a wife, when I thought he would never look up from his silly scientific experiments long enough to even think of it. And if Damien is our most reliable courier to bring her home, then Damien it shall be, because I want that gel brought back here."

"Oh, Mama. You know her money is her only recommendation."

She laid down her embroidery again. "I know no such thing, and shame on your vulgar tongue!" She pressed the back of her hand to her forehead. "Sometimes I wonder how you and Harold could possibly be brother and sister. He would never say such a thing to torture me. Harold is such a polite boy."

Violet had to work hard not to roll her eyes at her mother's melodrama. "I'm only being honest, Mama. The estate is not performing as it should, and I can't bear another reduction in our spending."

Lady Osulton picked up her embroidery again and resumed her stitching. "Don't talk about that, Violet. You know I don't like it." A moment went by before she spoke again. "The fact is, Harold has taken a fancy to someone, and I am greatly relieved. I don't care where she comes from, and I have every intention of welcoming her into this family like one of our own. She will provide us with an heir, after all. I only want what's best for this family, Violet. That's all. I don't care about the money."

"Of course you don't, Mama."

But it was generally understood by all members of the prestigious Osulton household that Violet—wanting a substantial dowry of her own to snare the best husband possible—most certainly did.

The storm raged on, and the cottage creaked and groaned like an old ship. Damien sat on the floor, slouching against the wall sipping coffee out of a tin cup, his long legs stretched out in front of him, one bent at the knee.

He gazed at Miss Wilson's profile in the firelight while she sat before the hearth, quietly watching the flames dance, and wondered why Harold had neglected to mention that she was unimaginably beautiful.

"I have found the perfect woman," he had said with a dumbfounded, besotted smile when he'd returned from America. "She is so good, I believe she must be a saint. She is polite and obedient with her parents. She is agreeable and genuine. I don't believe she is even capable of having a bad thought. She is purity and goodness and perfection personified. And I, heaven help me, am in love."

For some reason, Damien had imagined she would be plain. She was many things, but not that.

Regarding the other qualities Harold had described, Damien couldn't argue. Harold had been right. There was something sweet and angelic in her nature. Damien knew it now, even though he had just met her in the most strange and bizarre circumstances. The woman exuded virtue.

He disregarded the virtue for a brief moment, however, to let his experienced gaze roam free down the full length of her body. She had long, graceful legs and a curvaceous figure. With freckles and full lips and long, curly, honey-gold hair, she was the kind of woman who could make a man dream of things that were—in a polite manner of speaking—quite the *opposite* of pure and saintly. Which was ironic, he thought, feeling slightly amused as he imagined the men who must have salivated over her in the past—and gone to confession straight afterward, whether they were Catholic or not.

Damien took another sip of his coffee. Truth be told, if she were any other woman besides his cousin's virginal fiancée, he would likely be sharing the chair with her right now—holding her on his lap, offering comfort in the form of gentle caresses and soft kisses. They were stranded alone in a remote cottage, after all, and she'd been through a terrible ordeal. It was a most palpable opportunity, and he was a man who enjoyed women.

As he continued to watch her, however, he came to the opinion that she wouldn't require his consolations anyway. There had been no tears today. No hysterics. She'd remained calm and clearheaded through all of it. In fact, she'd earned his respect the instant she'd announced her name, while holding a chair up over her head.

A gust of wind whistled down the chimney and shook the flames. Miss Wilson sighed. Damien looked at the tattered dress she wore and imagined what she would look like in her opulent Newport mansion, covered in silk and jewels. She was probably desperate for her maid right now.

"I suppose this isn't what you're accustomed to," he said, just before he raised his coffee cup to his lips. "I'll wager that right about now, you'd love to run screaming back to your gold-plated bathtub in New York."

She tilted her head at him. "I beg your pardon, Lord Alcester. I hope you don't think I am overindulged and have never known hardship."

Enticed by her unexpected response, Damien rested an elbow on his knee. "You're not?"

"No," she replied somewhat tentatively.

How damnably charming she looked. He raised his eyebrows, waiting for her to continue.

"I don't mean to be defensive," she said, "but I wouldn't wish you to be misinformed about your cousin's future wife. Or to entertain prejudices about Americans in general."

He narrowed his gaze, suddenly in the mood to toy with her. She was certainly an attractive plaything. "But I thought all American heiresses were overindulged."

She paused, as if taken aback. "That is not so, my lord. Not so at all. In fact, I'll wager that I've survived worse circumstances than you have. I can't imagine you've ever gone hungry, or went around without shoes on a regular basis each summer—indoors *and* out."

"Without shoes?" He had to concede. She had him with that. She also surprised him with her "wager." Perhaps there were tiny embers of wickedness smoldering somewhere in the depths of this perfect angelic creature after all.

She seemed to suddenly comprehend the intricacies of her argument, and squeezed her eyes shut. "Perhaps I shouldn't have said that. You English already think we are beneath you as it is."

"*You English?*" he repeated, drawing his dark brows together, feeling very pleasantly intrigued by their conversation. "Clearly *we English* are not the only ones with prejudices. Tsk tsk, Miss Wilson. What is the world coming to when people of different nationalities cannot get along, I ask you?"

She stared at him for a few seconds, looking surprised until she realized he was teasing her. Then she smiled. It was a dazzling smile— sweet and scintillating at the same time, and so very genuine.

It was the first time Damien had seen her

smile, he realized. She'd been nervous and uncomfortable until this moment, looking at him
as if he were something to be feared. Perhaps
now she would relax.

He, on the other hand, felt his own relaxation
slip.

Damien dropped his gaze to his coffee, suddenly understanding very well why Harold
had been so taken with her. Not only was she
magnificent in every way a woman could be,
but there was something elusively indefinable
about her as well—a sensual, earthy nature that
seemed to glow with warmth. A man like
Harold, who was shy around women, would be
seduced by such natural charisma.

When their smiles died away, she returned to
the thread of their conversation. "I suppose
Harold described my summer home in Newport to you," she explained, "and it didn't
sound at all like I had to go without shoes."

"He told me about your diamond-studded
champagne glasses."

She was suitably embarrassed and lowered
her gaze, shrugging as if to apologize for the
glasses.

Damien seized the opportunity to glance
down at the lovely fullness of her bosom beneath her thick, wool bodice. He experienced a
pang of guilt, because she belonged to his
cousin, but it was quickly overcome when he returned his gaze to her face and made a solemn
vow to keep it there.

"We didn't always have money," she said innocently, which charmed him, because she was not even remotely aware of his lusty interest in her bosom. "Papa earned his fortune on Wall Street when I was ten." She stared pensively into the fire. "Sometimes when I look at my life, it seems like it's divided in two. Before the money, and after. So you see, I'm not quite as overindulged as you think. At least, I wasn't always." She inhaled and let the breath out slowly, looking faintly reminiscent.

"I miss those old days," she said. "I used to enjoy running about barefoot. I still do on occasion, when I'm alone in the woods, which unfortunately is very rare. But *please*," she said, her bright smile returning, "keep the part about my running about barefoot to yourself."

He inclined his head, trying not to become too diverted by the enticing image of her doing *anything* barefoot.

"But perhaps I owe it to Harold to tell him," Damien said. "He doesn't know he's about to marry a wood nymph."

Her responding smile made his breath catch.

She let her head tip onto the chair back and gazed into the flames again, looking tired. Damien allowed her some peace, though he couldn't tear his gaze away from her enchanting profile. As he stared at her, he contemplated their situation.

If she were a different woman, and these were different circumstances, he *would* find a way to have her tonight. In his arms. Crying out his name as he took her to the heights of passion.

But she was *not* another woman, so he would *not* have her. Tonight, or any other night. There was no point in even thinking of it.

"It's getting late," Lord Alcester said, rising to put another log on the fire. "You must be tired. I can help you up the stairs if you wish."

Adele watched his broad back as he set the log on the charred remains of another, and used the poker to stir the heat. She felt a tremor of panic. She did not want to go back upstairs. She'd been locked in that room for three days, and her kidnapper was up there. Dead.

Lord Alcester leaned the poker against the stone hearth and turned to face her. He stared down at her for a long moment. "I'll move the body," he said, as if he'd read her thoughts.

She considered it, but the sickening dread remained. "I would rather not go back up there. Could I sleep down here?"

He gazed at her for another few seconds, and she recognized a flicker of sympathy and compassion in his eyes—an expression that eased the tension in her shoulders.

He nodded. "I'll bring the bedding down."

He immediately went upstairs, and she listened to the sounds of his movements across the floor, then his boots tapping slowly back down the stairs. He reappeared with the hay tick, dragging it across the floor and setting it down a safe distance from the fire. He took the blankets and shook them out on the other side of the room, then spread them on the tick.

"You can sleep here," he said. "I can go upstairs, or I can sleep in the chair, whichever you prefer."

"The chair, if you don't mind."

He nodded, then held out his hand to her. "May I assist you?"

She gazed at his large, rough-looking hand and set her own inside it. He helped her up, and she crawled onto the makeshift bed and got in. She pulled the blanket over her, while he helped straighten it around her feet.

"I'll be glad to leave here tomorrow," she said, lying back and looking up at him, so tall standing over her.

He smiled gently. "I know."

He knelt in front of the fire again and used the poker to move the log, making sure it was catching the flame. Then he sat down in the old chair. Adele closed her eyes and tried to go to sleep. For about fifteen minutes, neither of them spoke. The only sound in the room was the crackling of the fire. Then Adele opened her eyes again and looked at her rescuer. He was staring at her.

"I can't sleep," she said. "I haven't been able to sleep at all over the past few days."

He shook his head. "Neither have I."

"Would it be all right if we talked?" she asked.

He didn't say anything for a second or two. "What would you like to talk about?"

She thought about it, then rolled onto her side and rested her cheek on her hands. "Tell me about Harold's home—Osulton Manor. Have you been there many times?"

"Been there?" he said, sounding surprised at her question. "I was raised there."

She leaned up on her elbow. "You grew up with Harold?"

"Yes. We're like brothers. You didn't know that?"

"No. Harold and I didn't have as much time to talk as we would have liked," she explained. "Do your parents live at Osulton as well?"

"My parents died when I was nine. That's why I was sent to live with Harold's family."

"I see. I'm very sorry."

He looked into the fire. "I suppose my life is divided in two, as well."

Adele nodded compassionately at him. "Do you still live there?" she asked.

He seemed to require a moment to think about how to answer that question. He tilted his head from side to side. "I'm residing there temporarily, because I've rented out my London house for the Season, and I'm looking for tenants for my country house as well."

Because of the money problems, she presumed.

The conversation died for a few minutes. The wind whistled through the chimney, and the flames danced chaotically.

Lord Alcester leaned his temple on a finger and stared down at her. "Tell me how you met Harold."

Adele was glad to resume talking. She had

spent too many days alone upstairs to enjoy any kind of silence now. "We met in Newport," she replied, lying back on her side again. "As you know, he had taken a holiday in America over the winter, and my mother heard of his visit and arranged a ball in his honor. It was quite the affair," she added, smiling. "Every Knickerbocker in New York was scrambling for an invitation."

"Knickerbocker?"

Adele smiled again. "Would you like the long, drawn-out explanation?"

He gestured with his hand. "We certainly don't have much else to do."

She sat up, leaning back on both arms. "All right then. Let me describe the social hierarchy of America to you. There is a very defined line between Old Money and New. I—as you may or may not know—am *New* Money. My father earned his fortune almost overnight, and as I mentioned before, took us from our one-room cabin in Wisconsin to a mansion on Fifth Avenue quicker than you can blink. To get to the point, Old Money is inherited, and those who have it are called Knickerbockers because most of them are descended from the early Dutch settlers who wore knee-length trousers. Like you, they can trace their family's heritage back through generations. They live in Washington Square in plain brownstones, and consider themselves the social elite, while people like us are vulgar because we build showy mansions in the newer neighborhoods. And I will admit, our house is exceedingly showy, but that's my mother." She shifted her weight to lean on one arm. "She loves everything to be grandiose."

Lord Alcester's lips turned up in a grin.

"I think you'll like her," Adele continued, lying back down. "Or at the very least, find her amusing. She doesn't put on any airs and sometimes ignores or protests certain social graces that have no practicality, which I suppose is why the Knickerbockers give her such a difficult time."

Lord Alcester leaned forward to rest his elbows on his knees, his gaze intent upon hers. "I honestly had no idea there was such a pecking order in America. I had thought it was a classless society."

"On paper, perhaps," she replied, tossing an arm up under her head again, "but if you could walk in my shoes in Newport for one day, you would feel the divisions as clearly as you feel your own here in England. It's like walking into a brick wall sometimes."

He leaned back again, his dark eyes studying her with a serious intensity that unnerved her. "I am much enlightened, Miss Wilson. Was Harold aware of all this when he attended your ball? I can't imagine he was."

"No, I don't believe so. And I certainly wasn't about to tell him." She recognized her blunder as soon as she said it, and felt her cheeks pale. "Oh."

Lord Alcester smiled and crossed one booted leg over the other. "Don't fret, my dear. Your secret's safe with me. It wouldn't have mattered to him anyway. In his eyes, you're either English or you're not."

It should have been Lord Alcester's turn to go pale, but he brushed it off with a clever retort. "In your case, you are most decidedly *not* English, and thank goodness for that, or I would be immensely bored right now."

The flattery came a little too close to a flirtation, Adele thought, feeling a surge of butterflies in her stomach. She was reminded of his reputation with women, and felt a sudden measure of uneasiness.

"So how did you go from a ball to a proposal?" he asked, bringing the conversation back around to her and Harold. She wondered if he'd recognized her unease.

Adele looked up at the ceiling, determined to focus on the questions instead of the man. She thought about how quickly she and Harold had become engaged, and could attribute it to one very obvious catalyst.

"When you meet my mother, I'm sure you'll notice that she is very ambitious and often impatient about getting what she wants. She has spared nothing to be accepted by the Knickerbockers in New York—and she's managed to accomplish that since my sisters married a duke and a marquess. When she decided Harold was the one for me, she was equally determined."

"*She* decided?"

Adele tried to explain. "Well . . . yes, she was the one to suggest that he would be a good match for me. My father came into the picture then. He was impressed with some of Harold's ideas about chemistry, and I believe he would like to be involved in one of Harold's experiments—something to do with a new type of dye. He sees business potential there."

"Does he indeed? Harold didn't mention that to me."

"Well, it's all just in the idea stage. At any rate, my mother held a few more assemblies and invited Harold, and it wasn't long before we both realized that she was right, and we were very comfortable with each other. I liked his sense of tradition, and he liked my—"

"Yes?" He leaned forward, radiating an intensity she'd never seen in a person before. Lord Alcester was a very potent human being, she realized, and she supposed that was why he had such a reputation. Women were no doubt attracted to such a strong personality and such a handsome face to go with it. Even Adele found him intriguing, and certainly unnerving as well. He was her future cousin by marriage, however, so she would just have to get used to him.

"Well . . ." Her insides jangled. "He said he thought I would fit in here in England, and I *believe* that is why we were drawn to each other. Compared to other American girls my age, I am perhaps more reserved than most."

He studied her for a moment. "You don't seem sure that's the reason."

She shrugged. "Well, I suppose I can only

guess why Harold approved of me. He didn't actually *tell* me."

Lord Alcester sat back again. "He told *me*. Would you like to know what he said?"

"He told you?"

"Yes. We're not only cousins, we are close friends as well."

Adele found it odd that they were so close, considering how different they were in every way. Harold was gentle and never threatening, while Lord Alcester had an unmistakable hard edge to him. And he was very different with women.

Lord Alcester rested his temple on a finger again. "Harold told me he admired your goodness. He even went so far as to say you might be a saint."

Adele plucked at the woolly blanket over her legs. "Ah. A saint."

His brows drew together. "That doesn't please you?"

Adele wet her lips. "Lord Alcester, it's strange. People have always told me how good I am, how agreeable and dependable. They look at me and they think I can do no wrong. Even my parents have always thought that. I don't know why. I don't know where it started. I certainly didn't *try* to be a well-behaved child. I just was. At least, compared to my sisters, who were always trying to get me to do mischief with them. The point is, I don't know why I am perceived that way. I don't consider myself overly righteous. Sometimes I even feel like an impostor."

"Have you ever done anything you knew was wrong?"

She considered the question carefully. "Not really. I've made mistakes, of course. Everyone has."

"Have you ever *wanted* to do anything wrong?"

A vivid memory of a red candy stick came swirling into her mind. She had seen it at the mercantile in Wisconsin when she was nine or ten, but she'd had no money.

"I once thought about stealing something when I was a child," she said. "A candy stick."

"But you didn't."

She shook her head. "No, I didn't. It was very tempting, though," she added with a smile. "It was the brightest, most colorful candy stick I'd ever seen, with a cherry drawn on the tag. I knew it would fit perfectly into my pocket, and no one would know if I was sneaky enough. I kept staring at it, imagining how I would hide it and keep it secret from my sisters. I picked it up and held it in my hand."

He smiled and nodded, seeming to understand. "But you didn't take it," he reminded her.

"No, I put it back. So maybe I *am* a saint," she said, mocking insight. "If you could have seen that candy stick—"

"I'll bet it was delicious."

She sighed. "I've always wondered."

They watched the fire for a few more minutes until Lord Alcester stood. He picked up the cushion from the chair and tossed it onto the floor close to the fire, but a few feet away from where Adele lay. "I think if I'm to sleep, I'll need to stretch out," he said.

Adele shifted to get more comfortable. "The floor won't be too hard? Or too cold?"

He lay down on his side, facing her. "Not at all. This is a fine pillow, and my coat is warm. I'm just glad to be able to finally take a breath and close my eyes." He stared at her for a few seconds. "Good night, Miss Wilson."

"Good night." Adele lowered her head onto the pillow but continued to watch him in the firelight. She had to admit she was intrigued by him, and wanted to know more about the way he lived, which was so different from the way *she* lived. He seemed very different from Harold as well, yet they were close. She would like to know why and how.

I'm just glad to be able to finally take a breath and close my eyes . . .

She pondered that. He was glad because he had been on a mission to rescue her. He'd had to contend with the prospect of facing a kidnapper, or the prospect of finding her harmed. Or dead. He had worried over that prospect.

And now, he had fulfilled his duty to Harold. His cousin and friend. She turned her thoughts to *him*. Her fiancé . . .

Adele could only assume that Harold had been worried, too. She did not know because he had not come himself, but surely he had lost sleep as well. She certainly had. She was exhausted. Yet tonight, like the past three nights in this house, she did not want to close her eyes.

This ordeal had been very difficult. She would be glad to return to her normal, safe life.

Waking to the budding light of dawn the next morning, Damien opened his eyes. He lay on his side, looking at Miss Wilson across from him. She was still asleep, facing him, her cheek resting on her hands, the blanket pulled up to her chin. Her lips were parted slightly, and her breathing was slow and steady. It would be best, he decided, if he could rise without waking her, and simply leave as he had said he would, to fetch a coach and driver.

He leaned up on an elbow and looked around. The fire had gone out sometime during the night, and the cottage was cold. Damien blew into his fists to warm his hands. Miss Wilson made no sound, so he quietly rose to his feet.

He stood gazing down at her moist, full lips in the early light of the morning. Thick locks of curly, golden hair were spread out around her on the rough-hewn floor. Damien noted the delicate shape of her face, her tiny nose, and the soft, smooth texture of her skin.

She was astoundingly beautiful. He had known it last night in the firelight, and the gray light of dawn did not diminish it in the least. Harold must have been enormously distracted by something to have forgotten to mention such a thing.

Damien wondered suddenly if Harold realized how lucky he was, and if he'd been fighting lustful thoughts ever since he'd met her in America last spring.

It was difficult, however, to imagine Harold having lustful thoughts about anything except his chemistry experiments. He had never described Adele—or any other woman, for that matter—in such a way. But he got a certain lusty look in his eye when bubbles started to form in a beaker.

Harold should have come, Damien thought suddenly with a slight twinge of reproach as he thought about what Adele had gone through. How could Harold have trusted this important task to someone else, even if that someone was Damien, his cousin and best friend? How could Harold sleep at night, not knowing if his beautiful fiancée was dead or alive? He, at the very least, could have accompanied Damien.

But Damien supposed that Harold had always preferred to keep his head in the sand, and likely always would. Damien and the rest of the family even helped Harold bury his head on occasion. They had often dealt with certain household problems themselves, keeping Harold in the dark, knowing he would have preferred it that way.

Damien felt guilty all of a sudden for thinking badly of Harold, his friend, who was a kindhearted and principled person. Like Adele. Perhaps they were a good match. Damien swept the critical opinion away.

When it didn't appear that Miss Wilson was going to stir anytime soon, Damien combed his fingers through his hair and rubbed his face. He went outside and fetched a fresh bucket of water for Adele from the well, then brought it back and set it down gently in front of the chair. He stared at her for another few seconds, admiring the slender curve of her hips and the feminine shape of her hands. He imagined her as a girl, staring longingly at that candy stick, and felt an odd mixture of amusement and pity. He wondered how many cherry sticks she had resisted in her life, how many she had never tasted. Then he thought of Harold again. Harold would probably be very pleased that she had not taken the candy stick.

Damien, on the other hand, wished he could get her one. He wouldn't steal it, of course. He would pay for it. He would just like to see her face when she tasted it. He'd like to watch her eyes. And her tongue and lips.

He shook his head at himself, and headed for the door, keeping his footsteps light. It was probably a good thing they were leaving here today and heading back to civilization. Because Damien was beginning to find Miss Wilson far more appealing than he should.

Chapter 3

Shortly before noon, Adele went outside to meet Lord Alcester, who was riding into the yard on his big, black horse. He swung down from the high saddle and landed gracefully on the ground. A coach was behind him, rumbling slowly up the hill.

His hair was like a wild mane around his face, his coat blowing in the wind. It was difficult to imagine that this man was related by blood to her fiancé. They were so remarkably different in every way. Harold had red hair, and though he was tall, he was very slender, with small hands. Damien's hands were huge. They were a horseman's hands.

"You shouldn't be out here," he said. "You'll catch your death."

59

"I've been stuck in there for three days. I couldn't stand it anymore."

He glanced down at her feet, which were bare. "Isn't it a little chilly to be a wood nymph this morning?"

She met his smiling gaze and recognized the power of his charm. It was no wonder he had so many eager lady friends. "You know I have no shoes."

"Yes, I know. There are stockings and shoes for you in the coach, which isn't far behind."

She turned and saw it slowly rolling its way up the hill. Lord Alcester was very good at taking care of things, she realized. It was easy to rely on him. "Thank you."

She limped beside him while he led his horse to the trough.

"I know this is unpleasant business, Miss Wilson, but someone will be along to collect the body after we're gone, and we'll have to speak to the magistrate in the village tonight. He's already given me his word he'll keep it quiet, and I trust him. Will you be able to discuss it?"

"Of course."

"How is your wound, by the way?" he asked.

Immediately, a vision of his hands on her leg jolted her. She forcefully pushed the recollection away. "It feels a bit better this morning. It's not so difficult to walk."

His eyes were downcast as he watched his horse drink from the nearly overflowing trough. The wind blew a part in his thick, black hair and revealed dark brows against his sun-bronzed skin. If Adele were an artist, she would paint him as Michael, the warrior angel. She had seen a statue of Michael in Paris once, when she had spent time there with her sisters, learning to speak French. She had never forgotten it. She often dreamed about that statue.

For some reason, she thought of Lord Alcester's mistress at that moment, the famous actress. From what Sophia had said, the woman was very beautiful and very liberal. She enjoyed taking lovers, and by all accounts, she was just the kind of woman Lord Alcester desired. Theirs was purportedly a passionate love affair.

It was hard for Adele to imagine any woman being so free, not worrying about duty or correct behavior. To even *think* about such a woman— to have any connection to her whatsoever— seemed strange for Adele, who had led an exceedingly sheltered and proper life. She didn't even *know* anyone who'd had a "lover."

She supposed, however, that many women would forget what was proper when tempted by a man as attractive as Lord Alcester. He was like no other man she had ever met before. Everything about him was interesting and alluring— his eyes were seductive, his lips sinful. She might be innocent, but she could at least recognize *that*.

"I also sent a wire to Harold," he said, "to inform him that you're safe, and that he can expect you in two days."

"I hope he'll pass that message on to my mother. She must be worried sick."

"From what I understand, your mother has

been in London with your sister, and she'll be traveling by train to meet us in two days. We'll travel by coach and check into an inn this evening. We'll tell everyone we encounter that you are my sister-in-law." Lord Alcester tethered his horse to the post next to the trough. "And I'm pleased to say you can anticipate a hearty dinner by a warm fire this evening."

"I can hardly wait."

Lord Alcester walked to the edge of the yard. "Here comes the coach."

A few minutes later, it pulled up in front, and Adele limped toward it. She climbed in, pleased by the interior of the vehicle with its soft, blue upholstery. A box with a ribbon around it sat on the seat.

Lord Alcester stood at the open door, his large, masculine hand gripping the latch. "Shoes and stockings," he said.

Adele picked it up and held it on her lap. "Thank you."

While she gazed at his handsome face in the sunlight, she felt almost entranced. In an effort to distract herself, she peered out at his horse, still tethered by the trough. "You're lucky you get to ride."

"You like to ride?" he asked, sounding surprised.

"Yes. I sold my hair when I was seven to keep my father from selling our pony when we couldn't afford to keep her. I just couldn't live without her, or without the freedom to explore the woods where we lived."

He lifted his chin, gesturing toward his own horse. "We have something in common. I've been leasing out my London house to keep *him*."

Adele's eyebrows lifted.

"Do you still have that pony you loved so much?" he asked.

"No. She died when I was nine. I explored the woods on foot after that. Until we moved to the city, of course."

He hesitated at the door for a moment. "You'll be glad to hear that Osulton is surrounded by forest, and the stable is stocked with thoroughbreds."

"Really? Harold didn't mention that. I can't wait to get there."

He nodded. "Signal if you need anything."

"I will."

Lord Alcester closed the door. She watched him from the window as he waved to the driver and strode toward his own horse. He swung himself up into the saddle and led the way out of the yard.

The coach slowly turned around, and before Adele knew it, she was rocking back and forth on the seat as they made their way down the hill and back to real life. Though she wasn't sure anything would ever be completely normal again.

Osulton Manor

"He found her! She's safe and on her way home!"

Eustacia waved the telegram over her head as she dashed into the brightly lit conservatory. Or rather, the brightly lit *laboratory*, as it had been cleared of plants a number of years ago and lovingly dedicated to the pursuit of chemical science.

Harold lifted his gaze from the beaker of bubbling liquid that stood before him. His protective eyewear was covered in steam, so he pushed the large glasses off his face to rest on top of his curly, red hair. "I beg your pardon, Mother? Did you say she was safe?"

"Yes! Yes!"

"Are you referring to Miss Wilson?" he asked.

His mother skidded to a halt before him. "Of course I am, you silly, silly man! She's safe! Damien has procured her!"

He took the telegram that his mother held out to him and read it. "Well, that is indeed good news. I told you Damien was the right man for the job."

"Yes, you were right as always. He no doubt put that despicable kidnapper in his place and . . . Well, let's not go into that. We know how Damien can put up a good fight. The point is, they're on their way home! They'll be here in two days."

"Two days. You don't say."

"I do say, Harold. You'll have to get a haircut."

"Yes, I believe you're right."

"And we must plan a special dinner in Miss Wilson's honor. She is the future Lady Osulton, after all. Would roast lamb do? Or do you think she would prefer beef? I believe Americans are beef eaters, are they not? You were there. You should know. Or perhaps they eat so much of it, it's become a bore. Oh, Harold, what should it be?"

Harold looked down at his beaker. The bubbles had disappeared. "I don't know, Mother. You decide." He slid his protective eyewear back down over his eyes and leaned close. "What the devil happened?" he muttered to himself. "They were there a minute ago."

That evening at the inn, after Adele had bathed and spoken to the magistrate, she prepared for supper. She had to don the same homespun dress she'd been wearing for the past three days, but at least she felt clean.

She left her bedchamber and went to the dining room. A movement to her left caught her eye, and she spotted Lord Alcester making his way across the room to greet her. He offered his arm. "Good evening, Miss Wilson. Our table is this way."

He had bathed, too, and shaved. His hair, still damp, was slicked back off his face. He looked . . . Well, he looked . . .

Different.

He escorted her to a table in the far corner. It was clothed in white, with a vase of fresh daisies in the center next to a bottle of wine. A candle burned in a small jar.

Adele stopped before the table and stared down at it. "I can't begin to describe how good it feels to be among civilized people again, and to look at such a lovely table laid out with such care." She gazed up at him. "I've been eating turnip and beef in a pan for the past three days."

He nodded with understanding, then moved behind her to pull out her chair. "Then it will be my pleasure this evening, Miss Wilson, to provide you with what you've been missing. I'm happy to report that the food here is excellent. *Everything* is done with care." He took his seat opposite her. "I took the liberty of ordering a bottle of wine. I hope you'll join me in a toast."

"I'd be delighted."

He poured her a glass, then lifted his own. "To life and marriage."

"To both."

Over the next hour, they discussed light topics—the artwork in the dining room, the population of the village and surrounding areas, the weather, of course, and the route they would take to reach Osulton Manor in the most efficient time.

Soon the food arrived, and they enjoyed their dinner while the pink hue of twilight streamed in through the lace-covered window and lent a relaxed, magical atmosphere to the room. Their conversation relaxed as well, as they meandered into more personal topics, without ever realizing the transition had occurred.

"So you know how Harold and I met," Adele said, recalling her curiosity about this man the night before when she had watched him falling asleep. "Now tell me a little about yourself, Lord Alcester. You wear no wedding ring. How have you managed to avoid marriage for so long?"

It was a bold question, she knew, but she didn't feel quite herself. This was not her life, she supposed. It was "Adele on an Adventure."

"It's been no small feat, I assure you," he replied. "Both my aunt and my grandmother would like to see me attached as soon as possible, and they become more and more determined each year. I predict my aunt and your mother will get along famously. They'll be two kindred spirits, matchmaking to their heart's delight."

Adele imagined what his life was like as an English nobleman, where a sense of duty was probably fed into his veins from infancy onward. "I suppose it's your goal in life, isn't it, to make a good marriage and produce heirs?"

Good God. Produce heirs? She was feeling bold, not scandalous. Perhaps she'd had too much wine.

"Yes, exactly. Not to put too fine a point on it, but I had best get to it. I'm not getting any younger." With a wicked grin that made her squirm in her chair, he picked up the bottle and tipped it over her glass, but she firmly held up a hand.

"No, thank you, I've had enough. Please feel free to finish it."

He didn't argue. He poured the rest of the wine into his own glass and took another sip. He didn't seem the least bit affected by it. Quite unlike herself.

"Don't get me wrong," he said, "I adore my

aunt and grandmother, and nothing would please me more than to make them happy, but I have yet to discover the one woman who makes me . . ." He paused. The candlelight flickered between them. "The one who makes me want to be a husband. I don't want to marry just anyone and be miserable. That doesn't do anyone any good."

"Well, happiness is indeed an important thing to consider," she said, feeling a great need to bring her fiancé into this conversation. "*Harold*, for instance, has made me indescribably happy on so many occasions."

"Has he indeed? In what way, may I ask? Perhaps I should consult him in matters of romance. It sounds as if he could provide some helpful advice."

Adele stared at the electrifying glimmer in his eyes that almost seemed to challenge her. She noticed suddenly that they were both leaning forward with their elbows on the table. She sat back and couldn't help reaching for her wine again.

"I hardly think *you* need advice, my lord. I know about your reputation with women." She surprised herself with that comment.

"Do you, now? Where in the world would you hear such a thing? Does news like that reach America?"

"My sister told me. She mentioned it in a letter when Harold was still in America."

"Well." He took a deep swig of wine, then casually shrugged.

"You're not denying it," Adele said, shocked in some ways, but not in others. Lord Alcester didn't seem all that concerned with what was proper. He was like no one she'd ever met.

"No, I am not denying it, because it's all true. I am without a doubt the worst scoundrel in London. You had best keep your distance."

He smiled with riveting splendor, and *boom*, there it was in full force. The pounding allure that her sister had described, and she herself had witnessed on so many occasions leading up to this one. The sweet, seductive power that even Adele—inexperienced as she was with men—could recognize. The very qualities that made him notorious. A strangely pleasant, dizzying haze moved over her thoughts as she stared at him.

The server came and took their plates away. As soon as she was gone, Adele became aware of her heart beating shockingly fast. An unfamiliar thrill was rippling through her veins.

She didn't like it.

Feeling shaken by her body's response to Lord Alcester, she thrust the haze away and forced her thoughts back to their earlier conversation. "Perhaps you haven't married because you simply haven't met the right woman yet," she said, struggling to recover her calm. "When you do, everything will seem effortless, and you will defy your reputation and find the happiness that you seek."

She saw his Adam's apple bob. "I'm not sure," he said, his voice low and husky, "that I will ever be able to know true happiness, Miss Wilson, even if I encountered Venus herself."

She stared at him across the table, bewildered by this surprising declaration, and more than a little curious about his meaning. "Why would you think that?"

He said nothing for a moment or two, then he drummed his long fingers on the table. "There is no good reason for me to think it, Miss Wilson."

The server arrived at that moment, and asked if they wished to have dessert—apples and cream.

Lord Alcester leaned back in his chair. "Apples sound delicious."

She realized she'd been staring blankly at him. "No . . . no, thank you, I couldn't eat another bite."

"Tea? Coffee?"

She shook her head. The server went away. Lord Alcester rested both hands on his thighs. "It seems our dinner has come to an end."

Though she couldn't possibly eat any more, Adele had to confess, she didn't want their dinner to end. She wanted to keep talking to him. Proper decorum, however—and the sensible, warning voice in her brain—required her to politely agree and bid him good night.

He helped her up from her chair. "We'll get an early start tomorrow," he said, "and meet your mother by noon the following day if the weather holds. Is seven too early for you?"

"Seven is fine. Thank you, Damien, for everything you've done."

Too late she realized she had used his Christian name, when she should not have taken such a liberty. Again, she blamed her indiscretion on the wine and hoped that he hadn't noticed, when she knew very well that he had.

His eyes were warm. The seduction was gone now. "It has been my pleasure, Miss Wilson."

Relieved that he had made things respectable again—because she had been quite unable to make them respectable herself—she smiled one last time, then retired uneasily to her room.

Damien lay in bed that night with his arms up under his head, staring at the ceiling and remembering the conversation he'd had with Harold less than a week ago . . .

"I've never given you advice before, Damien. God knows it's usually the other way around. I feel clumsy even thinking of it, but here it is: Your creditors have been getting more aggressive lately, and things seem to be coming to a head. Maybe it's time you looked for a bride."

Damien had known that was coming. He'd been considering it himself. "A wealthy bride, you mean."

"It wouldn't be difficult. Not for you, with all your appeal with the ladies. Certainly, if I could do it . . ."

"You think I should go to America," Damien had said.

"Yes, I do."

"But you know how I feel about marriage for profit."

Harold had stiffened. "Unfortunately, it's my duty as your closest friend to try again to convince you that not all arranged marriages end badly like your parents' did. Some can turn out very well. I'm sure mine will."

"I would prefer not to leave anything to chance," Damien had told him.

Harold sank into a chair. "All that aside, Damien, I know how wretched your financial situation has become, and that's perhaps the point of this conversation. There was another creditor here today . . ."

Damien rolled over on the bed as a heavy weight pressed upon his chest. He reconsidered his cousin's suggestion. If there were other women like Adele Wilson in America, perhaps Damien *should* consider it. It would solve a host of problems, to be sure. Money problems, for one.

And after today, there were other problems, too. More than once this evening, Damien had found himself staring across the table at Adele and not just admiring her as he had in the cottage, but truly wanting her for himself. She was so good. She was the perfect woman. Nothing like Damien's own mother.

He wondered selfishly how much Harold really wanted Adele. How disappointed would he be if he lost her? Was there a chance her father's business interest in his experiments was what fueled their hasty engagement? Or had Harold, for the first time in his life, fallen in love? It was not unlikely, Damien thought, now that he had met Adele and seen for himself the full measure and depth of her beauty, both inside and out.

Damien shook his head at himself. He should not even be pondering such a thing. Harold's happiness mattered to him very deeply. Though perhaps at times, a little too deeply. Everyone had always said so.

Regardless of his feelings of loyalty toward Harold, however, his thoughts darted immediately back to Adele. He imagined her in her bed. He imagined going to check on her. What would happen if he did? Would he stay very long? Would she be glad to see him?

He cupped his forehead in his hand and squeezed his eyes shut, and cursed aloud. "Bloody hell." He was overwhelmingly attracted to her.

You should not have sent me, Harold. You should not have sent me . . .

Chapter 4

Damien woke to the sound of a scream in the night, and was out of his bed and into the hall before he'd even realized he was awake. Another scream rent the air—a woman shouting, "Get out!"

Adrenaline speeding through his veins, he ran to Adele's door and jiggled the knob, but it was locked. He slammed his shoulder against it, again and again, until it gave way and opened, smacking against the inside wall and bouncing back.

Damien crossed the moonlit room in two swift strides and took hold of Adele, who was flailing on the bed. He wrapped his hands around her upper arms. "Adele, it's me, Damien."

She sat up and shoved him away and began to slap at him, smacking his face and arms and shoulders until he had to put his arms up in defense.

"Adele, it's Damien. Wake up!"

She continued to slap at him for a few more seconds, then stopped suddenly. She sat very still, staring at him, and it was only then that Damien noticed the sound of footsteps in the hall and raised voices.

He grabbed hold of Adele's arms again. "You were dreaming."

She continued to stare at him. He could see her face in the dim moonlight that beamed in the window, and recognized the look of terror in her eyes. She bowed her head and covered her face with her hands. "Thank God."

She leaned forward to rest her head on his shoulder, and all at once, his body began to ache with the most unsettling need to draw her up onto his lap, cocoon her in his arms, and press his lips to hers to kiss away the terror. He blinked a few times, feeling very uneasy.

He sensed the presence of others in the doorway behind him, then the sound of heavy footsteps pounding down the hall and entering the room.

"Are you all right, miss?" a male voice asked. "Do you know this man?"

Damien didn't even bother to turn around to see who was asking, not when Adele was still trembling. All he could do was sit on the edge of the bed and touch her the only way he could. He cupped her head in one hand and ran his other hand up and down her damp back.

Adele nodded and sat back. She wiped the sweat from her face. "Yes, I know him. I'm sorry. I didn't mean to cause such a disturbance."

"Do you need assistance?"

"No, but thank you." She looked into Damien's eyes. "This man is my protector."

There was a curious silence, then whispers.

"You can all go back to your rooms now," she said shakily. "Again, I'm sorry to have awakened you."

Reluctantly, the spectators ambled out of the doorway, still whispering. Damien kept his eyes on Adele the whole time. Her breathing slowed, and she wiped the perspiration from her face again.

Damien reluctantly stood up to leave also— *because he knew that he should*—but he stopped when she took hold of his forearm. Her grip was tight, her palm clammy.

He gazed down at her in the dim moonlight, and his chest heaved with dread. There was some truth to his reputation, after all. He enjoyed making love to beautiful women, and his sexual instincts were presently on high alert, because Adele was, in no uncertain terms, beautiful. More than beautiful. She was exquisitely lush and fresh and innocent. She was nothing like Harold's deficient description.

He glanced down again at her slender hand

on his arm, and felt the warmth of her fingers. He was *glad* she had stopped him. *Glad*. Because he didn't want to leave.

But the gladness turned almost immediately to concern, because he found himself speculating again about Harold's true feelings for her. *Would* he be that disappointed to lose her?

It was a selfish thought. Things would get complicated if he didn't put a quick end to this attraction and leave now.

She gazed up at him with pleading eyes. "Please don't go."

Damien shook his head. She had no idea what she was saying and who she was saying it to. He was a man of questionable repute. A man who desired her. She should not be so trusting.

"Please stay, Damien," she said. "I don't want to be alone."

Bloody hell. His desires were stirring, and all he could think was, "Harold who?" Adele was glowing with perspiration and begging him to stay with her in her bedchamber. She had no idea she was stoking such a dangerous fire.

Damien's gaze fell to the top of her shift and the smooth expanse of her neck, and he clenched his jaw. He imagined trying to explain an indiscretion to Harold. He imagined Harold's reaction. Then he felt a painful ache deep down inside himself—an ache that came out of the past, from a day when he was only nine.

Damien remembered the look on his father's face when he'd told him what his wife—Damien's own mother—had been doing and where she had gone. He remembered his father's sobs and tears. Then he remembered his own tears, not long afterward, when his mother and father were each lowered into the ground.

No. It was not something Damien could do.

Then he noticed that Adele was squeezing her hands together in her lap, and he knew she was still afraid of the nightmare. He felt a stirring of compassion in his gut, and tried to focus all his attention on that.

He swallowed hard, and told himself he would try to ease her fears, but he would make it clear that he could not, under any circumstances, spend the night in the same room with her. Neither his conscience, nor his integrity, would allow it.

Moonlight streamed in the windows and gave the room a spooky, unearthly glow while Adele sat waiting for Lord Alcester's reply. She gazed up at him standing shirtless before her.

Tantalizing memories stirred in her mind, as she was reminded of statues of nude men she had seen in Paris. She recalled the muscular curves that had mesmerized her, the width and breadth of the shoulders, and the finely chiseled faces. Damien was no less magnificent standing before her now. He could be a god. A great work of art.

Her eyes swept over the smoothly rippled muscles at his abdomen, and she marveled at the sheer brawn of his upper arms. A most surprising shudder of delight pulsated through

her. This—the real flesh and blood of a man—
was far more stimulating than a stone statue.

Her innocence exploded to the surface of her
being at that instant, and she realized again
how little she knew about herself—and life. Before this day, she had not been remotely aware
of sexual desire and how it could influence or
overwhelm a person physically with its intensity. She had not known the true meaning of
temptation. A candy stick could not compare to
this.

Feeling dizzy from the awesome display of
maleness that stood before her, she inhaled
sharply and tried to gather her thoughts. "I
can't be alone," she told him.

For a few awkward seconds, he stared down
at her. When he finally spoke, his voice was
deep and quiet. "It wouldn't be right, Adele."

She wasn't sure if he was referring to the
strict code of behavior they both lived by, where
an unmarried lady such as herself would be ir-
reparably ruined if the people in the inn discovered she'd had a gentleman in her bedchamber
at night—or if he was referring to something
else more specific. More personal. Something
unspoken. Something to do with the open way
they had interacted at dinner.

"I don't care," she said, thinking only of what
she needed right now. Him. His protection. His
calm.

She realized suddenly that she had just taken
hold of his arm again. His skin was smooth and
warm. She wanted to run her thumb over the

tight bands of muscle, but she resisted the urge. It was only the second time in her life she'd had to fight hard against something she wanted, something she knew she shouldn't have— something that would be wrong.

He sat down and gently pried her fingers off his arm, then set her hands on her lap, away from him. He was going to tell her she would be fine if only she would lay her head down on the pillow and draw up the covers. That's what her mother always used to say when Adele had had nightmares as a child.

But he didn't say that. "What was the dream?" he asked.

She wet her lips. "I dreamed he came back."

"Your kidnapper?"

"Yes. He took me out of my bed, and since that night, I haven't been able to sleep."

"He won't be coming back," Damien said. "You can be sure of that."

Looking down at her hands on her lap, she nodded. "I know. At least my mind knows it, but when I dream, it feels real. How will I ever feel safe enough to fall asleep again?"

He covered her hands with his own. "You've been through an ordeal, and it's only natural to feel the way you do, but it will pass. Your peace of mind will return a little more each day, every time you wake up safe in your bed."

"How long do you think it will take?"

"It's hard to say, Adele."

Somehow, they'd fallen into the habit of using each other's Christian names. It wasn't proper, she knew, but she couldn't imagine it the proper way.

"But I'm exhausted," she said, and her voice broke.

Damien's large, warm hand came up to rest on her cheek. Before she could stop herself, she covered it with her own, reveling in the feel of his soft touch upon her skin, and exploring the strong bones of his hand.

She felt safe *now*, even though her heart was racing and she was, in many ways, flirting with another kind of danger altogether. She was playing temptress with a rugged, wild, hot-blooded man who took great pleasure in the seduction of women.

It was like nothing she'd ever done before. Adele's sisters would dip into these uncharted waters, not she. *She* was sensible Adele Wilson, who never misbehaved.

Feeling as if she were floating in someone else's body—a reckless adventurer, perhaps?—she closed her eyes, while he stroked her cheek with his thumb and stirred hungry, unfamiliar longings inside her body. She had no idea where they would lead her.

She didn't want him to stop, but she knew, any second now, he would. Because this was wrong. Wrong, wrong, wrong, and they both knew it.

But oh, how good it felt, and how painfully deprived she would feel when he stopped.

Quickly, he slid his hand out from under hers. "Adele, don't."

It was a clear warning.

"I'm sorry," she replied, feeling as if a glass of water had been splashed in her face. She shouldn't have clutched at his hand like a woman starving for affection. He had meant to offer her comfort and understanding, and she'd tried to take more.

She forced herself to think of Harold. She was engaged to Harold. She wanted to marry Harold.

"I'm just upset," she said. "That's all. And scared."

"You need to sleep." He said it as if it were an explanation for her behavior just now.

She knew he was about to leave—which was of course what he had to do. He couldn't stay here with her all night.

He continued to stare at her as if he were struggling with what to do, then he laid a hand on her upper arm. "Try to get some rest. No one is going to harm you tonight."

Anxiety pooled in her belly. "You're not going to stay?"

"You know I can't do that."

She had the distinct feeling again that there was more to his refusal than simple propriety. It was the unspoken reason again . . .

"You'll be fine," he said, standing. "I'll be right down the hall, sleeping with one eye open."

She nodded because she had to, but her hands were still shaky.

He walked to the door and took hold of the knob to close it behind him, but the knob fell off. He tried to move the door. One of the hinges dropped to the floor with a noisy clang.

Adele sat up on her heels. "It won't close?"

"No."

Practicalities sank in. "I can't sleep here without a lock on the door."

He glanced up at her briefly. He was not pleased. He returned his attention to the broken door, swinging it to and fro, then shook his head. "It'll need a new hinge."

"A new hinge?"

His voice was low and controlled. "You can have my room."

"But—"

"No buts. Come." From across the room, he held out a hand to her.

She knew she had no choice but to comply, and was reminded of the way she had felt when she'd first seen him at the kidnapper's cottage. He was not to be reckoned with that day, and he was not to be reckoned with now. He was tense and in no mood to argue with her, though she wasn't exactly sure why. She wasn't sure of anything where he was concerned.

Regardless, she climbed out of bed barefoot, and crossed to him. With his hand at the small of her back, he escorted her down the hall to his room. He opened the door for her, and she slowly walked in and looked around.

This was a man's bedchamber—the place where Lord Alcester dressed and shaved. It smelled of sleep.

Her gaze drifted to the bed, where the sheets

and covers were tangled together and spilling over the side, onto the floor. There was an indentation in the pillow. His clothes were tossed over a chair in the corner. There was an empty brandy glass on the bedside table. She could see the remaining traces of amber liquid in the bottom.

She looked back at the unmade bed again. A tingling thrill quivered through her. She was going to lie in that bed and put her face on the pillow where he had just been sleeping.

"You'll be safe," he said, moving past her to pull the blankets up and tidy the bed. "The lock on the door works, and so does the one on the window. There's no one under the bed." He checked, just to be sure. "And I'll be listening."

He moved to the chair and picked up the shirt he'd worn at supper, and quickly shrugged into it. He relaxed a little after he did that, though he still seemed tense and a trifle impatient with her.

"Thank you," she said, not wanting him to think she didn't appreciate everything he was doing for her. But still, she wished he did not have to leave.

He crossed to the door and paused there a moment. "You'll be fine here, Adele. I promise."

Without another word, he walked out and left her alone.

She stood motionless in the center of the room, listening to the sound of his footsteps tapping down the hall. A second later, everything was quiet.

She crossed to the door and turned the key in the lock. Struggling to remind herself that

Damien was still nearby, she moved to the bed and pulled the covers back. She gazed down at the white sheets with the moonlight spreading upon them—wrinkled and billowy in places from having been slept on this very night. She swallowed hard and climbed in, pulling the heavy blankets up over herself and resting her arms on top of them.

There was still warmth from his body down where her legs were. She lay flat on her back and stared at the ceiling for a moment, then turned onto her side and closed her eyes. Damien's musky, masculine scent permeated her consciousness and swirled through her senses.

She pressed her face into the soft feather pillow and breathed deeply, filling her lungs until she could hold no more of him, then she did it again and again and again, squeezing the pillow until she felt satisfied, and fell asleep.

But only for a little while. The rest of the night was a stressful affair filled with many swift, frightful awakenings.

Chapter 5

Adele descended the stairs the next morning, her eyes burning from lack of sleep. She went to the dining room. Lord Alcester rose from the table they'd shared the night before and crossed the room to greet her.

She remembered with a shocking, tingling quiver how he had looked the night before in her bedchamber—surreal, like a god in the moonlight. Powerful and beautiful.

He looked beautiful again this morning, she thought with another disturbing shiver of anticipation. He wore the same shirt, waistcoat, tight riding breeches, and black boots as he'd worn every other day, but today Adele was more aware of his size and strength. She had seen it for herself last night.

"Good morning, Miss Wilson," he said coolly, with a slight bow.

Adele couldn't deny her disappointment at seeing him return to his formal manner and call her "Miss Wilson." But she supposed it was best.

He escorted her to their table. As soon as they sat down, he said, "Did you sleep at all?"

"Not much."

His chest rose and fell with a deep intake of breath, as if he felt that he had failed somehow. "You will no doubt be glad to join your mother, and arrive at Osulton Manor. There was a telegram from her this morning." He reached into his breast pocket and handed it across the table to her. She read it quickly:

> *Overjoyed to hear you are safe stop*
> *Will celebrate soon stop*
> *Love Mother stop*

Adele's heart relaxed a little as she read the words. It was a small connection with reality— a reminder of her real life. She read the telegram two more times, then looked up to see Damien's concerned eyes staring intently at her, his brows drawn together. His dark gaze held her captive, and her pulse fluttered alarmingly.

"What is it?" she asked.

"I'm sorry if I was short with you last night. It was inexcusable of me."

The gentleness in his voice as he delivered such a sincere, honest apology shocked her. She had to struggle to come up with a reply.

"You weren't short with me. You were helpful."

"You're being polite. The fact is, I shouldn't have left you alone when you were distraught. I should have listened to you when you told me you couldn't sleep. Last night you called me your protector, and I was hardly that when I walked out on you like an irritable dog."

She inclined her head curiously, and spoke without thinking. "Why *were* you irritable, Damien? Did I do something wrong?"

He stared at her across the table.

She didn't know why she had asked him that question, with such an intentionally innocent tone of voice, as if she had no awareness of the fact that there could be something inappropriate simmering between them—which was why she suspected he had been bad-tempered.

She was putting him on the spot, wanting to know if the attraction she had been sensing was real, or if it was all in her mind. She was challenging him to acknowledge it.

The server arrived and poured coffee. Damien leaned back in his chair, looking slightly relieved to have been spared answering the question.

As soon as the server was gone, however, the question continued to dangle in the air between them. It could not go completely unanswered. That in itself would have revealed something was amiss.

Damien's gaze swept restlessly around the room, and she sensed he was displeased with her again.

"You did nothing wrong," he finally said. "I was the one who behaved badly. I was tired. Like you, I haven't slept much the past few days, and I apologize for my unforgivable irritability."

Adele nodded to thank him for his reply, then she picked up her coffee cup and took a sip. Even if he did feel an attraction, she thought, he would never acknowledge it. He, too, was loyal to Harold, and she at least respected him for *that*. Yes. If he were not, she would think him the worst human being in the world, and despite what she knew about his reputation, she did not think *that* of him. He had not tried to seduce her. He had been nothing but a gentleman since they'd met.

Though she herself had not always had the heart and mind of a lady. A part of her wanted something very wicked, and she wasn't sure she would have the strength this time to put the candy back if she went so far as to actually take it in her hand.

Throughout the whole of the day, the coach lumbered jerkily over moors and dales and hilly green pastures, stopping around noon to change horses in a quaint village inn, where they had a bite to eat.

Adele had dozed off a few times in the coach, but the slightest bump or jostle awakened her with a start, and each time it would take a good ten minutes for her heart to settle down again. So when they stopped again, late in the afternoon, Adele had a glass of wine, hoping it would help her sleep. She filled Damien's flask with a little extra to take with her as well.

It was early evening when the creaky vehicle rumbled into another small village and pulled up in front of an inn much smaller than the one the night before. Adele should have been hungry, but she didn't feel well enough to eat. Her stomach was rolling from the long drive, and consequently, she felt nauseated and had very little appetite. None in fact. But she certainly did feel sleepy from the wine.

As soon as they slowed to a stop, Damien opened the door of the coach and peered inside. "We've arrived. How are you?"

She took his hand and stepped out onto the dusty lane. "As well as can be expected. I slept a little along the way, though it was rather bumpy this afternoon. Did it rain? I seem to remember raindrops pattering away on the rooftop, though I don't know when that was."

Still holding her hand, he stopped in the street. "No, it didn't rain." His eyes narrowed as he stared down at her and lowered his voice. "Are you feeling all right?"

"I feel fine."

He hesitated, then took a step closer and leaned down to her ear. He was so tall, so much of a man, she shuddered at the overwhelming nearness of him. She found herself looking closely at the texture of his coat collar, and the details of the seam at his broad shoulder. She loved the way his thick black hair curled in a large wave at his neck.

She was almost close enough to touch her lips to that neck. She imagined how it would taste. Salty perhaps.

"Your speech was slurred just now, Adele."

She felt the heat of his breath in her ear, and it sent the most delightful array of gooseflesh down her entire left side. She closed her eyes and imagined what it would feel like to wrap her arms around his neck and just dangle.

"Slurred?" she asked, remembering clumsily that he had just tried to tell her something.

"Yes. If one didn't know better, one might think you were intoxicated."

She felt her brows lift in surprise. "Good heavens! Intoxicated! I only had a little wine. Two glasses at most." Though she felt strangely giddy.

He held a finger up to his lips and took a full step closer—*yes, closer*—crowding her in the most exhilarating way. Their bodies almost touched. It was shocking and breathtaking and undeniably wonderful. She could smell the faint scent of his cologne.

"Shh," he whispered. "I know you had only a little to drink. I am of the opinion, however, that, my dear, you are suffering from an acute lack of sleep, which has given the wine an extra kick."

My dear. That was all she heard.

The next thing she knew, she was blinking up at him, feeling dim-witted and completely unable to remember what he had said after *My dear*.

My dear. His voice was like sweet syrup. Sweet and yummy. She would like to lick it.

He glanced over her head, up and down the street. "You need a bed, Adele, and it is imperative that you close your eyes when you get there."

She felt dazed, looking up at him. The strong line of his jaw was so lovely. Lovely, lovely, lovely. He would make a handsome statue on the chest of drawers in her room in Newport.

Ahhh, Newport. How she missed the gulls and the smell of the sea.

"It smells funny here," she said, wrinkling her nose. "Like sheep."

She felt nauseated again. And dizzy. Still a little giddy, too.

Suddenly, Damien's arm moved around her waist, and then she was floating toward the front door of the inn. No, not floating. She was being carried there. By a handsome black knight in not-so-shiny armor.

He smelled like the outdoors. Fresh and clean and manly—though there was a vague aroma of horse mixed in with the cologne she'd smelled earlier. Some horses were very manly. Yes. He was a stallion.

No, he was a knight. A stallionish knight with big, sturdy hooves.

She sighed and rested her face against the rough wool of his black coat, feeling it scratch her cheek. Her eyes were closed now. She sighed most happily. Wasn't life wonderful? *Yes, yes it was* . . .

Carrying Harold's snoozing, deadweight fiancée in his arms, Damien followed the innkeeper up the stairs to her room on the second floor. She was mumbling something about her sister now, asking why she had wanted the blue bowl, when the white one was closer.

Damien carried her into the bedchamber and laid her down gently on the bed, careful not to wake her. He sat down beside her and moved the fallen locks of hair away from her face. She moaned softly.

"She hasn't slept in four days," he told the innkeeper. "She's been ill." It was the only explanation he could come up with, as he didn't want to give away the details of their situation.

"Is she all right now?" the plump little man asked.

"Yes, she just needs to sleep."

He gazed down at her freckled face in the gray light of the afternoon. She smiled and moaned again and rolled over on the bed toward the wall. The sound of her throaty, feminine voice and the gentle curve of her hips beneath her skirts sent a wave of desire through Damien's tired, exhausted body.

He imagined for a moment what life would be like—what this moment would be like—if she belonged to him. If she did, he would lie down beside her and hold her, and he would stay with her all night until she woke up the next morning, feeling rested and more herself.

"Should I bring soup?" the innkeeper asked, startling Damien out of his thoughts, and thank God for that.

Damien stood. "Perhaps later, after she's had a

chance to sleep awhile." He reached for the wool blanket at the foot of the bed and covered her.

"She's your sister-in-law, you say?" the man asked.

Damien met his gaze squarely. "Yes."

The man inclined his head. "So I presume you'll be wanting another room?"

The man was perceptive. He was checking to see if some other arrangement might suit Damien better. Another arrangement certainly *would* suit him better, but he would hold tight to his integrity. Though it was squirming like a wet fish in his hands.

"Yes, another room would be most appreciated."

"My wife is preparing one now." He left the room and closed the door behind him with a quiet click.

Damien moved to stand over the bed where Adele lay sleeping, and let his gaze drift lazily over the exquisite, appealing length of her body. *Yes, if she were his . . .*

That very instant, something thumped in the next room—probably the innkeeper's wife making the bed—and Adele sat up. She gazed vacantly at Damien's face for a moment or two before she spoke.

"Did I sleep? Is it morning?"

He sat down beside her again. "No. You've been asleep for only five or six minutes."

"Five minutes?" Her voice revealed her utter disbelief. She was hopelessly discouraged. "Why can't I sleep?"

He ran his hand down her arm. "You need to relax and know that you're safe."

"I *want* to know it. When I'm awake, I know he's not coming back, but when I go to sleep . . ." She took hold of Damien's lapel between two fingers.

She was touching him. Touching his clothes . . .

"Please stay here tonight," she said. "No one will ever know. I won't tell. This is the last night of our travels, and tomorrow I'll be with my mother and sisters. Everything will be normal then. But I can't meet Harold looking and feeling the way I do. *I can't.*"

She gazed up at him with bloodshot, puffy, pleading eyes, and his blood burned like fire through his veins. It was all he could do to keep from pulling her close and pressing his lips to hers.

For a long moment, he gazed at her in the fading light of the day while he fought to subdue his desires. God, he wanted to make love to her. He wanted to kiss the warm, supple flesh of her body and hold her naked in his arms. He wanted to bury himself deep into the heat between her thighs.

There it was. In plain terms.

He squeezed his eyes shut and pressed the heel of his hand to his forehead. He thought of Harold. Then he thought of his mother, who had betrayed his father. His father had died. His mother had died, too. So much of what had happened that day had been Damien's fault. He had been the one to tattle on his mother. He'd had no tact; he was only nine. His father had not taken the news well. The situation had exploded.

Then he thought of Harold again, who trusted him absolutely. Harold, who, for the first time in his life, had not only fallen in love with a woman, but had found the courage to propose to her. And he'd asked for Damien's help to bring her home.

No. There would never be *anything* between Damien and Adele. *Never.* She belonged to Harold. She was to become Damien's cousin by marriage. He could not feel what he was feeling. He could not devastate Harold. He could not. He had to bury this.

"Please, Damien," she said. "All I need is one good night's sleep, then I'll be myself again. You need only spend one night in a chair, with a promise that you won't leave. A good night's sleep will cure me, I'm sure of it. I just can't think straight now. My eyes hurt, and I can't seem to differentiate between what's real and what's a dream."

"Neither can I," he whispered, feeling more than a little exhausted himself. It had been a long few days—first with the disturbing news of the kidnapping from Harold, then with his own quest to find Adele and bring her home safe to his cousin.

His fight was gone. He couldn't do it anymore. He closed his eyes, tipping his head forward to rest upon hers. He still held both her hands in his. They were warm and clammy.

"Please just stay in the room while I sleep,"

she whispered, and he reveled in the feel of her wine-scented breath on his face.

He couldn't argue anymore. Maybe it was exhaustion. Maybe it was adoration. Who would ever know?

But what did it matter *why* he couldn't argue? All that mattered was that if he slept in the chair in the corner, everything would return to normal tomorrow. Adele would remember her life and become the woman Harold had proposed to. She would be ready to go home to him. Damien would deliver his cousin's fiancée to him as he had promised. Then he'd be on his way.

He shook his head at the verdict that was about to cross his lips. "All right, I'll sleep in the chair."

"Do you promise? I must have your word. I must be able to trust it." There was force in her voice. Grit and resolve. She would not be lied to.

"I promise."

She immediately fell back onto the pillows, but continued to hold his hand. "Thank you, Damien. I'll make it up to you somehow. Honest, I will."

Then she closed her eyes and fell asleep almost instantly, leaving him tense and worried, and wondering how he was going to resist collecting on that promise. Especially in the hours to come.

Chapter 6

The innkeeper knocked on the door a short time later, and delivered a key to Damien for the other room, which had been prepared for him. Damien thanked him, and asked that both he and his wife refrain from knocking on this door again through the night, as his sister-in-law was struggling to sleep and could not under any circumstances be disturbed. They would not likely be taking any supper.

The innkeeper gave a sympathetic nod toward the bed. "You have my word, sir. I hope she'll feel better in the morning."

The helpful, discreet man walked out and closed the door behind him.

Damien spent the next fifteen minutes sitting in the blue chintz chair, grappling over his

promise to stay and contemplating the worst
temptation of his life: he desired his cousin's fiancée. He couldn't stop thinking of her; he
wanted to lie with her, to hold her. He wanted
her wholly and completely, in every way a man
could want a woman, even while he knew it
would betray the cousin whom he had always
felt a need to protect.

Damien sat forward and covered his face
with his hands. He despised himself. He knew
he had to resist and bury this madness, but he
had not yet done so.

Just then, Adele woke again and sat up. Instinct pulled him out of his chair, and the next
thing he knew, he was sitting on the bed again,
wondering how the hell he had gotten across
the room so fast before his brain had had any
say in the matter.

"Go back to sleep," he whispered, hoping,
praying that she would.

"Is it morning yet?" she asked. Her eyes
looked as if someone had poured salt into them.

"No. It's been only fifteen minutes since the
last time you woke."

She rubbed her eyes. "You've been here the
whole time?"

"Yes."

She tugged at the collar of her dress, buttoned
tight around her neck. "The bed is spinning. And
I'm not comfortable. I need to get out of this."

Jesus. Perhaps this was some kind of test,
Damien thought. If it was, he would pass it. He
would.

"What do you need?" he asked.

She glanced around, looking almost confused, as if she didn't know where she was. "Nothing. I just need to take this off." She began to unbutton her bodice.

"Adele," he whispered quickly, curling his hand around hers to stop her. He heard the warning in his voice. "*Wait*."

Her bloodshot eyes met his, and her forehead crinkled with frustration over her fatigue. *Wait for what?* he asked himself, realizing he'd needed her to stop only because he wasn't ready. Wasn't ready for this to be harder than it already was. He took a second to steel himself. He told himself she probably wouldn't remember this. She was half asleep, and the wine was certainly having an effect.

"How can I help you?" he asked, because no matter how difficult this was for him, she needed his help and he would give it to her, because he wanted her to sleep, and sleep well, so things would be normal again.

"Help me unbutton this."

He clenched his jaw. *Unbutton it.*

He hesitated, then took a deep, slow breath. He would focus on the task, nothing else. Carefully, he reached down and put his fingers on the tiny covered button under her chin, and one by one, with his heart pounding like a steel mallet in his chest, he unfastened them.

"You're good at taking care of people," she said sleepily. "You're very gentle."

He said nothing. The bodice fell open in

front, and he caught a glimpse of white under-garments beneath. He found himself compar-ing this moment to all the other moments in his life when he had gazed upon a woman's under-garments. There had been many times, but he had never felt like this.

"Would you be so kind as to look away?" Adele asked, her voice weak and listless as she began to shrug out of the bodice, hardly giving him a chance to react.

He stood and went to the window, looking out at the darkening sky. He was completely worn out. He would be glad when night fell. Then he wouldn't be able to see her. He would go to sleep himself, then he would wake up and it would be morning and he would take her di-rectly to Harold.

He heard the sound of clothes rustling and the bed creaking. "I'm finished," she said. He turned, and she was under the covers, lying on her back.

Damien returned to the chair. He sat for about an hour, trying to fall asleep, but couldn't. All he could do was watch Adele in the dim light and imagine with a deep, physical yearn-ing what it would be like to lay beside her.

A short time later he heard footsteps in the hall. He stood up and opened the door. The innkeeper's wife was passing by.

"Pardon me," he said. "Would you send up a glass of brandy?"

"Certainly," she replied with a polite smile.

Five minutes later, she delivered a tray with two glasses and a full bottle. He would only need one glass, of course. But he was very grateful for the full bottle.

Chapter 7

S omewhere low, in the cavernous, darkest depths of night, Damien became drowsily aware of a soft feather of a kiss on his cheek. Still half absorbed in what felt like a hazy dream, he didn't fight to open his eyes. His consciousness crouched low in the pitch black . . .

The seasoned lover in him responded with a primitive, highly sexed instinct. He turned his head on the pillow, meeting the sweet, teasing kiss with his mouth. It was only then, as his hand came up to brush the long, curly hair away from her face, that he moved fully from sleep to wakefulness, and realized whose lips these were and whose bed this was. His eyes opened. Then he remembered. He had sat down and stretched out beside Adele not long ago. He had just wanted to be comfortable for a minute or two . . .

Gracious lover that he was, he promptly brought the kiss to a graceful and polite finish before he spoke. "Adele," he whispered firmly, pushing her back and inching away from her while he struggled to squeeze a tight fist around the neck of his desires. He abruptly leaned up on one elbow. "Wake up."

But as he said the words, the selfish being that lived in his nether regions was raising a disapproving eyebrow at his all too righteous sacrifice.

"I'm awake," she replied.

He stared down at her for moment. "You were kissing me."

She lay very still. "I . . . I'm sorry. I just wanted to thank you."

For a man who had shared beds with many interesting and experienced women, he found himself staggered, and most assuredly out of his usual range. He was staring down at complete, absolute innocence—virginal and naive beyond any imagining. And so beautiful, she knocked the wind right out of his lungs.

He gazed off to the side and raked a hand through his hair, feeling almost shaky, and still problematically aroused. "I suppose I was kissing *you*. I don't know." He shut his eyes.

Her warm hand cupped his cheek again, and she turned his face toward her. "It doesn't matter. Please, just lie down. Stay. I slept better with you here."

He knew he should get up and return to the

chair on the other side of the room, but something prevented him from doing it. It was the selfish being in his nether regions—the part of him that wanted her, no matter what the cost, no matter who got hurt. He just couldn't get up and walk away. Not now. His body wouldn't let him.

He put his arm around Adele, and she snuggled closer to him. They lay there for a moment in the silence, while a voice in his head kept saying over and over, *You shouldn't be doing this.*

Damien was intensely aware of her slender hand resting upon his chest, as she moved a finger back and forth over the rough wool of his waistcoat. Was she experimenting? Was she curious? Or did she honestly have no idea how dangerous this was?

Damien clenched his jaw. Adele lightly nuzzled her nose over his cheek. He didn't move. The clock seemed to stop ticking, and instead his body was pounding in its place.

For a moment more, he stared at the ceiling in the darkness, then the lover in him somehow gained a foothold. All at once, physical response dominated thought, and he turned his head to the side again. His blood quickened, and the being in his nether regions smiled like a red devil. Before he had a chance to consider right and wrong, he was rising up and rolling on top of her in one smooth, fleeting blur of movement and consciousness.

She wrapped her arms around his shoulders and held him tight, though she didn't know enough, thank God, to wrap her legs around him.

He devoured her soft lips; her enthralling, silky tongue; and her deep, wet mouth. He became lost in darkness and sensation, out of control with a burning need to possess her, and completely oblivious to the tenets of obligation and loyalty.

He pulled her closer, more snugly to his feverish, roused body, while inside his bones, from the depths of his memory and his childhood, he sensed disaster in the offing. He dragged his lips from hers. He rested his head on the pillow over her shoulder. "God, help me," he whispered.

"You're so heavy, Damien," she said, ignoring his plea, or perhaps just not understanding it. "No one could take me when I'm under you like this."

"*I* could take you."

"But I'm not afraid of you."

"You should be."

They both went still.

"I know this is wrong," she said shakily, "but I can't stop myself."

"I'm having a similar problem." He lay quiet and still for a long, agonizing moment. "You're in bed with me, Adele, and I'm not made of stone." He buried his face into the hair at her neck. "Push me off."

She made no move. She lay beneath him, clutching on to him. "Not yet."

He lay still, too. For another long moment.

Then he found himself bending to the whim of his sexual needs again, inhabiting a place where his principles lost contact with the workings of his body, and he gently thrust his hips through the clothing that served as a barrier between them.

Once. Very slowly . . .

Then again. Slowly. Gently. Long and gradually.

If this were real sex and there were no trousers binding him, no shift protecting her virtues, he would be deep, deep inside her.

"Am I hurting you?" he whispered. "Your wound?"

"Only a little. I don't care."

He was breathing hard now. Quite unable to stop himself, he slid his hand down to her knee and up under the flimsy cotton fabric of her shift, up the outside of her thigh to her bare, fleshy hip. She felt like heaven—soft and warm and succulent.

With his face still buried at her neck, and his eyes squeezed shut amid the battle that was raging inside him, he stroked her soft skin. How easy it would be to slide his hand around to the front, into the damp depths between her thighs, and discover for himself whether she was a virgin or not after the kidnapping. He could answer the question now. Set her mind at ease.

If, on the other hand, she *wasn't* a virgin . . .

A host of possibilities—both glorious and horrendous—loomed wickedly in his brain. What if he made love to her, and they let people presume it had been the kidnapper? *God*. No. He couldn't believe he was even contemplating such a thing. What was this woman doing to him?

Still breathing hard, he turned his face away from her on the pillow again. He let out a breath. His mind fought hard against his body, now trembling with a fierce need. She felt so good, so supple and inviting beneath him.

He'd never wanted a woman like this before. Perhaps because he wasn't used to waiting and wanting. He only engaged in this sort of thing with women who were ready and willing. But no, it was more than that. It was deeper than that.

Adele's long legs began to slide apart on the bed beneath him, opening, making a cozy place for him between her thighs. She truly had no idea, not the faintest, of the peril she was placing herself in.

He knew, however. He also knew with a crushing wave of frustration that it was long past time to stop. "Don't do that, Adele. Don't spread your legs. Push me off. Now."

Her body tensed at the harsh tone that was now a command rather than a request, and a second later she obeyed. Her small hands moved to his chest, and with open palms, she pushed. He rolled off her onto his back.

"I'll stay in the bed so you can sleep," he said, his voice deep and husky, "but don't touch me again. Do you understand?"

She nodded. "Yes."

He turned his back on her. He was angry. Not at her. She'd been through an ordeal, and she just wanted to be held. She needed affection. Caring. He had taken advantage of that innocence and vulnerability. He had been very weak.

He was angry at the situation, at himself for letting this go too far. And he was angry with Harold for sitting idly back with his head in the clouds, while Damien saved the day as he always did. Harold should have saved it himself. *He* should have been Adele's hero. He had known how beautiful Adele was. He should not have expected Damien to be made of stone.

Damien closed his eyes and vowed to keep his back to her for the rest of the night, no matter how badly she needed to be held. After tomorrow, what Adele needed would be Harold's problem. Damien would have his own problems to deal with. He would have to forget about Adele, and he would have to live with the regret over his weakness and lack of honor tonight. Not unlike the adulterous mother he didn't care to remember.

Adele gradually became aware of the backs of her eyelids growing brighter, and felt her mind awakening, little by little, from the murky oblivion of a long, deep slumber. Conscious thoughts began to form. It wasn't dark anymore. It was morning. She had slept. But what a headache she had.

She opened her eyes and looked up at the white ceiling, remembering suddenly that she had kissed Damien somewhere in the depths of night, and he had lain on top of her in the bed.

Just the thought of it stirred her senses to the thrilling memory of his warmth and heavy weight, and the feel of his lips and tongue when he'd kissed her with an open mouth.

The thrill was crushed quickly, however, by a heavy, devastating awareness of what she had done, what she had wanted, and what she had let herself do. Thank God Damien had stopped things when he had.

Even so, she would never be the same again. She now understood more completely the true basis of attraction between men and women. She felt as if her eyes were now open to a whole new world—a world of men and their so-called charm. It was all about lips and hands and the sweet promise of physical pleasure.

She also understood Damien's famous allure, and the reason he was able to have any woman of his choosing. There was something seductive and special in his eyes, in his body, and quite frankly, in everything about him. Last night, he'd drawn her to him like a magnet, and she had been pulled in, much to her dismay. It was shocking to think she had lost all sense of right and wrong, and had not been able to find the strength to fight against a temptation.

She felt suddenly nervous and afraid, because she would never be the Adele she was yesterday. Or thought she was. What would her parents think if they knew what had happened last night? Could she blame it on the wine? No, it wasn't just that.

She glanced to her left. There was Damien.

Still. Her heart began to pound with uncertainty and apprehension. He was asleep on the bed beside her, lying on his back with his head turned in the other direction, still wearing the clothes he'd been wearing yesterday—the loose-fitting white shirt, black waistcoat and trousers, and boots.

Just then, he stirred. He inhaled deeply and turned his head toward her, then opened his eyes and looked directly into hers. They both lay there, just staring at each other. Adele didn't know what to say. Her stomach was rolling. She wanted to disappear.

Damien leaned up on one elbow and gazed down at her. There was a shadow of stubble on his face. He looked very much like the rugged warrior he had been when he'd rescued her at the cottage—disheveled, rough around the edges, virile. She tried to ignore the strange fluttering in her belly and the astonishing, overwhelming urge to touch his cheek as she had last night in the dark.

His gaze went from her eyes down to her lips, then back up to her eyes again. "Damien," she whispered, with no idea what she wanted to say. She just needed to say his name. She was confused. She felt the urge to cry.

He shook his head and whispered in return, "No, Adele, don't."

She fell silent. This was agonizing. He rose quickly from the bed. He faced the window and raked his fingers through his hair. Adele leaned up on both elbows. She watched him while he stood with his back to her, not ready to leave just yet.

He faced her squarely. "Adele . . ."

His dark brows drew together, and his voice lowered a notch. Adele fought to control her breathing. She didn't know what he was going to say to her. She couldn't bear this.

"Last night," he said, "I promised you discretion. I promised I would not tell anyone what happened between us. I am a man of my word, and I will honor that promise, as long as it is still what you want."

What was he getting at?

"Yes, it is," she replied, hearing the thunderous crash of reality in her ears. They were going home today. She would see Harold, her mother, her sister. Last night suddenly seemed like a delirious dream, now laden with regret—a dream they could not take back. She was so ashamed.

"Then I *will* have full responsibility for what happened," he said. "You are an innocent, I am not. I knew what I was doing, and from my perspective, I took advantage of you. You, therefore, should harbor no guilt."

Her eyebrows pulled together and she sat up. "You did not take advantage of me. You were the one who put a stop to what was happening. Remember? So neither should *you* harbor guilt. In fact, what happened between us was more my fault than yours. I have felt very alone the past few days, and I needed to be close to someone. I was scared and exhausted. That's all. You took care of me last night, Damien, because I wanted you to. So you may relax." She paused and sat back. "Although I thank you for the kind offer to take the blame."

He nodded reluctantly and turned to the window.

"Should we tell Harold?" she asked.

He whirled around. "No. Definitely not. Last night was a temporary madness. It should be forgotten."

A temporary madness. That's exactly what it had been, but for some reason that made no sense, it hurt to hear him call it that. "But you and he are close," Adele said. "Can you live with a secret between you? Because I'm not sure I can, not if I am to be his wife."

"You would hurt him to ease your own guilt?"

She swallowed uncomfortably. "I . . . didn't think of it that way."

"Well, that's the way it is. Believe me. I've told you before that I am protective of Harold, and I don't want to see him hurt because of *my* weakness. I will live with the guilt. Besides, this is not real life. Once we're back at Osulton, things will be different, and I'm sure we will both deeply regret our indiscretion here."

She nodded. "All right."

"And it would be best for everyone," he continued, "if both you and I never spoke of this to each other again, not even privately. Especially privately. Such a rapport between us would not only be inappropriate, it would be . . ." He paused. "It would be dangerous. I'm a dangerous man, Adele. You think you're safe with me, but you're not. I'm not like Harold. He should not have sent me."

She stared at him, speechless. "No, he was right to send you. I'm alive, aren't I? And we're almost home."

He walked to the door, shaking his head. "I'll return to my room first, then arrange for breakfast to be sent up to you. I'll see you downstairs in an hour." He paused in the doorway. "I'll deliver you to your mother today, then you'll be reunited with Harold a few hours later. I'll never mention any of this again, Adele. You have my word. We'll forget it ever happened."

He walked out and closed the door behind him.

BOOK TWO

The Reckoning

Chapter 8

The Osulton coach, with an impressive liveried driver at the reins, rolled swiftly and smoothly across the lush, green English countryside behind a thunderous team of galloping grays.

Inside, Adele sat quietly with her mother, Beatrice, her sister Clara, and baby Anne, while a second coach was coming later with their maids, their luggage, and Anne's nurse.

Adele had met her mother two hours ago at a village inn. As soon as Damien had dropped Adele off in the reception room and had been assured that her mother was indeed in the building, he had taken his leave without waiting to be introduced, and had ridden off in another direction.

Adele had been glad to see him go, very glad and very relieved. Yet at the same time, she had been mystified by the frustrating well of misery that curled like a snake around her gladness and relief.

She should *not* be mourning their parting, she told herself for the umpteenth time as the coach passed through the village just north of Osulton Manor. She was promised to *Harold*, and besides, Damien was not the kind of man she would ever want to marry. Yes, he had been her hero during their journey together, but in real life, he was in love with his mistress and was known to be irresponsible. She had to keep her head on straight about what had happened between them, and accept what he said as true: it had been a temporary madness.

So she anticipated her approach to the manor with the sensible hope that she was at last returning to the real world and the familiarity of her life. The adventure, thank heavens, was over.

Upon peering out the window, however, she discovered most disagreeably that one's expectations could often be lost in the wind. As the carriage passed through the massive stone gateway—which, emblazoned with a dramatic coat of arms, resembled the Arch of Constantine in Rome—she recalled telling Clara that she did not crave adventure. She only wanted to marry the man who had proposed to her, and move forward through life as she had intended.

Now she was facing another astonishment. This place—this massive country estate—was nothing like what she had expected or imagined. She had thought she would be living in an ivy-covered cottage in the English countryside, in the Tudor style perhaps, because Harold, as it were, had described his home as an "old and quaint country house."

Quaint? Perhaps Harold needed a new dictionary.

Osulton Manor was no quaint country house. It was a great, white palace, baroque in style, with large flanking octagonal turrets and a spectacular center skyline of smaller cupolas and domes. It stood on top of a high hill, surrounded by wrought iron fences and ancient English oaks that watched over the property like great lords themselves.

It was a palace fit for kings and queens, and Adele would be mistress of it all. She felt an unexpected tightening in her chest, as if this entire continent were pressing down upon her. A strict manner of behavior beyond her years and experience would be expected of her. How in the world would she learn all that she needed to learn to run a household on a scale such as this?

She pulled her gaze from the window and stared blankly down at the floor of the coach. Harold had not prepared her for this. He had made it sound like nothing. "You're very charming," he had said. "And that's all it takes, really."

She sincerely doubted it.

Then there was the matter of her virginity. She had not forgotten about that. Every so of-

ten, the fear hit her like a snowball in the face.
She hoped it would not be an issue.

They crossed a bridge over a rectangular pond
that reflected the house and trees, then rolled to
a stop in front of a central rotunda, which served
as the formal entrance. Adele noticed the large
glass structure around the side of the house, and
surmised it was a conservatory. She imagined
what it would look like inside. It would be filled
with green leafy plants and flowers. She felt her
spirits lift slightly. She told herself there would
be other things to look forward to as well.
Damien had mentioned the fine stables and the
forest. Surely, she was just nervous.

"Here we are, girls," her mother whispered,
as if all the proud ancestral ghosts of Osulton
were listening from above. "Sit up straight,
now. Here they come."

"You're making her nervous, Mother," Clara
whispered, trying not to wake baby Anne.

"I'm fine," Adele replied, which, of course,
she was not.

People stood outside on the steps, waiting for
them. A footman wearing navy knee breeches,
ivory stockings, and shiny buckled shoes
opened the door and lowered the step, then
reached in to take Clara's hand. Their mother
was handed out next, and then Adele.

Adele peered out from under the wide brim
of her green, plumed hat, and searched over the
strange faces on the steps, all of them staring at
her. Evaluating her.

Then she saw Harold. *Ah*, familiar Harold.

She was back. Centered. Her fears and tensions drained away at last. She met his gaze and smiled. He smiled in return, with his usual exuberant enthusiasm.

That's what she had admired about him the first time she'd met him, she recalled. He always looked so pleased and eager to see her. He possessed the friendly excitability of a child, and he always made her feel at ease.

He stepped away from the rest and descended the stairs to greet her and her mother and sister. "Lady Rawdon, welcome. And Mrs. Wilson, it is indeed a pleasure to see you again." He turned toward Adele and spoke more slowly, with more care. "And of course, Miss Wilson. Adele, I should say." With a flourish, he raised an arm to display his home. "Welcome to Osulton Manor."

Adele smiled. "Thank you, Harold. I'm so glad to be here at last."

"Yes, yes, of course you are. Come, meet my family. *Your* family, before long, eh?"

She nodded and followed him up the stairs to where the others were waiting.

"Lady Rawdon," he said to Clara, "may I present my mother, Eustacia Scott, the Viscountess Osulton."

The two shook hands.

"Lady Rawdon," Eustacia said, "it is a pleasure indeed. And this must be baby Anne! What a darling!" She admired Clara's daughter.

"And Mother," he continued, "may I present Beatrice Wilson, and her daughter, my betrothed, Adele Wilson."

The viscountess—a plump woman with curly red hair like her son—stepped forward, and displaying her good breeding, offered her hand to Adele's mother first. Adele paid careful attention to this English manner of introductions, for it was something she would be required to understand fully. Rank meant everything, which was why Clara had been attended to first, before their mother.

Eustacia shook her mother's hand. "Welcome to our home, Mrs. Wilson."

She clasped Adele's hand last, but held on to it for a bit longer. "My dear," she said, "I have waited too long to make your acquaintance. We are most pleased to welcome you into our family."

Adele couldn't have predicted the relief she would feel upon meeting her future mother-in-law. Previous to this moment, she had recalled with more than a little anxiety the sufferings of both her older sisters, Clara and Sophia, who had been forced to contend with women who despised Americans and had not approved of their sons' marriages. Sophia had in time won the respect and love of her mother-in-law, the dowager duchess, while Clara had never been able to do so. Adele, it seemed, would not have to face that challenge.

"Thank you, Lady Osulton. I'm pleased to meet you, too."

"You are going to be my daughter-in-law, so you must call me Eustacia!" she said, with the same jolly enthusiasm that characterized her son. "Now come and meet Harold's sister."

Clara and her mother were dealt the honors first, of course, then Adele was introduced. "This is Violet," Eustacia said.

Adele shook hands with the young woman. Violet was as dark as night, resembling a certain other member of the family.

"Now let us go inside and get you settled," Eustacia said.

Adele felt as if she were being carried away on a huge wave. She walked into the house with the others, and stopped in the center of the round entrance hall. All along the interior pale, stone walls of the great rotunda stood classical busts and statues of Greek and Roman gods and emperors. Over her head was a frescoed ceiling—the top of the dome depicting a man atop a black horse, holding a spear over his head.

Adele gazed in awe at the bright colors and the graceful, sweeping lines. There was movement in the artistry. The fact that she could almost hear the thunderous clatter of hooves and the victorious battle cry of the great warrior stirred her senses.

Harold moved to stand beside her. "It's the first Viscount Osulton," he said, "victorious in battle. He was awarded his title and this house in 1715 by King George I. Just think, America wasn't even a country then."

Adele, who felt suitably low to the ground at that moment, smiled warmly at her fiancé. "I'll look forward to seeing the rest of the house, Harold. Perhaps you can tell me more about its history."

"You will learn every detail, my dear, as you should. But there is plenty of time for that. Now, we must see you all to your rooms, so you will have enough time to dress for dinner. We have invited a few other guests, you see, to celebrate your arrival. Some of the local squires. The Earl of Whitby is also here—who is a friend, I believe, to your brother-in-law the Duke of Wentworth," he said, referring to Sophia's husband. "My cousin Damien, Baron Alcester, will be dining with us as well."

At the mention of Damien's name, Adele stiffened. She had known that in order to avoid a scandal, they were all to act as if nothing out of the ordinary had occurred over the past few days. All members of the family had been informed of that. Her familiarity with him was not to be mentioned. Adele was to meet him as if for the first time.

She had not expected it to be tonight. She had thought he would stay away. She had thought she would have time to grapple with her desires.

Harold gestured toward the grand staircase, framed at the bottom by two massive, fluted columns. "I am sure you will approve of your accommodations, ladies. They are—may I be so bold as to say?—fit for queens. You shall have everything at your disposal as you prepare for this evening, which will be, I assure you, most exhilarating."

Adele made her way soberly to the stairs. If Damien was to be in the drawing room tonight, exhilaration was something she would prefer to avoid.

Chapter 9

It was late afternoon when Damien finally emerged from his rooms. He had bathed and felt clean at last after far too many days spent sleeping in his clothes. He went immediately to see his grandmother.

As soon as he pushed through the door, she clapped her hands together and wheeled herself away from the table where she had been reading the newspaper, to meet him halfway across the room. "At last! Give me a kiss, you devil."

Damien clasped her frail, trembling hands in his, and bent forward to kiss her on the cheek. He straightened, then tipped his head at her. "A new perfume, Grandmama?"

"Why, yes . . ." She fiddled alluringly with a

tendril of snowy white hair that had fallen out of her chignon. "What do you think?"

"It's wonderful on you, but you've always had exquisite taste. I hope you realize you'll have to fight off the gentlemen this evening."

She slapped his hand. "Oh, you naughty flirt. Come and tell me about London. Are you still tangled up with that actress?"

His grandmother—who knew nothing of the kidnapping and thought he'd been in London all this time—wheeled herself back to the table.

Damien seated himself across from her, stretching one long leg out in front of him in a lazy sprawl. "Yes, and by God, she has talent."

His grandmother smirked. "You are a wicked scoundrel, Damien. Just like your grandfather. Until he met me, of course."

He smiled affectionately at her.

"So tell me, what do you know about this heiress Harold has brought over from America? I told him not to go, you know. I told him he'd be purchased like a stud at market."

"And he most definitely was. For a very good price, I might add."

She clicked her tongue at him. He grinned and sat forward.

"Have you met her?" his grandmother asked.

Damien hesitated. "Yes." He sat back again.

"I heard the gel's father wants to fund one of his experiments. Is it true?"

"I believe so."

"Go into business together!"

Damien smiled and raised his eyebrows.

She leaned forward and rested an elbow on the table. "What about *you*, dear boy? Isn't it time you found a wife, too? Essence House has been empty too long. I understand Harold's American gel is related by marriage to the Duke of Wentworth. He has a sister, does he not? Lady Lily, I believe? A pretty little dark-haired cupcake?"

"I do like cupcakes."

"I'm quite aware of that, young man." She leaned back again, gazing into Damien's eyes with scrutiny. "From what I hear, this particular cupcake has exceptionally rich frosting. The duke is a wealthy man. Surely, you must be considering such a practical quality in a young woman. Times have been difficult lately, have they not?"

Damien stood and walked to the window. "Yes, they have."

"It would be a very advantageous match."

Damien sighed. "I'm sure the duke would be immensely pleased to marry his sister off to an impoverished rake."

She grinned at him. "If she has hot blood in her veins, she would probably make her brother's life miserable if he didn't agree to it. You have that effect on women, my boy, and don't pretend you don't know it. You could have any woman you wanted if you set your mind to it."

Hands clasped behind his back, he continued to gaze out the window. "Not *any* woman, Grandmama."

She was quiet for a moment, then her eyes turned serious. "Promise me you'll *try* this Season, Damien. I know you too well. These eyes may be old, but they can still see when you are troubled. I know the desperate state of your finances, and I've known it for some time now."

With a sigh of resignation, he turned away from the window to face her. "Yes." Though there was so much more to it than just that.

"I also know how you feel about marrying for money or position, and that cynicism has held you back."

He merely nodded.

"Please, *promise* me," she said. "You mustn't continue to let the deaths of your parents stop *you* from living. You deserve happiness. You were just a boy when they died. It was not your fault."

Damien gazed down at his grandmother, looking so much older than she had the last time he'd seen her, only a few weeks earlier.

He bent forward to kiss her on the cheek again, taking her hand in his and kissing it as well. "I promise, I will try," he said with genuine sincerity, because he loved his grandmother very much, and he knew she was right.

Then he went to dress for dinner.

The green Huntington Room, where Adele was staying, overlooked the east garden, which contained the celebrated Chauncey Maze.

It was, to be sure, a fascinating view, for the green hedges of the maze were unlike any other hedges she had ever seen depicted in photographs or paintings. The mazes she had seen and explored in her lifetime were always square and symmetrical, while this one sported an indiscriminate, paisley design. It was quite decidedly erratic, and would be a challenge to the most enterprising of minds.

The loud dinner gong rang, and Adele swallowed nervously. She and Clara and her mother met in the wide corridor to make their way to the drawing room.

"I liked Harold very much," Clara said, looping her arm through Adele's. "He had a certain warmth about him. Not at all pompous, like some people can be."

Adele pulled her sister close as they walked. "Oh, Clara, you have no idea how relieved I am to hear it. I was dreading the possibility that you might disapprove of him. I didn't want to have to argue with you."

"Disapprove?" their mother said haughtily. "Surely not!"

Clara smiled. "You won't have to argue with me, Adele. I admit that I pictured an older man for some reason. I'm pleased that he's young, and he seems exceptionally lively. I believe the two of you will be very well suited to each other. And how can I hide the simple fact that I am thrilled you will be close by? We will be separated by a mere train ride, rather than the unbearable expanse of the Atlantic."

Beatrice quickened her steps to keep up with her tall, long-legged daughters. "Oh, must you rub salt in the wound, Clara? The Atlantic will now separate me from my youngest daughter.

My baby! The dearest, most sensible of my brood! How will I ever manage the heartache?"

Clara smiled mischievously at her mother. "You will manage just fine, Mother, when Mrs. Astor invites you to all her balls and waits with bated breath while you take your time to reply."

They found their way to the formal drawing room and quietly entered. Eustacia was quick to greet them at the door. "Welcome! Welcome!"

Adele looked around at the dark red velvet wall coverings that repeated the paisley design from the Chauncey Maze, the matching velvet chairs and settees, the spectacular gold ceiling carved with intricate swirls and leafy patterns. With her educated eye, she recognized the French style of Louis XV.

She didn't see Damien anywhere.

"Please come and meet our other guests," Eustacia said, then she added with a whisper, "And Harold's grandmother is here— Catherine, the Dowager Baroness Alcester."

Adele glanced across the room at an old woman in a pushchair. Her snowy white hair was pinned up in a loose, elegant bun, and her black, high-necked gown complemented her coloring. She was slim, with high cheekbones, and she wore dainty drop earrings. Adele suspected she had been a great beauty in her youth.

Eustacia escorted them to her. "Mother, we have some new guests."

The older woman raised a pair of gold spectacles to her eyes with slender hands that trembled. "The Americans," she said cheerfully. Her head trembled as well.

Eustacia was about to begin the introductions, when Catherine interrupted. "I daresay, they're all lovely. Do you gels know what a stir you and your fellow countrywomen have been causing in England?" She turned slowly to look up at Eustacia. "Times are changing, are they not?"

Adele and Clara exchanged smiles.

Catherine nudged Eustacia. "Well, get on with it. I want to know which one of these Yankees is to marry my grandson."

Eustacia made the presentations. When it was Adele's turn, Catherine raised her spectacles again to get a better look. She smiled and leaned back. "Now I understand what all the buzzing was about. You, my dear, are a cupcake!"

Adele laughed. "A cupcake?"

"Yes. Tell me . . ." She leaned forward, as if to ask a secret. "Do you plan to raise your flag outside?"

Adele laughed. "No, my lady."

"What about the country dancing you people do? Are you going to make us learn that? I understand someone shouts out the steps."

Eustacia bent forward to speak loudly in her mother's ear. "Adele is not like most Americans, Mother! She won't be *shouting!* She's very polite, you'll soon see! One would almost take her for an Englishwoman!"

Adele tried to take the remark as a compliment. She wanted to fit in, after all.

Catherine raised her shoulders to her ears and peered up at her daughter. "The only one shouting at the moment is you, Eustacia. I'm not deaf."

She winked at Adele, who decided she was going to like Harold's grandmother very well.

Eustacia led them across the room toward a handsome, golden-haired gentleman in the opposite corner, who was conversing with Violet.

"Lord Whitby, may I present Lady Rawdon, Beatrice Wilson of New York, and Adele Wilson, my future daughter-in-law."

"Ah, yes," he replied, turning and bowing toward them. "But we have met before, Mrs. Wilson, during the Season a few years ago, and of course at the wedding of your eldest daughter, Sophia. I am an old friend of the duke's."

Adele's mother beamed. "Yes, of course! Lord Whitby! I remember your charming toast at their wedding! And the beautiful red roses you sent to Sophia not long after her London debut."

Adele winced, for she remembered those roses. Sophia had described them in one of her letters. Whitby had clearly been making his romantic feelings for Sophia known, but he had lost out to his friend James, the duke, who had later become Sophia's husband.

Leave it to her mother to mention that.

Whitby smiled rakishly, unruffled by the reminder. "Your memory is most impressive, Mrs. Wilson. I believe at your daughter's wedding, I referred to our newest duchess as a rose, for which England was to benefit from the careful American transplantation."

Adele's mother blushed. "Oh, Lord Whitby. You are too kind. Too kind."

They discussed light matters for a few minutes, then Eustacia guided them toward the other corner of the room, where Harold stood with his back to them. He turned when he sensed their approach.

"And here with Harold," Eustacia said, "we have my nephew, Damien Renshaw, Baron Alcester."

Adele—caught off guard by the sudden shock of his appearance as he stepped out from behind a tall, potted tree fern—sucked in a quick breath. She hadn't thought he was here.

A shudder passed through her. He looked so different. He wore a formal black dinner jacket with a white waistcoat and white bow tie, and his raven hair was slicked back in the most flattering way, complementing the strong, masculine lines of his cleanly shaven jaw and the fiery intensity of his dark eyes.

He was the perfect London gentleman, bowing politely with his hands clasped behind his back. Adele, however, had seen the rugged warrior who simmered beneath.

"Lady Rawdon, it's a pleasure," he said, bowing first to Clara. He greeted Adele's mother, then turned his beautiful gaze toward Adele and raised an eyebrow.

"And what a pleasure indeed to meet *you*,

Miss Wilson. Allow me to deliver my best wishes on your engagement to my cousin."

She was momentarily speechless, for it felt hypocritical to behave in this manner. She had woken up beside him in her bed that very morning, yet here they were, both of them, pretending they had never met.

The most outrageous part of it all was that half the people in the room knew the truth. They were aware of her kidnapping and Damien's heroic rescue and escort across England. They knew that Damien had bandaged her thigh. They knew he had brought her to the inn where she had been reunited with her mother and sister.

Adele tried to keep her knees steady as she offered her hand to Damien and went through the motions of *meeting* him. Her blood skittered through her veins at the warmth of his touch. She prayed the others wouldn't recognize how flustered she had become beneath the surface of her casual civility.

"I'm honored, Lord Alcester," she said, as indifferently as she could manage, realizing, however, that what she felt for Damien Renshaw was anything but indifference. Now—back in the real world and in the presence of all these other people—she knew.

What she felt for Damien Renshaw—notorious rake and loyal cousin to her fiancé—was not a "temporary madness," nor was it the stuff of fantasies or fairy tales. What she felt for Damien was real, very real indeed, and one way or another, she was going to have to deal with it.

Chapter 10

After a formal dinner, during which Adele sat gratefully at the opposite end of the table from Damien, the ladies retired to the drawing room for coffee, while the gentlemen remained at the table to enjoy their claret and cigars.

"Come and sit with me, Adele," Violet said, patting the sofa cushion beside her. "It's time we became better acquainted. We're going to be sisters, after all."

Adele rose from the chair on the other side of the room to join her future sister-in-law, who looked ravishing in a low-necked gown of magenta silk, trimmed with black lace. Her dark hair was pulled up in a most flattering bun with loose tendrils curling around her temples.

"Harold is so happy you're here at last," she said, leaning to pick up her coffee cup. "He absolutely adores you. I've never known him to be so deeply in love."

"Thank you, Violet."

"You must be pleased to be reunited with him as well."

"Oh yes."

Violet lowered her voice to a whisper and touched Adele's hand. "I can't imagine what you must have suffered the past few days. I said a prayer for you every night, and we were all so relieved to hear that Damien had found you. You must tell me everything. Was it as horrible as I imagined?"

Adele swallowed uncomfortably. "How horrible did you imagine it?"

"Well, to be kidnapped and held prisoner is one thing, but then to have to travel alone across England with a man like Damien. You must have been terrified."

Adele leaned forward to set her cup down on the table. "I wasn't terrified of Damien. Or . . . was that what you meant?"

She could have kicked herself.

Violet gazed intently at her for a moment and narrowed her eyes, then smiled and waved a hand through the air. "Oh, of course you wouldn't be terrified of Damien. He's family. Though with *his* reputation, a lady should never be too careful. I daresay, it was a good thing we managed to keep it secret, or you'd be ruined for sure." She laughed.

Adele didn't know what to say.

Violet covered her mouth with a hand. "Oh, I've shocked you. I was only joking, Adele. I adore Damien like a brother, and I didn't mean to offend."

"I'm not offended," Adele replied, working hard to keep her composure. "My sister had mentioned that Damien was slightly—" she stopped. "Oh, I don't remember what she said. It's not important. All that matters is that I'm here now and I'm safe, and Harold and I are to be married."

Violet squeezed her hand. "Yes, and I hope you'll let me help with the plans. I can show you all the best shops where you can choose your flowers and everything else. It's going to be such fun." Her voice took on a playful tone. "I only hope we can keep Mother from insisting upon using the family seamstress. She'll want to make you look like a big glob of clotted cream with bows."

Adele smiled, though her chest hurt.

"Don't worry. I won't let her do it. I want everything to be perfect for you and Harold. He's my only brother, after all, and my favorite person in all the world. You couldn't ask for a better husband, Adele. He's the most decent man you'll ever know. Don't ever forget that."

Adele picked up her coffee cup, and knew that he was indeed the most decent man she would ever know, and she was very lucky. She also knew that she had to be sensible in the coming days, keep her feet on the ground, and be very careful with her decisions.

* * *

"No, I don't know the Earl of Whitby very well," Clara said to Eustacia, who was glancing across the room at her daughter, Violet. "I met him at my sister's wedding, but I've not had the pleasure of his acquaintance since then. I was married just last Season, you see, and from what I understand, the earl has been in California until recently."

Eustacia handed Clara a cup of steaming coffee with cream. "Yes, that trip to California is what I'm wondering about. I assume he was looking for an American wife." She met Clara's gaze. "Not that there's anything wrong with that, of course. You girls are charming and lovely. I only mention it because I think Violet might have caught his eye. She does look stunning in that gown, don't you think?" Eustacia gazed proudly at her daughter.

"Yes, she does. She'll do very well this Season, Eustacia. I wouldn't be surprised if she receives a dozen proposals."

Eustacia sipped her coffee. "One will do fine," she replied with a somewhat anxious smile. "As long as it's the one she wants."

Later, the gentlemen joined them for an evening of music and entertainment—all except Damien, who sent his apologies, explaining that he had a business matter to attend to.

Adele was relieved. She hadn't been sure she could keep up the pretense of never having met Damien before. Nor had she been looking forward to spending an evening not only hiding her feelings of attraction, but struggling to bury them as well.

Violet played the piano and sang a charming rendition of "Home Sweet Home." Shortly thereafter, a game of charades began, and much giggling ensued. Afterward, Adele found herself alone with her fiancé at last, in a quiet corner of the drawing room.

"Harold, I'm so sorry to have caused so much anxiety for your family these past few days," she said. "I can't bear the thought that I was such a bother."

"Nonsense," he said with a smile, in his usual friendly manner. "You're here now, and that's all that matters. Tomorrow I will take you on a tour of the house and gardens, and you'll feel like you've lived here your entire life."

She felt her shoulders rise and fall with a contented sigh. "That would be very nice, Harold. Thank you."

"And I believe," he said, "that my mother is bursting with ideas about our nuptials. I hope you'll humor her by listening. She mentioned lilies in the church, and she was most curious to know what you Americans like to eat. I daresay, she's eager to please. She sees it as her duty to bridge the gap between our two cultures and smooth out your conversion."

Adele swallowed. "It's not as if I were changing religions, Harold."

He laughed awkwardly. "No, no, of course not. I only mean to say that some things will be very new for you. I hope you will feel free to turn to Mother with any questions you may have. It is imperative that you learn all about our English ways."

"I certainly will, but I hope I will be able to turn to *you*, too, Harold, for we are to be husband and wife."

He blushed, then laughed out loud. "Quite so! Quite so! I will be happy to answer any of your questions, Miss Wilson." His blush brightened. "Adele! I keep forgetting."

She smiled, finding his nervousness endearing. How comfortable she felt when she was in his amenable company. There were no nervous butterflies. He was everything she remembered him to be.

The party ended shortly after two A.M. Adele and Clara walked together to their rooms, which were conveniently located across from each other in the Huntington Wing.

"Will you come in for a little while?" Adele asked, hoping Clara wasn't too tired.

"Of course. We haven't had a chance to talk yet, have we? Not without Mother listening in. And Seger will be arriving tomorrow, so I will no doubt be pleasantly *occupied* most of the day."

They both smiled. Adele knew all too well the fire that burned between her sister and her husband, Seger.

"You are just as naughty as ever, Clara. That's probably what Seger loves most about you."

"That, and my brown sugar buns. He's still

appalled that I haven't shared the recipe with Cook. I insist on making them myself, and the servants still haven't figured out what to make of a marchioness in the kitchen. They never seem to know where to stand when I'm there. They hustle about in a panic, trying to fetch things for me."

Adele laughed and led the way into her bedchamber. Clara sat down on the bed, while Adele removed her pearl necklace and laid it down on her night table. "Clara, can I ask you something?"

"Of course," Clara replied.

Adele faced her sister and paused before speaking. "Why have you always tried to talk me into having adventures, when I've constantly told you I don't want them?"

Clara smiled gently and thought about her answer. "I suppose I always wished that you would let go of your inhibitions every once in a while. I worried that you might be repressing your passions, and that you might eventually explode. Because I certainly would, if I were as perfect as you all the time."

Adele snickered. "Explode?"

"Yes. Though you have never shown any signs of unhappiness or discontent. So all my life, I've told myself that you're not like me, and I shouldn't expect you to have to 'let go' like I must do sometimes. We're different, that's all, and I accept that."

Adele thought about the way she had felt in bed with Damien the night before. She had definitely been repressing passions, passions she hadn't even known she possessed.

"Yet you keep trying to make me 'let go,' as you put it," she said. "On the ship, you wanted me to have a Season."

Clara shrugged apologetically. "Old habits are hard to break."

Adele turned to face the mirror again, and pulled the pins out of her hair. "Maybe you still believe I'm repressed."

Clara didn't say anything.

"I've begun to wonder," Adele said, "why I have always been so well behaved, and so different from you and Sophia. Was I born this way, or did something make me this way?"

"Maybe you should ask Mother that question." Clara leaned back on the bed and put her hand on something. "What's this?" She picked up a note that lay on Adele's pillow and handed it to Adele.

It was written on the Osulton stationery.

Miss Wilson,

I took the liberty of arranging for the Osulton family physician to visit you tomorrow, at ten in the morning.

D.

Adele's pulse began to beat erratically, all because of a simple note. A note from *him*. And of course the knowledge that someone would be examining her intimately tomorrow, and finally telling her whether or not she still possessed her maidenhead. "Oh my."

Clara slipped it out from between Adele's fingers. "Someone's coming to examine your leg," she said cheerfully. "That's very wise. You don't want to risk an infection. Wait—who's D.?" She stared at the note for a few seconds. "That must be Lord Alcester."

Clara looked up at Adele, who couldn't seem to feel her tongue at the present moment, which made no sense. It was just a note about a doctor's visit—a visit she had been readily anticipating.

But the note had been private, meant only for her, and it had been written in the finest hand . . .

"Oh," Clara said softly. "You were on a first name basis."

Adele knew that somehow, without her ever saying a word to Clara, Clara suddenly understood everything.

"I see." She gave the note back and stood up, pacing behind Adele. "I must say, I was quite surprised when I met him this evening."

"Why?" Adele asked.

"Because he's so handsome. Why didn't you mention that?"

"I'm engaged to Harold. I don't notice whether or not other men are handsome."

Adele wasn't sure why she was denying this to Clara, who already seemed to know the truth. Perhaps it was because every instinct Adele possessed was telling her to deny it to herself as well. And she was so used to being good.

She continued to stand before her night table, slowly removing her earrings, until Clara stopped pacing behind her. "You don't have to be that way with me, Adele. I'm your sister."

Adele crossed the room to fetch her dressing gown. "I'm not being *that way*. Honestly, I care nothing about what Lord Alcester looks like. Don't you remember what Sophia said about him? That he keeps mistresses with questionable reputations? *I* certainly remembered, and I made the connection as soon as he told me who he was. I could hardly find a man like that attractive, Clara, no matter what he looks like. You know me better than that."

"But he rescued you—quite heroically—then tended to a wound on your thigh."

"I'd been shot. We had no choice about the thigh. Believe me, I didn't feel a thing except pain."

Too late, she realized how defensive she'd sounded just then, and faced her sister, who was looking at her with a sympathetic expression. Perhaps the "discontent" Clara had mentioned and feared was finally revealing itself. Perhaps this was a small hint of an explosion. Adele felt a sudden wave of apprehension move through her.

"Don't, Clara," she said firmly, holding up a hand. "I'm fine. I'm in love with Harold, and he's the one I want to marry."

"But—"

"No buts. I know you have very romantic notions about passion and adventure—and I will be the first to admit that Damien is a handsome man—but we've had this conversation before. Damien might have come to my rescue, but he is not my knight in shining armor. Harold is. Harold sent him, after all."

"Yes, I know, but—"

"No buts!" she said again. "I don't want to talk about it anymore. Damien helped me, and I am grateful for that, but he's not the kind of man I would ever want to marry. That's the end of the story."

Clara—quite surprisingly—gave in. "All right. I won't mention it again."

"Thank you."

Clara yawned. "I think I'll check on Anne now, then go to bed."

She walked to the door, but paused and glanced uncertainly at Adele before she left. As soon as the door closed behind her, Adele picked up the note and read it again, then thought about Damien arranging for the doctor. He had spent some time thinking of her and her needs, in particular about her worries regarding a most intimate, personal matter. She imagined him taking the time to make the arrangements—riding to see the doctor, explaining things as discreetly as possible. He had not forgotten about her.

Warmth swelled inside her belly. She wondered curiously if he had told Harold about the examination. A part of her—a part that she didn't want to face—hoped he had not. She liked knowing it was a secret they shared, just between the two of them. And she couldn't imagine discussing it with Harold.

Chapter 11

❧ ❦ ❧

Down by the lake—which this morning was a dead calm reflecting the trees and the sky with astounding clarity—Damien eased his horse from a gallop to a walk.

He hadn't realized how badly he'd needed some time alone in the woods, just breathing in the fresh air and the scent of the leaves on the ground. It calmed him, it always had, and this morning, he had needed to relieve some tension.

Two letters had arrived for him yesterday. One had come from Henderson, his steward at Essence House, saying that one of the tenant farmers had packed up and left without so much as a note saying why, and something had to be done because the rent was due and the estate couldn't weather another loss in income.

Damien had written back to him, instructing him to manage the finances as best he could for a little while longer. Things would improve soon, Damien had promised. He didn't say how, but he did tell Henderson to discontinue the search for a family to lease the house, because Damien planned to return as soon as possible after the London Season came to a close. He assumed his steward would guess that he intended to bring home a bride.

As he wrote the reply, however, Damien envisioned himself wearing a stiff bow tie every night during the Season, attending dull London balls and assemblies, and bowing politely to dozens of simpering, bejeweled debutantes.

He had not enjoyed penning the note.

The other letter, doused in perfume, had come from Frances. She wanted Damien to return to London as soon as he could manage it, because she was "utterly bored" with her current theater production. She wanted a distraction.

Damien headed back to the house and spotted his grandmother's open carriage on the lane. She was out for her usual morning drive. He trotted up beside her.

"Damien!" she said. "I was hoping I would meet you. I have a bone to pick with you, young man."

"A bone, Grandmama?" he replied over the clatter of hooves and carriage wheels.

"Yes. You kept a secret from me yesterday. About your adventure."

Damien glanced uneasily at the driver of the carriage.

Catherine noted his concern and tapped her cane. "Stop here, Regan. Would you fetch me some daisies? Just over there, that's right."

The driver set the brake, hopped down, and left them alone. Catherine squinted her eyes at Damien. "Why didn't you tell me?"

His horse took a few restless steps sideways. "Who let it slip?"

"Adele's mother, Beatrice. She can't keep a secret, that one. Delightful sense of humor, though."

They both looked up at the house on top of the hill.

"It was nothing," Damien said.

"Please, you needn't pretend it hasn't been intriguing for you, rescuing Harold's fiancée from a kidnapper and bringing her home like a hero to deliver her into the arms of her betrothed. Very romantic, don't you think?"

He shook his head at her.

She smiled mischievously. "I heard she was shot, too. Truly, it's the stuff of novels. And you were so good to bandage her leg. Her *thigh*, I should say. Good heavens, if you weren't future cousins, one might go so far as to call it scandalous."

"It really was nothing, Grandmama."

"Of course it wasn't. And I'm sure you kept your eyes closed the entire time."

Damien leaned forward, resting an elbow on

his knee. He grinned at her. "You know you're a thorn, Grandmama?"

"I know," she replied, smiling. "But you need a good painful prick every once in a while, Damien, to remind you you're still alive." She turned toward her driver, still picking daisies. "Call him back, will you? He'll get stung by a bee."

"Regan!" Damien shouted, waving him back. He returned and handed the bouquet to Catherine, who patted him on the arm.

"Thank you, you're a dear."

The carriage lurched forward and they started back toward the house. "All right," she said, "let's change the subject. I had a good time last night."

"I heard you were up until two."

"Yes. We played charades and Violet sang, and received an overwhelming round of applause. She loved it, of course. It's a shame you missed it."

"I had things to do."

"Did you now?"

"I did."

He felt his grandmother's intrusive gaze digging into him.

"She certainly is lovely," she said.

"Who?"

Catherine gave him a knowing, sidelong glance. "Adele, of course. I like her demeanor. She has no pretensions. She was nervous meeting us, but she didn't try to hide it under an aloofness that's so common among some people. She was very warm and friendly. I can see why the American gels are snatching up all our young men. Clara, her sister, was just as lovely."

"I suppose," he replied.

Catherine leaned over the side of the carriage to tap his knee with her cane. "Oh, stop, will you? Didn't you get to know her?"

"Not really."

They looked up at a bird flying overhead, and rode in silence for a few minutes.

"Do you think she'll be happy with Harold?" Catherine asked.

"I wouldn't know."

"She mentioned she loves to ride."

"Did she?"

"Harold hates it."

Damien shook his head again. "There are more important things in a marriage than a shared interest in horses and a love of the outdoors. People connect in many different ways."

"I didn't mention a love of the outdoors," his grandmother said. "I think you know her better than you let on."

Damien pulled his horse to a stop, and she went on. On any other day, he would have ridden the rest of the way back to the house with his grandmother. But today—given the subject matter of their conversation—he preferred to stay behind.

Adele sat up on her bed and watched the physician close his black leather bag. He must be a very skilled man, she thought, feeling more than a little impressed. After he'd checked her

bullet wound and changed the bandage, he'd
taken one brief look at her down *there*—a look
that lasted less than a second—and said simply,
"All is well." He'd not even touched her.

Though she was still embarrassed by the
sprawling nature of her reclining position just
now, her immense relief overshadowed it. All
was well.

She rose to her feet, resisting the most un-
English urge to jump up and down and kiss
him. "Thank you, Dr. Lidden."

She escorted him to the door, but could not let
him leave without learning something first.
"This is certainly good news. May I ask if you
will report the results to Lord Osulton?"

The doctor stopped and looked down at her.
He had the kindest, warmest blue eyes. "Lord
Alcester requested the strictest confidentiality
on my part. *You* are the only person I am responsible to, Miss Wilson. Unless, of course,
you *wish* me to inform Lord Osulton."

So Harold still knew nothing. Damien had
been discreet.

Adele gazed up at the doctor. Should she tell
him to go and speak to Harold? Dear Harold
hadn't mentioned any concerns about this sort
of thing, but how could he possibly initiate such
an intimate topic of discussion?

He must be wondering, though. The whole
family must be concerned . . . .

"I believe, Dr. Lidden, I would in fact prefer
that Lord Osulton know all the particulars of
my condition. We are to be husband and wife,

after all. Please tell him why I was concerned—
because I had been unconscious during part of
my kidnapping—and assure him that all is
well."

The doctor smiled. She sensed he was relieved to be spared the necessity of keeping a secret from the family. "I will go and speak to him
right away," he said, bowing to her before he
walked out.

"I beg your pardon?" Harold said, straightening from his bent-over position at his lab table
and pushing his protective glasses up onto the
top of his head. "What did you say?"

Dr. Lidden cleared his throat. "I said, my
lord, that Miss Wilson was not compromised
during her kidnapping. I've just examined her,
and you can be confident that there will be no
confusion regarding a male heir, if one were to
be a product of your marriage in the near future. Do you understand my meaning?"

Harold laughed nervously. He pulled off his
glasses, dropped them onto the stool behind him,
and moved around the long table to screw a lid
onto a jar. He closed it tight, then laughed again.

"You can actually discover these things?" he
asked. "I say, it's quite a science, isn't it?
Though not a science I would likely enjoy." He
gestured toward the bottles behind him,
stacked on shelves against the glass wall of the
former conservatory. "Are you a man of science,
Doctor?" Harold blushed and laughed again.
"Of course you are. What a dimwitted ques-

tion." He paused and shifted his weight from one foot to the other.

"So you say she's healthy?" he went on. "Well, that is good news, isn't it? Good news indeed."

He turned around to face the opposite wall, as if looking for something to do, then faced the doctor again and lowered his voice to sound more like the lord he was supposed to be. "That'll be all, Lidden. Thank you for your time."

Dr. Lidden bowed and walked out, shaking his head as he climbed the steps that led back into the main part of the house.

Damien sat back in the saddle and watched the doctor's carriage roll by on the lane. It was done. He had examined Adele.

Damien's shoulders heaved with a deep sigh. He could not comprehend the inappropriateness of his curiosity. He had instructed the doctor to keep the matter private between himself and Adele, but now Damien wished he had told the man to report back. Damien wanted the assurance that she had not been harmed when she'd been unconscious, and it was killing him now—*killing* him—to leave the matter alone and stay away.

Chapter 12

From her window on the second floor, Adele watched Dr. Lidden walk out of the house, climb into his carriage, and drive away. She turned and looked at her door, expecting to hear a knock at any moment. Surely, Harold had been relieved to hear the news that she had not been harmed in *that* particular way during her kidnapping.

She waited, and waited, and waited some more. Still, he did not come. Perhaps he was afraid to. Perhaps he felt uncomfortable discussing such things.

Adele sighed, remembering what a sensitive man Harold was. She remembered how he had rescued a spider in her Newport drawing room once, while the ladies were screaming, and had set him free out the window. That was the moment she had decided Harold was the one for her. He had not squished the poor creature under his boot. He was a sweet, nonthreatening man.

She decided at that moment to seek him out instead. She wanted to share her happiness with someone. Who better than her husband-to-be?

She met the butler in the main hall, and asked where Lord Osulton might be.

"He's in the conservatory, Miss Wilson," the butler replied.

What a perfect place, she thought. She had been looking forward to seeing the plants and flowers.

She made her way through the gallery and down a long corridor, then finally found the entrance to the conservatory, flanked by graceful statues of the human form. She didn't let herself stop to look at them. She did stop, however, rather abruptly, at the top of the conservatory steps.

There were no plants. The entire room had been converted to a laboratory. There were five or six tables covered with bottles, scales, funnels, and flasks, and papers strewn about. Tall bookcases filled with reports and journals stood in front of the glass windows, blocking the view of the garden. It was not what she had expected—which characterized her life in general over the past week.

Slowly, feeling almost heartbroken, she descended the stairs, looking around at the jars and bottles full of liquids and powders, all with hand-printed labels. Adele cleared her throat. "Harold, I was hoping to talk to you."

His smile seemed slightly strained. "What about, my darling?"

Adele tried to keep her voice casual when, in actuality, she felt very awkward. "Did Dr. Lidden come to see you?"

"Dr. Lidden? Yes, yes he did."

"And he told you that everything was fine?"

The smile disappeared from Harold's lips, then it returned—a forced, nervous grimace. He picked up a crucible and moved it to a new spot on another table. "Everything is fine. Yes. Glad to hear it."

A wave of disappointment slowly made its way through Adele. She had imagined he would take her into his arms and express his relief. She had thought he might kiss her.

"So, what do you think of my laboratory?" he asked, abruptly changing the subject. "We had it converted two years ago."

She had to work hard to shake herself out of her expectations, forget about the subject matter that was "fine," and show interest in this passion of his. She moved more fully into the large room and looked up at the glass ceiling. "What did you do with the plants?"

"To be honest, I don't know what they did. It wasn't my concern, really. I was more interested in where the tables would be placed. The light's fabulous, isn't it?"

"Yes, it certainly is."

He gave her a tour of the laboratory and

showed her a chemical heating lamp that a local tinsmith had made—which Harold admitted he was very proud of. He showed her his alkalimeters, his acidimeters, his hydrometers, his eudiometers, and his pestles and mortars and gas tubes. He was particularly proud of his collection of scientific circulars.

As soon as he had shown her everything, an uncomfortable silence settled over them.

"Well, I should leave you to your work, then," Adele said, laboring to sound cheerful. "Perhaps later, we could begin the tour you suggested."

"Tour?" he asked, looking slightly baffled.

"Of the house and gardens. You said you'd show me around."

His face split with a huge grin. "Oh yes! A tour! I would be most happy to do that, yes!" He glanced around at the papers lying about. "Just give me a few minutes to finish what I'm doing here. Why don't I come and fetch you in an hour?"

Adele nodded. "That would be very good, Harold. Thank you."

She picked up her skirts and climbed the steps, telling herself that she would feel better in the days to come, after she and Harold had time to be alone and talk, and become more at ease with each other.

Adele stood on the front steps and watched Clara dash into the arms of her handsome husband, Seger, whom she had not seen since she'd left England over a month ago.

"I missed you!" Clara said, as Seger swung her around. "Next time, you're coming with me!"

"Next time, I definitely will," he replied, pressing his lips to hers and kissing her deeply for everyone to see.

Adele gasped at the display and felt the others gasp, too, then they all looked away, pretending not to notice, except for two footmen, who enjoyed the spectacle and nudged each other.

Clara took her husband's hand and walked up the stairs to introduce him to everyone. It was hardly a dignified moment. Adele heard someone whisper, "*Those Americans*."

While Seger met the family, Adele noticed a rider coming up the hill. It was Damien. He circled around to the stables at the back of the house.

A short time later, Clara and Seger retired to their rooms to spend time alone with baby Anne, and everyone else dispersed. Adele was left in the main entrance hall with Harold.

"Perhaps I could take you on the tour tomorrow," he said. "I'm in the middle of a very complex experiment and I would like to return to the conservatory. Tomorrow would be better."

Adele wondered why he continued to call it a conservatory when it was quite another thing. She kept her opinions to herself, however. "That would be fine, Harold. Tomorrow."

He hurried off to finish what he had begun.

Adele stood alone in the center of the round entrance hall, and felt a longing to be outdoors. Though she was disappointed that Harold wished to work on his experiment today, she was still so very pleased and happy about the doctor's news earlier. She wanted to run. And she wished she could share her news with someone.

Adele glanced toward the front door and remembered seeing Damien not more than a few minutes ago, riding back to the stables. She remembered what he'd said to her before he'd left her bedchamber at the inn—that it would be dangerous for them to speak to each other, especially alone.

But surely, she could just tell him this one small bit of news. She couldn't very well leave him to wonder about it.

For a moment or two, she dithered over what to do, then gave in and decided she would break the rule just this once. It wouldn't be such a terrible thing. She would just tell him the news, then return to the house.

She ventured out the front door and made her way along the lane that circled the house, her leather boots crunching over the clean, white gravel. The air smelled of roses and clipped green grass. She glanced down the hill to the woods, and longed for the smells down there. A leisurely ride would certainly clear her head today. Perhaps Harold would finish his work early, and be willing to join her later.

She walked to where the stables were located at the back of the house. She didn't see anyone around, so she quietly entered the largest building where the doors were flung open, letting the sun stream onto the wide, plank floor.

Inside, the strong smell of hay and horses wafted to her nostrils, and she breathed deeply, basking in it. She had been too long in a cabin on a boat, and then trapped in a tiny cottage with no escape. Her bones were kicking to enjoy freedom, her heart longing to gallop.

Thinking of that kind of freedom made her remember her conversation with Clara the night before, when Clara had used the word "repressed." An unfamiliar tension curled around Adele's muscles. She realized that the only time she felt truly "free" was when she went riding or running in the woods. It was a natural place where everything was real. There were no expectations in the woods. No rules to worry about.

Adele wandered down the long row of stalls, stroking the horses' soft, silky noses, enjoying the sounds they made as they nuzzled her palm. Just then, she heard a voice. A man's voice. Damien's voice. Her heart began to race.

She contemplated the frustrating response. She had thought she would be able to subdue her feelings when she saw him, but here she stood, suffering from yet another attack of improper exhilaration—and she hadn't even *seen* him yet. She'd only heard his voice in the next stall.

Perhaps this hadn't been such a good idea, she thought, feeling apprehensive and anxious all of a sudden. She turned to leave.

He was talking to his horse, she realized suddenly, stopping again. What was he saying? His voice was too low and gentle to hear. She listened for a few seconds, then couldn't help herself. She turned back and peered around the corner.

He was feeding an apple to the horse. She could hear the crunching sound; she could even smell the apple. It reminded her of home, of their orchard in Wisconsin. Then she noticed a bucket full of juicy red apples just outside the stall.

Damien picked up a brush and began to groom his horse. She thought *she* was the only one who groomed her own horse. Her mother constantly said, "That's what servants are for," but Adele liked to do it. She had done it since she was a girl and she did not wish to give it up. It was the only thing she did that her mother disapproved of, though she had long ago stopped mentioning it.

Adele watched Damien for a moment. He had taken off his riding jacket and wore a black waistcoat over a crisp white shirt. His raven hair looked windblown and artless, spilling down onto his collar as it had when he had first burst into her room to rescue her at the isolated cottage.

He had two looks, she realized—the wild, rugged warrior and the elegant London gentleman. She believed she liked the warrior best. It was more *him*. Organic and untampered with. It was the look that fascinated her.

She found herself mesmerized by the sight of

his large hand holding the brush, smoothly stroking the horse's shiny coat. Damien's muscular arm and shoulder moved with grace. The strength and breadth of his back was indeed something worth looking at.

"I don't suppose you'd like to help," he said casually, and it took Adele a few seconds to realize with horror that he was talking to her.

She cleared her throat and, quite suitably embarrassed, stepped out from behind the post. She fought to contain and hide the tension she was feeling. "It appears I've been discovered."

He glanced her way and grinned—a most wicked, seductive grin—and her body seemed to melt into something resembling warm, sticky molasses. She put her hand on the post to keep from toppling over into the next stall.

He turned his attention back to what he was doing—stroking his most fortunate horse—and Adele managed, at last, to breathe. She searched her muddled brain for the reason she had come here.

"I . . . I thought you might like to know what happened with Dr. Lidden."

Damien froze mid-stroke. He stood still for a few seconds, and the stable seemed very quiet. He lowered the brush and walked toward her. His boots swished over the hay.

Adele felt the power of his approach like a fire moving closer and closer, soon too hot to bear. She took a step back and sucked in a breath, hoping he hadn't noticed, but knowing he had. Of course he had.

"And?" he said, stopping before her.

She smelled his cologne. It was so potently familiar. It assaulted her senses like a storm. "And all is well," she replied shakily.

His broad, muscular shoulders lifted with a deep intake of breath, then he whispered, "Thank God."

"Yes, thank God," she repeated.

He stood before her, saying nothing. She didn't know what to say either. They had vowed to keep away from each other once they'd arrived here.

"And everything else is all right?" he asked. "You're comfortable here? You have everything you need?"

She nodded quickly.

"Good," he said.

Still he didn't turn away. His horse nickered. She would nicker, too, if she were waiting for Damien to finish rubbing her down.

"I'm glad you came," he said, in a soft, husky voice. "I was thinking about you."

Feeling an onslaught of deep and potent yearning, she gazed up at his dark, devilish eyes and strove to be sensible. She thought of all his mistresses. She thought about his reputation, and the fact that he was Harold's cousin, and she was engaged to Harold and did not want to jeopardize that fact, for she was happy with her choice. It was the *right* choice. The temptation she felt around this man was dangerous, and she had no business feeling hot and impassioned in his presence. She would never want to marry *him*.

Why, then, could she not make the feelings go away? Why could she not resist the wanton desire to see him, and the urge to stay here with him and do more than just talk?

Adele breathed faster. "I was thinking about you, too. I mean . . . I wanted you to know that everything was fine."

They stood there, saying nothing, just staring at each other, and Adele thought her heart was going to give out. His gaze moved all over her face—from her eyes down to her lips, where he lingered a moment, then down her body to her feet and back up again.

It felt strangely as if he had touched her in all those places. She felt weak and exposed, standing before him—a man who clearly possessed a great deal of experience and command when it came to women. It was no wonder he'd had so many mistresses. She suspected most women would tumble into his arms quite happily when faced with *this*.

"So now I've told you," she said. "I should get back to the house."

He tilted his head at her. "Yes, you should."

Her lips parted. "All right then," she said, feeling utterly ridiculous. "I'll go."

She turned and left the stable, but felt his eyes watching her the entire way out.

Chapter 13

Still in her nightgown, Adele left her bedchamber and went to her mother's room. She knocked softly, for it was still early, and entered. Her mother was asleep with her mouth open, snoring.

Adele knelt by the bed and whispered, "Mother?"

Always a light sleeper, Beatrice woke. She gazed drowsily at Adele, then lifted the heavy covers. "Adele, darling. Get in. It's chilly."

Adele climbed into the warm bed and lay next to her mother. It reminded her of the days in Wisconsin when the family used to sleep together in the one room cabin. They'd had no servants to light a fire in the morning, so they often snuggled close in bed.

Adele faced her mother for a few minutes before she spoke. "Can I ask you something?"

Beatrice opened her eyes again. "Of course."

"You and Father always said I was the most well behaved of your three girls. I never got into trouble, and I'm trying to understand why I was so different from Sophia and Clara."

Her mother rested a hand on Adele's cheek. "You were different from the moment you were born. Even as a baby, you never complained when I put you to bed. You went to sleep. When you were a little girl, you were always happy and very independent. You didn't seem to need to fight against anything."

"But I fought against Sophia and Clara. I tattled on them. I didn't like it when they broke the rules."

Her mother thought about that for a moment. "That happened in New York. You didn't do that so much in Wisconsin. You usually went your own way."

"I changed when we moved?"

"Well, you were growing up."

Adele thought about her life, how she'd always felt it was divided in two. First, she had been "Adele in Wisconsin," who had loved her pony and went riding alone in the woods. Then she had become "Adele in New York," who had loved her parents and wanted to please them, and often felt frustrated with her sisters, who did what they wanted when she could not.

Why couldn't she?

"Do you think I was born with this personality, to be good?"

"We are all born with a natural disposition."

"But can that disposition change?"

Her mother's brow furrowed. "Is something wrong, Adele? Are you not happy? Has your ordeal—"

"No, I'm very happy, Mother. Please don't worry. I just want to understand the person I'm supposed to be."

Beatrice smiled. "You're supposed to be you. And you're perfect, Adele."

Perfect. There it was again. That word. It had never made her uncomfortable before. But now, since she'd been kidnapped, and since she'd let Damien kiss her and lie with her in the darkness, she felt as if she might be an impostor, and the walls all around her were closing in, threatening to squeeze the breath out of her.

Over breakfast the next day, Adele smiled and took part in the animated conversation about her nuptials. Her mother and Eustacia sat together at one end of the table, clucking like hens, while Violet sent amused, knowing glances Adele's way.

The family seamstress was mentioned, and Violet practically dropped her teacup into her saucer. "Oh no, Mother, you must consider a designer in London. Or perhaps that Worth fellow from Paris. Adele's marriage to Harold must be perfect, and to be perfect, she must have the very newest fashion. Her sister Sophia wore a wedding gown by Worth, and she is a duchess, after all."

Eustacia's face lit up with interest, and Adele's mother beamed, nodding with pride. "Oh yes," she said. "It *must* be a Worth gown."

Adele glanced across the white-clothed table at her future sister-in-law, Violet, who looked very satisfied with herself and her suggestion. Adele, on the other hand, heard only the word "perfect," and felt a great pressure squeeze around her chest.

After breakfast, Adele asked where Harold might be, for she was looking forward to her tour of the house and gardens, and she didn't want to think about wedding plans anymore. They were becoming too complicated, and everyone seemed to be getting carried away with the details. Adele wanted only to begin her new life and get to know her fiancé better. She wanted to feel that this was her home, so she would finally be able to relax here. That's what mattered to her. Not the color of the bridesmaids' sashes.

She was told Harold would be in the conservatory. Or rather, the laboratory. She made her way there and entered. Her fiancé stepped out from behind a wall of bookcases. He saw her and jumped with fright.

"Oh, good gracious!" he said, resting a hand on his chest. "You surprised me, Adele!" He smiled awkwardly. "What are you doing here?"

Adele approached him. He wore a white apron with a dark stain on the front. As she came closer, she noticed he smelled like sulphur.

"You promised to show me the house and gardens today, Harold. I'm especially looking forward to a tour of the stables. I heard you have some of the finest horses in England."

He gave her a flustered look. "I was just about to begin something here. You see, I'm working on the idea I discussed with your father regarding a new synthetic dye." He gestured toward a number of jars on the table. "I am in the process of producing something artificial that I believe will be more practical than any natural concoction. It's quite exciting, don't you think?"

Adele looked at the bottles. "Yes, it's very exciting, Harold."

"Your father believes it has business potential." A long, awkward silence ensued. "Perhaps Damien could show you the stables," Harold said, sounding frazzled.

Adele's heart did a flip in her chest. "I beg your pardon?"

Harold turned. "Damien?"

Adele froze. There was a movement at the back corner of the conservatory, close to the far windows, behind the one tall potted plant that had managed to survive the renovation.

It seemed to Adele that Damien was always stepping out from behind something green and most inconveniently catching her off guard.

Hands behind his back, looking as if he had not wanted to be discovered, he stepped into view. "Good morning, Miss Wilson."

"Good morning," she replied, straightening her shoulders and feeling oddly defensive.

Harold smiled enthusiastically. "Yes, yes! This is most opportune! Damien is the best person to show you the stables. It's his doing, you know," Harold said proudly, "acquiring the best horses. He's very knowledgeable about that sort of thing. Damien, would you be so kind as to show my lovely betrothed to the stables?"

Another awkward silence ensued. Adele wanted to sink through the floor. Damien didn't want to show her the stables. He had not even wanted to be discovered.

"Of course," he said.

Adele put up her hand. "That's not necessary. I can wait, Harold. Truly. I wanted to see everything with *you*. Don't feel you have to entertain me. I don't want to intrude upon your experiments, and clearly, Lord Alcester was here talking to you before I interrupted and—"

"Don't be silly, my love!" Harold said. "Damien was bored anyway, weren't you, Damien? And he had just told me he wanted to go for a ride. Perhaps he could show you the estate as well. He knows these woods better than anyone, don't you, Damien? Always poking about outdoors."

Adele marveled at her fiancé's absolute trust in his cousin. Didn't Harold worry about Damien's reputation with women? Or how did he know Adele wasn't the type to swoon over Damien's good looks? Harold didn't know her that well, after all. Obviously, the concepts of swooning and gooseflesh had never occurred to him.

"Really," she said, backing away, "I don't mind waiting."

"No, no, don't leave!" Harold said with a rather desperate smile, taking a step forward to detain her. "In fact, I've been dreading taking you to the stables. I'm actually afraid of horses. I was kicked by one when I was twelve. Remember that, Damien? Nasty beasts, I daresay."

Harold was afraid of horses? He didn't like to ride? Adele hadn't known that. What else didn't she know?

"Please, let Damien take you," Harold said, "and I can show you the inside of the house later today."

Both Damien and Adele looked at each other. What could they say? To outwardly refuse to be together would suggest something out of the ordinary between them, and Adele certainly didn't want to admit to being uneasy around her fiancé's cousin. She should feel nothing but casual indifference toward him.

Damien took a step forward.

"There now," Harold said cheerfully. "This will give me time to finish my experiment, and I will be very content knowing you are in good hands, my dear."

Adele smiled nervously as Damien approached. Good hands. Good hands, indeed.

It was as if they had never met before yesterday.

Damien escorted Adele to the stables and gave her a polite tour, describing where each horse had come from and when it had been purchased or, if not purchased, bred here on the estate.

She nodded, vastly pleased to be discussing horses, which was a subject dear to her heart. It made it easy to avoid discussing anything personal.

She recalled her sister Sophia's letters describing how the English could behave in such superficial ways—all in the name of propriety. Sophia had wrestled with the frustration of it all, never knowing what any of them were truly thinking beneath the surface of their enormous reserve. Adele suddenly understood what her sister had endured. Adele was now acting as if there were nothing between herself and Damien except for the common link of Harold. And Damien was acting like someone else entirely. He was avoiding the teasing flirtations that she had, despite their inappropriateness, come to enjoy.

"Would you like to take a ride?" Damien asked, without making direct eye contact with her. A groom stood nearby, waiting for an official request.

"I believe I would," Adele replied, knowing that she should have said no, but she was positively desperate to escape this manicured palace and all the watching eyes. She just couldn't resist.

The groom immediately set to work, saddling two horses. A short time later, she and Damien were riding side by side down the hill, trotting across the green lawns. They rode in silence for some time, and Adele smothered any urge to talk and bring up anything to do with the time they had spent alone together.

Damien was certainly obliging the pretense that they had never met before yesterday. Perhaps it was best. Perhaps this was how it would be from now on. Out of respect for Harold, Damien would not be rakish in her presence. Yes, it was best.

They soon approached a lake and stopped to let the horses graze.

"Is that a teahouse on the island?" Adele asked, noticing a small, round building, painted white and surrounded by leafy oaks.

"Yes, but it's not an island, it's a peninsula," Damien replied. "We can get to it by riding to the other side of the lake."

"Can we?" Adele heard the excitement in her voice, and too late realized she should have been blasé about the teahouse and everything else, but she could only keep up this pretense for so long before she was bound to slip.

Besides, how could anyone resist exploring what looked like a secret hideaway in the forest? Though she didn't think it would be wise to explore it with Damien.

"Maybe another time," she said. "Perhaps I'll come back here with Harold."

He leaned forward and stroked his horse's neck, saying nothing for a few seconds while he gazed at her suggestively from under dark, long lashes. The corner of his mouth gave in to a lazy smile.

There. There was the Damien she knew—the

raw and earthy sexual being. He stirred something earthy in her as well—something unrefined. It tingled pleasurably through her as she sat on her horse in the cool, fresh air, and it validated her fears and uncertainties, confirming that Damien had an astonishingly powerful effect on her. It was true. It could not be denied. He made her feel things she did not feel with anyone else, things she had never in her life felt before.

"I doubt you'll get Harold down here any time soon," Damien informed her.

She gave him a sidelong glance. He smiled, his eyebrow lifting provocatively. What a wicked rake he was, when he slipped into those behaviors. And oh, how he excited her. She couldn't help smiling back, couldn't help enjoying the very foreign inclination to misbehave.

He turned his gaze toward the calm lake and surveyed the landscape. What was he considering? she wondered. Was he checking to make sure there was no one else about?

He glanced back at her, his dark eyes assessing. There *was* something between them still, she knew, even though they did not speak of it or, God forbid, touch each other. And it was understood that it would remain unspoken. For as long as they didn't ever acknowledge it openly again, or act upon it, they were doing nothing wrong. And they both knew where the line was drawn. The challenge, however, was in not crossing that line.

"You want to explore it now, don't you?" he

asked, sensitive to her desires as he always was. His husky voice touched her like a feather, tickled her skin, sent warmth through all her limbs.

When she didn't respond, he trotted off ahead of her. "Don't worry. I won't tell."

I won't tell. There were already far too many secrets where he was concerned. Far too many hidden, buried emotions.

Yet, against her better judgment, and for reasons Adele couldn't begin to understand, she could do nothing but follow him into the shady woods.

Chapter 14

He shouldn't be doing this, Damien thought, as he led the way through the trees and around the lake. He should not have suggested they ride on. He should have started back toward the house.

But he'd taken one look at Adele on her horse in the natural splendor of her feminine beauty, with her top hat perched at an enticing forward tilt on her head, and her luscious raspberry lips just waiting to be kissed, and he'd slid down the slippery slope of his less gentlemanly inclinations.

It was at that moment an instinct deeper than logic prevailed. It was the instinct responsible for his notorious reputation for being able to successfully seduce any woman of his choosing.

He did not, however, choose just any woman.

He had very particular tastes, and he always chose his lovers with careful, sound logic. Except for today, he thought irritably, when the opportunity to follow his more primitive desires had caused his body to respond promptly on cue with a most sizable and untimely arousal.

"I want to thank you for arranging for the doctor," Adele said, trotting up beside him.

He draped an arm across his pelvis.

"I wasn't sure how to handle that," she added. "I'm glad you thought of it."

He had thought of a great many things over the past few days.

"Did you tell Harold you were going to take care of it?" she asked.

Damien steered his mount around a fallen branch. "No."

She considered his direct, flat response. "Why not?"

"The subject didn't come up."

The sound of their horses' hooves tapping over the soft earth filled the silence. "I did talk to him about it myself," she said, "after I had the doctor explain the situation to him. I wanted Harold to know that I had not been harmed."

"What did Harold say?"

"He was relieved, of course, but I think he was a little uncomfortable talking about it."

Damien shifted in the saddle. He knew his cousin well, and he knew that Harold wasn't entirely comfortable around women, nor was he comfortable with anything to do with sex.

The truth of the matter was, Harold lacked experience, and Damien suspected he would be ill at ease on his wedding night. Painfully so. But it would be disloyal for Damien to express such an opinion to the woman Harold was going to marry. Instead, he would talk to Harold about it. He would prepare him for his wedding night, and tell him what to do.

The thought of that caused a sudden tightness in Damien's neck and shoulders. Could he do that? Tell Harold how to make love to Adele?

"I was surprised," she said, ripping him quite violently out of his thoughts, "when Harold suggested you show me the stables, given that we just spent so much time together."

"Harold trusts me."

"But how can he trust *me*? He doesn't know me as well as he knows you. It didn't even occur to him that I might be tempted by your reputed allure when it comes to women. Am I *that* predictably pure?"

He smiled at her, choosing not to answer.

"It's strange," she said, "that even though we're engaged to be married, sometimes I don't know how Harold really feels about me. Do you think he would be jealous if he saw us now, riding alone to the teahouse?"

Recognizing Adele's need for reassurance where her fiancé was concerned, Damien found himself wishing for the first time that his cousin had more finesse. Adele deserved to be adored. If she felt adored by Harold, she would not need to ask Damien these questions.

At the same time, he disliked the idea of her being adored by Harold. Though he loved Harold.

"I'm sure he would be," Damien replied.

But in all honesty, Damien was not sure. Harold probably wasn't even giving it a second thought. He was more likely leaning over a beaker right now, concerned only with what was going on inside it, which frustrated Damien greatly.

He told himself it didn't mean Harold didn't care for Adele. Harold was just being Harold. "He'll eventually relax around you," Damien said. "I know the man he is beneath the surface, and believe me when I say that he's a good man. Give him time. You'll have your whole life to get to know him as well as I do."

She shifted in her saddle. "I know he's a good man. You're right. I shouldn't try to rush things. I shouldn't expect to be intimate with someone I've only just met."

Yet he and she had only just met, and there was an incredible level of intimacy between them. Though at the moment, they were both working hard to keep it at bay.

They rode around the lake and arrived at the path that led to the teahouse. "Will it be locked?" Adele asked.

"Yes, but I know where the key is. Harold and I used to come here when we were younger, before he discovered chemistry. We spent many hours fishing right over there." He pointed to the log they once sat on. "Harold's father used to enjoy the outdoors. He was always hosting shooting parties."

"What about *your* father and mother? Do you remember much about them?"

Damien pulled his horse to a stop at the tea-house and swung down from the saddle. He went to help Adele. "My father was very much like Harold. Red hair and all. Eustacia was my father's sister."

"And your mother?"

"My mother . . . well, she had interests that didn't include me. I had no love for her, and to be honest, I don't remember that much about her. I never try to because when I do, all I feel toward her is resentment."

"You have no pleasant or happy memories of her at all?"

Adele's gloved hands came to rest on his shoulders, and he took hold of her tiny waist. She leaped down, landing with a thud before him, her skirts billowing upon the air.

They stood motionless, staring at each other for a few seconds while he thought about Adele's question.

"I suppose I do. I remember her holding me and singing to me when I was very small."

But he didn't like to think about that. It hurt to remember his mother's tenderness. It gave him a knot in his stomach.

"Were you close to your father?" Adele asked. "You see, I come from a close family and it's hard to imagine being a child and not feeling close to at least *someone*."

He finally let go of her waist and tethered the horses to a tree. "I suppose I was. We were very different, but we seemed to connect somehow. I suppose I knew he would do anything for me. I was loyal to him in return."

"Like you're loyal to Harold?"

The question made him uncomfortable. "Yes."

"When did you and Harold become so close?"

A memory flashed in his mind—an image of a day not long after his parents died, a month, perhaps. He had stumbled across some boys fighting at school, but it turned out to be boys beating on Harold. Damien had fought them off. He had felt very *useful* that day, after weeks of shame and regret, blaming himself for his parents' deaths.

With nose bleeding and eyes tearing, Harold had looked up at Damien from where he'd sat on the ground, huddled against a brick wall, and said, "You're my best friend, Damien. You'll always be my best friend."

Damien stood outside the teahouse with Adele and told her all about that day, and he saw in her eyes that she understood. He told her other things about their childhood as well. He explained how Harold had always been able to see when Damien was missing his parents, and had cheered him up with jokes or games. Damien gazed down at the ground, remembering so many little things . . .

The horse nickered, and both Damien and Adele went to pat him and talk to him. Then Damien retrieved the key to the teahouse from a jar nestled in a tree stump nearby, and returned to unlock the door. He pushed it open and gestured with a hand for Adele to enter first.

She walked into the large, round room bathed in sunlight, her black boots tapping over the wide planks on the floor. She wandered leisurely around the perimeter, looking out the windows at the lake, then she moved to the center where a large table stood—also round—with twelve Chippendale chairs.

Damien removed his hat, and closed the door behind him. "This was built in 1799, because of something Prince Edward, the Duke of Kent, said when he was a young man—that in a round building, the devil could never corner you."

"And do you believe that?" She turned her back on him and strolled around, looking carefully at the small paintings of landscapes on the walls.

He let his gaze sweep appreciatively down the length of her curvaceous body. "No. I believe he can corner you anywhere."

She nodded in agreement, looked around a bit more, then smiled at him.

"It's wonderful," she said. "I will come here every day, I'm sure of it, just to escape the . . ." She stopped whatever she was going to say, and glanced up very briefly at Damien before turning toward the windows again.

He took a slow step forward. "Escape the *what*, Adele?"

She faced him again, and smiled sheepishly. She shook her head. "Oh, I don't know. The perfection of it all. Everything is so manicured. Personally, I prefer something more like this. Something small and cozy and covered in ivy and overgrown grasses. I love how the branches dip down into the water just over there, and how the leaves over here"—she pointed at the window—"block the view slightly. It's natural and unpredictable."

She met his gaze and smiled warmly, and he felt a stirring deep inside himself. She was beautiful, there was no question about that, and he was attracted to her in a physical way, which was not unusual. That could be dealt with. But there was so much more.

Feeling on edge, Damien dropped his gaze to the floor. He had prayed these feelings would disappear after he returned Adele to Harold. He had prayed that he and Adele would both forget what had happened between them. But Damien could not. It was impossible. All he wanted to do now was pull Adele into his arms and just hold her. He wanted to take her to Essence House and show her the unkempt gardens and the cozy rooms that were full of mismatched pillows, and the stacks of books piled high on the floors, because there was no room left in the bookcases, and no one had ever wanted to part with the books.

Damien knew Adele would love Essence House, because she loved what was natural and unpretentious.

He feared suddenly that what he felt for Adele was more than just a passing lusty admiration for an attractive woman, and more than simply a desire for what was forbidden to him. Now that they were back in the real world, it seemed to be much, much more.

Damien squeezed his hat in his hands and felt a dark shadow, like a storm cloud, settle over him and inside him. It was a shadow of gloom. Shame. Dread. He couldn't move.

"What is *your* house like, Damien?" she asked, her expression bright with interest.

Not only could he not move, he couldn't speak, either. All he could do was stare blankly at her.

"Damien?" She sauntered closer. "*Your* house. It's called Essence House. Didn't you tell me that once? I looked the word 'essence' up in the dictionary this morning because I was thinking about it, and it means 'the real or ultimate nature of a thing, as opposed to its existence.' It means 'heart, soul, core, or root.'"

She continued to walk toward him in that carefree way, and he wished she would stop. "In my imagination, your house is very different from Osulton Manor," she said. "The way I see it, things aren't clipped. They are like *this*, aren't they?" She gestured toward the vista outside the windows. "Natural and overgrown and somewhat . . . messy?"

She laughed.

He didn't. He couldn't. "Yes, that's exactly what it looks like," he said flatly. "The truth is, I can't afford a gardener, and even if I could, I'd tell him not to touch a thing, because I love it the way it is."

She stopped her carefree sauntering directly in front of him, only a foot away, close enough that he could see the flecks of gold in her eyes and the individual hairs in her delicate brows. He could smell the clean scent of her skin. Though it wasn't perfume he smelled. It was soap.

Her hands were clasped behind her back. She was swinging back and forth like a mischievous child, gazing up at him with impish eyes. She'd never looked at him like that before—so playfully and flirtatiously. It was the Adele he'd always known existed deeper down. The Adele she had never let loose. This Adele—the carnal one—awakened his sharply honed instincts and impulses.

"I'm glad you keep your garden natural," she said. "I wouldn't want to ever think of you with your wings clipped, so to speak. I like the idea of you being wild, and soaring."

Damien fought to ignore the blood pounding through his veins. "Adele, you need to soar, too. Don't let them make you English."

Her smile faded, and her expression became serious all of a sudden.

God. He didn't know where that had come from. She was engaged to Harold. *Harold.*

"I didn't mean that the way it sounded," he said. "They're good people. They're my family."

She turned away from him and walked to the windows. She stood with her back to him, saying nothing. He set his hat down on the table, then moved around it and joined her, gazing down at her soft profile in the light reflecting off the calm lake.

She looked up at him. "Why *would* you say that? Is it because of what Eustacia has been saying—that no one would guess I'm American? That I'm practically English already? Do I mold and bend into any shape, fade into any background, rather than just be the real me? Or is it because everyone always says I'm perfect, and you're the only one who knows I'm not?"

He wasn't sure what to say, which was out of his realm of experience. He *always* knew what to say to women. He always knew what they wanted to hear, and he knew how to seduce the ones who wanted to be seduced.

But Adele, sweet Adele, did not want to be seduced. She wanted truth. She was unsure of her future, and she wanted him to tell her everything was going to be all right.

"Yes, it's just because of that," he said.

She gazed out at the lake again. There was not a hint of a breeze causing even the smallest waves. There were only random, circular ripples where the quiet fish bobbed to the surface.

"No, it's *not* just that," she said.

Damien's gut wrenched.

Then she turned to him and began to speak quickly. "Harold is a wonderful man, I know that. I just wasn't expecting so much grandeur. I had no idea I would be living in a house like this. I don't know what I'm supposed to do. How will I know when to curtsy or not to curtsy, or how to be a proper hostess? I'm not prepared for this. How will I ever manage? Do you think I made a mistake coming here? Or did Harold make a mistake, believing in me?"

"You'll learn," he said. "You'll learn all of it, because you're smart. Harold wouldn't have proposed to you otherwise."

"But do I *want* to learn it? Maybe it's too much. I've always done what my parents wanted me to do, but sometimes I think they may have overestimated me. They always said I was the most sensible and dutiful of their daughters, and I suppose that's what I've always thought I was born to be—sensible. I've been playing that role, but now I'm not so sure. I'm tired of this perfect life—the jewels and the shiny chandeliers and the astonishingly overwhelming wealth. I don't want all those *things*, I just want . . ." She gazed up into his eyes, looking almost frantic. "Sometimes lately, I find myself not wanting to be sensible. I've never felt that way before. I've never been tempted to do anything that was different from what was expected of me. I was content to just do what people told me to do. But since the kidnapping, I'm questioning that. And it scares me."

Her eyes were pleading. What did she want? Answers? Answers to what? Her place in the world? Her purpose? Her desires?

"There's a great deal in life you haven't experienced yet, Adele. That's all. You'll figure it all out in time."

"But I'm going to become someone's wife

soon. I am to choose my whole future, the rest of my life. What if I discover that's not what I'm meant to be?" She stopped talking and bowed her head and cupped her forehead in her hand. "Oh, listen to me. How very silly I must sound. I have cold feet, that's all, and I've been listening to my sister too much."

"What does she say to you?" he asked.

The pleading look disappeared, and Adele's voice took on a calmer tone. "She's always wanted me to go out and have an adventure before I settle down. But I already did that, didn't I?"

"Does she approve of your decision to marry Harold?"

Adele blinked a few times. "Oh yes. She likes him very much. Who wouldn't?"

"Of course," he replied.

Adele's gaze swept over his face, from his eyes down to his lips, to his hair and back to his eyes again. He simply stood there, letting her look at him.

"I'm sorry," she said, "for being so emotional. It's not like me to act that way." She paused, staring at his face as if she were pondering something. Then at last she added, "Sometimes I feel like I'm a different person when I'm with you."

He gazed down at her wet, ruby lips, glistening in the sunlight beaming in the windows, and an unexpected shiver of need coursed through him. She was unlike any woman he'd ever known.

Perhaps it was because she opened up to him and told him things she didn't tell other people. Or perhaps it was her innocence and her goodness.

No, it couldn't be. The only thing he thought about when he looked at her was everything that defied innocence and goodness. What he felt for her was dark and sinful and wrong.

She gazed up into his eyes and said with a deep, resounding sadness, "Damien, sometimes I worry that I don't really know who I am."

"*I* know who you are," he softly replied.

He stepped forward, closing the last bit of space between them, and took in a deep, liberating breath. *At last*, he thought, feeling a blazing hot surge of anticipation in his veins. But with it came shame and remorse—before he'd even done anything.

She looked into his eyes and shook her head, and he understood what she was saying without ever really saying it. *This is wrong*, she told him with her eyes.

It was wrong, he knew it was, but he could not stop. He could not.

He folded her into his arms and held her, as he'd held her on the bed when she'd had the nightmare. Only then he'd done it because he'd had to. He'd had to keep her safe when he was bringing her home to Harold. He'd been acting as her protector.

Now he had no excuses. They had arrived at Osulton. She was safe in every way but one. Because *he* should not be holding her. Harold should be holding her.

But still, Damien could not let go. He could not. His heart was pounding, racing out of control.

He pulled back, took her face in his hands, and kissed the tip of her nose, then her forehead, then he lowered his mouth to hers—softly, wetly, so achingly that it hurt inside him. Blood pounded in his brain. He swept his tongue into her mouth, and she made a little sound—a sweet, innocent whimper full of pleasure and awakenings.

Savoring the breathtaking sensation of her soft, luscious body pressed closely to his, and responding to the feel of her breasts crushed between them, Damien deepened the kiss.

Adele wrapped her arms around his neck, ran her fingers through the hair at his nape, and Damien's sexual impulses, like fire under a splash of kerosene, flared high with a gusty roar. He devoured her deliciously soft, supple lips with his own, and finally—*God, finally*—let himself cherish her.

Giving in to it—all of it—was like taking a cool drink of water, when he'd been almost dead from thirst. He couldn't stop guzzling. He wanted more and more and more.

He turned her in his arms and slowly backed her up against the wall, his lips never leaving hers. Harold could have been watching from outside one of the windows, and Damien wouldn't have been able to stop this. That's how badly he wanted her—with desperation and a fierce, fiery need more powerful than anything he'd ever known.

He had lost himself. He was doomed. Yet still he couldn't stop, because the pleasure was so good, and the need to touch her and hold her was so great, he thought he might suffocate if he let go.

Bending slightly at the knees, he thrust upward with his hips. She raised a knee to open to him, while she drove forward in return, applying an exquisite, stimulating pressure against his erection. Again and again, he bent at the knees and thrust upward between her legs, and each time, she let out a tiny whimper of delight.

It all came so naturally—this tantalizing, erotic dance that mimicked sex—even though they were fully clothed, upright against a wall.

Damien's senses reeled with a fierce, surging lust. He wanted so much more than this. He wanted to bury himself inside her and feel the hot wetness of everything she contained. He wanted to take her—in every way she could be taken—here and now on the cold, hard floor of this rotunda.

Sucking at the soft skin just below her earlobe, he let his hand drift up the side of her body to stroke the side of her neck. She sighed with pleasure, and the deep, husky sound of her voice, full of raw, sexual arousal, sent his heedless desires ramming hard against the crumbling wall of his self-control.

Feeling her hands cup the back of his head, he moved lower to kiss her neck, while he unfastened the top buttons at the collar of her bodice. *Adele* . . . He wanted to say her name, whisper it in her ear, but he didn't want to break the fragile spell. He kept quiet.

She moaned again, stroking his leg with hers, running her hands through his hair and making a terrible mess of it, while Damien dropped reckless, openmouth kisses across the moist, creamy skin just above her corset. He cupped her breast in his hand, lifting it, massaging it, suckling and wishing his mouth could reach her nipple, if only it weren't constrained beneath the tightness of her underclothes.

"Damien," she whispered, panting, as she tossed her head back. "Please, stop."

He heard the desperation in her voice, and realized she was pleading with him again, only this time for something very different from before. She was asking him to back away, because she didn't have the strength or the discipline to do it herself.

Damien labored to throttle his mounting desires, to choke them. Before his body had a chance to resist the order, he quickly stepped back and raked a shaky hand through his hair. Breath sailed out of his lungs as if he'd been punched. It was a reaction to his sexual desires being suddenly and swiftly interrupted by an instantaneous, stinging regret.

Adele stood against the wall. She gathered the top of her bodice in a tight fist and held it closed. Her cheeks were flushed. She looked shocked. Dismayed.

"*God*," he whispered. He was disgusted with himself.

Adele's eyes filled with tears. "How could we have done that?" Her voice was quiet with disbelief.

"It was my fault," he said shakily.

"No, it was my fault, too. Something inside me wanted you, but I don't *want* to want you."

Her statement hurt, even though he knew it was the way things were. He didn't *want* to want her either.

"Please go away," she pleaded. "Go to London until this passes. It's wrong, Damien, and we both know it. Please go away."

He stared at her sad, shimmering beauty in the brightness of the room as she pleaded with him to do the right thing.

He nodded, and walked out.

Damien strode to the house to leave a note to his aunt, to tell her he was leaving. He passed his cousin Violet on the way up the front steps. "Damien," she said, "where are you going?"

He did not stop to talk. "To London."

"But what about tonight? We've been rehearsing a scene from *King Lear*."

"It'll be stupendous, I'm sure." He entered the house and slammed the door behind him.

Violet remained on the steps, staring after her cousin, who seemed in a most impulsive hurry. *He is probably going to see that actress,* she thought, lifting her parasol over her head and turning to continue down the steps on her way to the garden, where she'd heard Lord Whitby had gone walking.

Lord Whitby. Violet inhaled deeply and sighed. He was so impossibly handsome, she couldn't bear it. She'd once heard that opposites were attracted to each other. Perhaps it was true. She did love his golden hair. Thank heavens he hadn't come back from America engaged to one of those heiresses. And thank heavens Harold *had* come home engaged to one.

Violet smiled. Fate was kind sometimes, was it not? Who would ever have thought Harold would manage such a thing, and secure Violet's own future? And secure it soundly, because she had always been able to pull her brother's strings. Now it would be the family's purse strings she would pull.

She glanced over her shoulder to where she had just met Damien a moment ago. He—on the other hand—had no strings to pull. He was no one's puppet. Lucky for her, the heiress still wanted to marry her trouble-free brother.

And thank God Damien was leaving.

Violet stopped. She stood motionless on the grass. Was she being selfish, she wondered, wanting Harold's marriage for her own advantage? She recalled what the vicar had said in church last week: "We must think of others before ourselves."

Perhaps she should try to be a better person, she thought fleetingly. One eyebrow lifted, and she gazed upward as she considered it. She pictured herself helping out in the chapel or doing something charitable. Could she help the vicar when he went to collect bread for the poor?

Then she thought of the horrid, cheap cologne he wore. Violet wrinkled her nose and started walking again. No, she didn't need to work at being a better person. She had been blessed with a pretty face, and very soon a full bank account. Besides, the vicar was annoying. Everyone said he was a nice man, but he had a squeaky voice. She certainly didn't want to end up married to someone like him.

An hour later, after Adele had returned her horse to the stable, she entered the house, her heels clicking as she walked quickly across the main hall to the stairs. She had just grabbed hold of the newel post, when she heard some-one at the top. Glancing up, she saw Damien.

Their eyes met, and they both halted where they were—she at the bottom and he at the top. She had not expected to see him. She had hoped he would be gone.

She considered backing off the step and stand-ing up against the wall to make way for him to pass. Or perhaps she could keep her head down and dash up the stairs, passing him without a word.

After a few seconds, Damien started hesi-tantly down the steps again, his eyes never leav-ing hers. All she could do was stand there, frozen in her place, waiting to see what *he* would do.

He slowed when he reached the step she

stood upon, and stopped beside her. Her heart was pounding; she half expected him to tell *her* to leave Osulton Manor. She was the outsider, after all.

But he said nothing . . . nothing as he took her hand and led her off the step and into the quiet, private confines of the library.

Chapter 15

Damien opened the library door, peered inside to ensure it was empty, then brought Adele in and closed the door behind him.

"We shouldn't be in here," she said, crossing the dark paneled room to stand in front of the window. "Not alone." She had to force herself to turn and face him with an appearance of confidence.

He had changed into city clothes—a crisp white shirt under a black jacket, and a long overcoat, open in front. Yet his wavy, black hair was in chaos, and despite the fine clothes, he had that wild, rugged look about him. His chest and shoulders were inconceivably thick and broad. He was a mountain. A windswept mountain.

When he finally spoke, his voice was deep

and controlled. "I need to say something to you before I leave."

He is going to apologize and say it will never happen again, she thought. *Then it will be over, and by nightfall, he will be in the arms of his mistress.*

She clung to the image of his mistress. It strengthened her will.

He took a step toward her. "Are you absolutely sure you should marry Harold?"

Adele stared at him, dumbfounded. It was not what she'd expected him to say. And why was he asking her this? Did he mean to convince her she should *not* be sure? Was Damien willing to consider fighting for her himself?

She imagined becoming his bride instead of Harold's, and a part of her basked euphorically in the notion that it could happen, that she could be loved, truly loved, by her wild, black knight. There. She'd admitted it. A part of her was indeed dreaming of such an end to this situation.

But no. She clenched her fists suddenly. She should not fantasize about him that way. He was not the husbandly kind. He was currently in love with a scandalous actress, and he had no loyalty. He went from woman to woman. Adele should not imagine him to be something he was not.

She reminded herself that he had unleashed her passions, certainly, but that wasn't necessarily a good thing. This change in herself was disconcerting and frightening. She didn't know what was on the other side of it, or how far it would take her. She didn't want to end up like Frances Fairbanks, promiscuous and not respectable and living for pleasure alone. Could that happen to Adele? Damien was a powerful temptation. He had enormous pull. Hence, he made her fear the possibility of tumbling into a dark abyss, a future full of regret. A life ruined, all because of a passionate, "temporary madness."

"I'm sure," she replied firmly, embedding herself in her determination not to be carried away by it.

He slowly crossed the room, growing closer and closer until he was standing in front of her with only a foot of empty space between them. Adele realized she was holding her breath. She had to consciously force herself to let it out slowly.

"I've spent the past hour killing myself wondering if I should tell Harold what just happened," Damien said.

Startled by the suggestion, Adele blinked up at him.

"Don't panic," he continued. "I would never hurt him for the sake of easing my own conscience. But I *would* hurt him to protect him." He began to pace around the room. "He lacks experience with women, Adele. He's innocent, and he's naive. What kind of wife will you be?"

The breath she'd been holding sailed out of her lungs in a single, thunderous heartbeat that shook her. So. He did not bring her in here to convince her to marry him. He brought her in here because he doubted her decency.

Though a part of her was having doubts about it herself, her pride nevertheless bucked. "Damien, I value my integrity, and when I speak my marriage vows, I will not take them lightly."

"But when I kissed you, you kissed me back."

Adele raised her chin.

"Maybe you're not as strong as you and everyone else thinks you are." He took another slow and careful step toward her. "That's what worries me. My mother was not faithful to my father, and their marriage ended very badly. I won't let that happen to Harold."

He crowded her up against the wainscoting. God, she could smell him. She could see the rough texture of the stubble along his jaw. She could feel the size and the weight of him, as if he were on top of her, which in a way, he was.

"I will never be an unfaithful wife," she said.

Breathing hard now, she gazed at his lips, so full, so soft-looking. Despite everything, she remembered what they felt like, what his tongue felt like inside her mouth.

"But you've been an unfaithful fiancée."

Her eyes widened. He was right. She *had* been. But that didn't make it any easier to hear, coming from him.

She felt angry all of a sudden. Life had been so simple before she'd met him. Adele defiantly raised her chin again.

"How dare you reproach *me*, when I had never sinned before I encountered you. If I have fallen from my pedestal, it was *you* who brought me down."

"Is that how you see me? As some kind of immoral snake?"

"Isn't that what you are? You bed scandalous women, you don't pay your debts."

Heated shock flashed in his eyes.

"And you betrayed someone you cared about," she continued. "What happened between us was about temptation and weakness, and now you're comparing me to your mother, who was an adulteress. It's all despicable. I'm sick over it. Everything between us has been immoral and I regret all of it."

Just saying the words was like a stake she was thrusting into her own heart. She had never been immoral before. She had always been good. And she hated to think that what they'd shared had not been tender and loving. There was a part of her that cherished what they'd done. *Cherished*. She'd felt cared for and safe in his arms. It broke her heart to think that it was dirty or shameful.

"You're too close, Damien," she said, laboring to stay focused.

Damien's eyes softened, and at long last, he stepped back. Adele grabbed hold of the windowsill beside her.

He stared at her for a long, excruciating moment. "Part of me wishes you were not so strong, Adele."

Anger and confusion all welled up inside her and burst forth like water breaking through a dam. "Why? So I would betray Harold and you could congratulate yourself for being right about all women being like your mother? That's why you haven't married before now, isn't it? You think all women are wicked and unfaithful, and you had to prove it with me. Harold told you I was saintly and you didn't want to believe it. You didn't want to believe that *you* might be afraid to love someone, afraid to trust someone like Harold trusted me. You didn't want Harold to have what you couldn't have, because it made you jealous. Jealous of him for being able to love and trust someone. You are deficient and you know it, and you want to pull someone down with you, and that someone is me."

Shock and fury coiled together within her. She could barely fathom what she'd just said to Damien. She'd never attacked anyone like that before—attacked his heart and soul in such a direct, cruel way.

But she'd needed to be cruel. She was angry with him. Angry with him for making her feel guilty and immoral, and for making her want him when he could not be had. She was angry with him because he was not willing to fight for her—to choose her over Harold and become the man she wanted him to be. To let go of his own misguided belief that no woman could be trusted. He was using this—these accusations about her integrity—to release himself from what would be a painful undertaking.

He turned and walked to the door. "No. Because this would all be easier to bear if I could think badly of you. I want to, Adele. I want to hate you, but all I feel is guilt, because you're right. I did bring you down."

He did not look back. He simply walked out.

Adele collapsed into a chair and struggled to catch her breath. *I did bring you down.*

Her heart throbbed painfully over all the hurtful words they'd just spoken. Damien did not respect or trust her. All he saw was her propensity to be just like his mother and cheat on Harold. He thought the worst of her. And Adele had told Damien he was deficient and immoral.

She didn't *want* to think those terrible things about the man who had saved her life, the man who had kissed her and held her in his arms, but they were true and she knew it. She had to accept it. She had to accept that he would never be hers. He would never be her prince charming.

She waited for a few minutes until she was sure he was gone, then she hurried from the room.

Violet, however, did not hurry from the room. She rose very slowly from the sofa she had been reclining upon—a sofa that faced the fireplace on the other side of the library.

She wanted to strangle Damien. Strangle him! Was there not one woman in England he could keep his hands off of? Harold's perfect, virtuous fiancée, no less?

Violet ground her teeth together and cursed her cousin. *Damn, damn, damn him!* She would not let it happen. She would not let Harold lose the one and only woman who had ever managed to lure his attention away from his precious laboratory long enough to get him to propose. Violet had never thought she would see the day, and if Harold lost Adele, it might be another complete lifetime before he looked up from his bloody experiments to take notice of

another woman. And what were the chances
the woman he noticed would be an heiress as
wealthy as Adele?

Slim. Very slim.

Violet stood up and walked out, resolving
that she would do something about this. She
didn't know what yet, but she would figure out
something, because she would not let those
American dollars slip so easily from her grasp.

Damien knocked on Frances's dressing room
door as he always did after a performance—
twice, then twice again.

"Come in, darling," she called to him from
inside.

He pushed the door open. The room smelled
strongly of the red roses that were lying about
in bouquets. Sparkling costumes were draped
over the backs of chairs, and decorative dyed
feathers stood in tall vases.

He walked in and closed the door behind him
with a quiet click. Frances swiveled around on
the stool in front of her mirrored vanity. She
wore only her chemise, corset, and stockings,
along with her stage paint and heeled boots.
She had taken the pins out of her thick, wavy
red hair, and it spilled wildly upon her shoulders. She knew that was the way Damien preferred it. She did not know, however, that he
would have preferred to see her without the
paint.

Saying nothing, Damien slowly sauntered
across the room, tugging at his neck cloth along
the way.

He usually smiled at her when they went through these motions after a performance, but tonight, he had no smile for Frances. He wanted only one thing, and that was all. He felt no need to charm. But she was not the type of woman who required it.

She slowly stood, meandering teasingly toward the red chintz sofa against the far wall, and sat down, leaning back. Damien came to a full stop in front of her, looking into her eyes while he finished loosening his neck cloth. He left it dangling around his collar.

She looked up at him for a moment, reading him, then she sat forward on the edge of the sofa cushion. The corner of her full mouth turned up in a wicked grin, and her green eyes sparkled mischievously.

"Someone's in the mood for something very naughty," she said, then proceeded to unfasten his trousers.

He closed his eyes, waiting to feel the desire flow through him as it usually did—a desire that he wanted and needed to feel tonight—but to his surprise and annoyance, a spontaneous reflex brought his hands up to gently take hold of her wrists.

Before he knew what he was doing, he had taken a well-defined step backward, and Frances was looking up at him with an expression of bewilderment on her face. "What's the matter?" she asked.

For a long moment, he had no answer, then at last he said, "Good God, Frances, I'm sorry."

She shook her head, not quite able to understand. He wasn't sure he understood it fully himself. He didn't understand anything about himself lately.

"Sorry for what?"

He took a few more steps backward, then turned away from her and fastened his trousers. "I shouldn't have come here."

Her voice took on a haughty tone. "Why not?"

"Because I would only be using you," he said flatly.

She stood. "I've never minded before."

Frances. She was like no ordinary woman.

He faced her again. "But it was different before. Before, I came for more than just the sex. We've always been friends, and you've known that."

Her eyes narrowed with anger. "So what's different now? It's not because of the bracelet, is it? I certainly didn't mean to become possessive, Damien."

"I know that."

"Then what's the problem? Are we not friends anymore?"

He hated this. *Hated* it. "I believe the time has come for us to be *only* friends, instead of what we are at the moment."

"Why?"

There was no point dragging this out. She deserved the truth—at least part of it. The rest he would keep to himself, until he could figure out how to deal with it. "Because it's time I found a wife."

Her jaw jutted forward. "That doesn't mean we have to stop seeing each other."

"Yes, it does." Because no woman would have him if he was still seeing Frances, and he *needed* someone to have him. He needed a wife of his own. The sooner the better.

Frances's head snapped back as if she'd been hit in the face with a ball. "I'd tarnish your reputation, you mean."

He said nothing.

"I have news for you, Damien. Your reputation was tarnished long before I invited you into my bed."

Her eyes flashed briefly with shock and fury before she turned without warning and picked up a pink perfume bottle from her vanity, and hurled it across the room at him, striking his wrist bone. As luck would have it, the bottle was open, and the lilac scent poured all over him.

He was still recovering when a tall, glass paperweight of a nude woman came whirling through the air and smashed into his face.

"Jesus!" He cupped his eye and bent forward.

"You deserve it, you bastard!" she screeched.

Damien straightened. He did deserve it, he knew it, so he was willing to let it go. But when a vase—much larger and undoubtedly heavier than both the perfume bottle and the paperweight combined—was launched at him, his generosity reached its limit. He deflected the vase, and instantly moved to restrain Frances.

He wrapped his arms around her from behind, took a few hits, but finally managed to calm her down enough to feel somewhat confident that she wasn't going to throw any more glass objects at him.

"I hope you rot in hell," she ground out, breathing hard.

"I'm sure I will."

He held her like that for a moment or two, feeling deeply ashamed. He had always been honest with Frances. They both knew what their relationship was about, but tonight he had come here to use her to relieve his own tensions and to suffocate his angst and confusion over another woman—a woman who was engaged to his cousin.

He had sunk very low.

Eventually, Frances's breathing slowed and her body began to relax in his arms. After a long, drawn out silence, she said, "I hate you."

"I know."

"You're a bastard."

"I know that, too." He rested his head on her shoulder, and let out a deep, miserable sigh.

She sighed, too. "Your eye is bleeding."

She stepped out of his arms and put her hands on his face to examine the gash at the top of his cheekbone.

"Look at this," she said, shaking her head. "You make me crazy, Damien. No man has ever made me crazy before." Her voice softened. "That's what I hate most about this."

Blood was dripping down the side of his cheek. He wiped it on the back of his hand.

"Maybe I'll be better off," she said, going to fetch a cold cloth. "Maybe we both will."

Chapter 16

Two days later, Adele sat in her bedchamber at Osulton Manor, staring absently out the window at the Chauncey Maze. Clara knocked softly and walked in.

"Seger and I and the baby will be leaving soon," she said. "They're loading everything onto the coach now."

Adele stood. The thought of her sister leaving sent a sudden, intense wave of emotion through her, and she had to fight the urge to cry—as she often had to do lately, whenever she thought about her family leaving her here alone, or when she thought about never seeing America again. It was not like Adele to cry. She had always been very strong.

She managed, however, to put on a brave face

217

for her sister, because she didn't want to lay all that on her shoulders. It helped when she reminded herself she would be going to London soon to visit her other sister, Sophia.

"I'm sure you'll be glad to get home," she said. "You've been away for a long time now."

Clara moved fully into the room and took both Adele's hands in hers. "I will, but I will also leave here feeling very worried about you. Are you sure you'll be all right? You don't seem like the same sister I knew back in New York— the sister who always had everything figured out. You've seemed sad."

Sad. Yes, Adele had indeed been that, which made no sense because she was surrounded by happy people, and she'd gotten what she'd wanted. Damien had gone back to London.

Since then, Harold had taken her on a tour of the inside of the house, Eustacia had taken her and her mother on a carriage tour of the estate and into the village, and Adele had spent many wonderful hours with Catherine, getting to know the elderly woman and enjoying her intelligent conversation. She had participated in each evening's activities, singing and playing instruments in the drawing room. Everything had been quite perfectly lovely.

"Does it have anything to do with Lord Alcester leaving?" Clara asked, hitting the mark as she always did.

Adele realized finally that she could not continue to keep this problem to herself. Her sister knew. She had always known. She had simply not pushed.

"Yes," Adele replied at last.

Clara's eyes warmed with compassion. She touched Adele's cheek. "You could have talked to me about it, Adele. I know that you think you have to hold everything together and be the perfect daughter and the perfect fiancée, but you *don't* have to be perfect. Nobody is. Come and sit down."

They sat on the edge of the bed. "It's a wonder you haven't exploded by now," Clara continued. "Tell me everything, and I'll see if I can help."

Adele nodded. "It started the first night, when he came to rescue me in the cottage." She recalled her first glimpse of him. "He burst into my room, strong and forceful and extraordinary looking, and he saved my life. I was grateful, but at the same time wary of him, because everything about him was frightening. He'd just killed a man. Then later, I remember wishing that it had been Harold who had come, because somehow I knew Damien and I would experience things together that we should not experience."

Adele described the conversations they'd had and the trouble she'd had sleeping. She told Clara about Damien sharing her bed.

"He knows me, Clara. He sees inside the real me, and he has made me see inside myself, too. And it happened after three short days. When I'm with him, I say things and feel things that I've never felt before. I open up to him completely, and because of that, I find myself doubting my relationship with Harold."

"You don't think Harold knows the real you?"

She lowered her gaze to her hands in her lap. "I don't think he really *sees* me, not the inner me. He talks, but he doesn't listen. I feel rather invisible when I'm with him. I feel like a shell of a person, whose only purpose is to nod and smile and agree with his opinions. Which is basically the person I was in New York."

"You're not that person now?"

Adele shook her head. "Ever since I met Damien, I've been questioning who I am, and I think I understand it now. I wasn't happy when we moved to the city. Our way of life was so strange to me, I didn't know what to do with myself, so I just did what people told me to do. I clung to rules and tried not to think about my life before. I couldn't bear the longing. And when Mother introduced me to Harold, I was content to marry him because I had begun to forget the person I was when we lived in Wisconsin. But then I met Damien and I became attracted to the wildness in him. He makes me remember our life before New York."

"And that was the real you?"

"Yes. I love the outdoors. I love to ride. I don't need jewels."

"But what does that mean for your future?"

"I'm not sure yet. One thing I do know is that I need to feel free and do what makes me happy. And that is to enjoy the outdoors more and find a *home* for myself—a place that's right for me.

New York wasn't right. I felt displaced and frustrated. I couldn't be myself there. I need to put my roots into the ground that is *right* for me."

"Will Osulton Manor be right?"

Adele considered that with great care. "Possibly. I love the countryside. I could become very attached to this place."

"But you need to become attached to more than just a place, Adele. You need to become attached to your husband."

"I don't know if I can."

"What about Damien?" Clara asked.

Adele shook her head. "We said some terrible things to each other just before he left. He compared me to his adulterous mother, and I told him that what we'd done was immoral. I don't know if we could ever get past that. What is between us definitely does *not* feel right. It feels wrong."

Clara squeezed Adele's hand.

"Harold is obviously the better man," Adele said. "He's reliable and decent and kindhearted, but I'm not sure we are compatible. I need to find out. I need to see if we can catch up to the level of intimacy that I had with Damien."

"Maybe you will never catch up."

Adele sighed hopelessly. "Oh, Clara, don't say that. I don't want everything to fall apart. Everyone would be so hurt and disappointed. I've promised myself to Harold, who is a good man. I've made a commitment to him, and I take my promises seriously. I can't break his heart, and certainly not for a man I could never trust."

"Because of his reputation?"

"Yes, and the things he said to me in the library. I'm not sure he's capable of being a good husband. He had a difficult childhood with tragic parents. He doesn't know what a happy marriage is. He has never been able to commit to one woman. He's jaded."

"You should listen to your heart, Adele—the organ that sees better than the eye. That's an old Yiddish proverb," she added. "You say you don't want to give up on Harold, but maybe you shouldn't give up on Damien yet, either."

Adele shook her head. "I would rather forget him. I believe he's with his mistress now—the actress. I know it shouldn't bother me, but to think of them together is like a knife in my heart. I want to get over this foolish infatuation. If you can help me with that, I will be eternally grateful."

Clara thought about it. "All right, here's what I suggest. Give yourself some time. Even a week can make a difference. I know I said that I wanted you to have a great romance, but I also know from experience that these things *can* be fleeting, especially where an unsuitable man is concerned. Now that Damien is gone, what you feel for him might simply pass, and you might realize you prefer Harold after all. If it does, everything will be very easy. If it doesn't, you can deal with it then. You'll be coming to London soon, and you can take the opportunity to see how Damien behaves. If he does something to earn your respect, you might discover that there could be more between you. Promise me you'll come to me if you still want him after a week away from him. I've been through this, Adele. I know what you're going through."

Adele hugged her sister. "Thank you. I will."

The balls and assemblies that were held over the next few days did not find Damien in attendance, as a black eye on account of an angry mistress was not becoming of a gentleman in search of a wife. Nor was he inclined to flirt when he was irritable most of the time because of his creditors and his London house tenants, who had taken it upon themselves to upgrade the stove in the kitchen and send him the bill.

He was irritable for other reasons, too. He was ashamed of the way he had lost all control in the teahouse with Adele, who, before she'd met him, had never done anything she needed to regret. He was ashamed of the way he had treated her in the library afterward, questioning her integrity, when Damien was the one at fault. *He* had kissed *her*. *He* had been the one to suggest they ride alone to the teahouse, even after she said she would prefer to return with Harold another day. He *had* dragged her down.

She must despise him now. She had every right to. Perhaps it was best.

He was also ashamed of betraying Harold's unwavering trust—Harold, his closest friend since childhood. He was ashamed for treating Frances badly as well. All in all, he was not proud of himself.

He spent many hours thinking about his future. He did not wish to continue along this low and sordid path. If he was going to be able to return to Osulton Manor and remain a part of the only family he had—and a decent, good family, it was—he needed a wife of his own. He needed to live a respectable life. But this was not a new wish. He had always wanted to rise above the disgrace that was part of his childhood and therefore part of him. He wanted a proper marriage—a marriage different from what his parents had had—and it had become more than clear lately that he could no longer put it off. Essence House needed funds. It needed its lord and master, and for other more heartfelt reasons, he needed a woman in his life. A woman he could love.

The following week proved slightly less trying. Damien's eye had begun to heal, his tenants paid their rent, and he was able to pay his creditors something to at least keep them from knocking on his door every other hour.

Regarding his regrets, he was still working at forgiving himself, which was not something he was particularly good at, but he was at least making an effort.

Consequently, he danced, he chatted, he flattered, and he charmed. He met many young women of good breeding, and many wealthy ones on a desperate social climb in an upward direction into the aristocracy. Some were American. Others were English, daughters of businessmen who had recently earned a substantial income, and looked upon an eligible baron as a most beneficial stepping stone.

So he kept busy and appreciated the many pretty faces that were new to the London Season. He had a goal, after all—to find a bride and bring her home to Essence House. And for Damien, a goal was always effective to keep his mind and body focused and disciplined. He thought very little about Adele.

Except on the rare occasions when he let down his guard, often when he was drifting into sleep. It was during those moments he thought of her, and felt a very deep and painful longing.

Chapter 17

For eight days, Adele did as Clara had suggested. She went on with her life as a guest at Osulton, and she waited. She waited for Damien to fade from her mind. She waited for Harold to do something wonderful and stir her passions. And she waited for the guilt over her intimacies with Damien to pass.

The guilt never did pass. Neither did the two other things happen. She'd said good-bye to Damien eight days ago, and she was still missing him and longing for him, despite all the hurtful things they'd said to each other. She was watching the end of the road, fantasizing about a black horse galloping up the hill with a dark knight on his back—a handsome, dark knight with wind in his hair, coming to rescue her again, from all her doubts and questions.

That never happened either.

On the ninth day when she woke up in the morning and gazed longingly at the window, she realized she had become utterly pathetic. Surely Damien wasn't pining away over her. He was the kind of man who could sweep one woman from his heart quite effortlessly—not that any one woman had ever truly been *in* his heart to begin with—and move on to the next. He was probably with his mistress at that very moment—in her bed, kissing her and holding her and laughing with her. Adele had pictured him with the beautiful actress more than once this past week, and each time, she'd been overcome with jealousy, even though she didn't even know what the woman looked like.

Adele needed to get over this. She sat up and told herself that she didn't need to be rescued, especially by a man like him. She was in control of her emotions, and her life at the current moment was as close to wonderful as it could be. She was engaged to a respectable and decent English nobleman, her family was proud of her, and she was surely the envy of most women in America, and probably England, too. She had been welcomed with open arms into her fiancé's family, and she would one day give birth to the next Viscount Osulton. Everything about her life was a dream come true. She *must* forget Damien.

She promptly rang for her maid, for she was ready to get dressed.

That very afternoon, however, in the closed

coach on the way to a neighbor's house for tea, Damien's name came up in conversation, and Adele felt her resolve flying out the window.

"Did you know that Damien had a black eye?" Violet said quietly, when Eustacia's head tipped to the side and she began to snore over the rumble of the rattling coach.

Adele's stomach lurched sickeningly as the coach went over a bump.

"Supposedly," Violet said, "it was his mistress who gave it to him. That actress—the Fairbanks woman." She shook her head at the sordidness of it all.

"What happened?" Adele asked, quite unable to resist asking.

Violet leaned in closer, seeming to enjoy the scandalous details. "She cut him with a glass, or threw it at him more likely. I'm not sure why, but I do know that they have a very turbulent relationship. It's not the first black eye Damien's received, I assure you, but he doesn't seem to mind. It doesn't stop him from seeing her, and others like her." She looked intently into Adele's eyes. "What do you think it is about women like her? Why are they so good at luring men like Damien into their beds? Maybe it's the risk and the danger. Or maybe if they're passionate in one way, they're passionate in others, if you understand my meaning. It's all a great mystery, isn't it?"

"Yes, it is."

The coach leaped over another bump, tossing Violet and Adele almost up off the seat cushion. Adele considered her relationship with Damien.

Was that what she had been to him? Something risky and dangerous, because she belonged to his cousin?

"But I suppose Damien is ripe for the picking for a woman who craves sin," Violet continued. "Have you heard the story about his parents?"

"Some of it," Adele said. "I know his mother had an affair."

"Yes, that's true, but there's more to it than that." She leaned closer and whispered. "Damien's father was so brokenhearted, he killed himself over her betrayal."

Adele stiffened in shock. "Damien's father?"

"Yes. Witnesses say he went looking for a fight in the worst part of London and provoked the other man. It was the very day they buried Damien's mother." Violet sighed. "Poor man. He was kind and decent like Harold. He even looked like him. He gave his heart to his wife, and she crushed it. She married him for his title and his money, then right away went out and spent as much of it as she could, mostly on her lovers."

"I had no idea."

"Well, from what I've heard, Damien is following in his mother's footsteps and hunting the streets of London as we speak, looking for a rich wife. He needs money quite desperately, I understand. Perhaps that's why Frances threw the glass at him."

He's looking for a rich wife? Adele had not known that. She had told Clara that Damien knew her in a way that Harold did not, and she had felt as if she knew him, too. Intimately. But she had not known this.

She felt very naive all of a sudden. Then her mind darted about at the ramifications. Was that why he'd kissed her in the teahouse? Had he thought he could steal her away from Harold, and get his hands on her marriage settlement? Had he hoped to make her believe that they shared a special connection, only to seduce her into leaving Harold for *him*?

No, she didn't want to believe that. Yet the doubts and suspicions were coming at her from all angles. Where Damien was concerned, nothing was ever straightforward. Everything about him—the things she heard, the way he treated her—made her feel wary. He constantly said he was loyal to Harold, yet he had kissed her. Obviously, he was not as loyal as he claimed.

But neither was she.

"Well, none of it is any great secret," Violet said. "I'm sure you would have heard all the scandalous talk eventually." She leaned closer to Adele—who was now feeling sick from thinking about all this—and touched her knee. "I beg your pardon for revealing so many horrid things, but I thought it would be best if you heard it from one of *us*, and I hope you will not judge Harold by the way Damien lives and treats women. Damien and Harold couldn't be more different. You chose the right man, Adele, I assure you, and I am so glad *you* are decent as well. You would never do to Harold what

Damien's mother did to his father." She gazed out the window.

The coach hit another horrendous bump, and Eustacia stirred in her seat. "Have we arrived?" she asked, looking around in a daze.

Violet patted her mother's knee. "No, Mother, we have quite a distance to go yet."

London
One week later

Adele peered out of the coach window and saw her sister Sophia, standing on the steps of her grand Mayfair mansion. Beside Sophia was her husband, James, the ninth Duke of Wentworth, widely known as one of the wealthiest men in London. With them were James's sister, Lily, and his younger brother, Martin.

Adele and her mother stepped out of the coach, and Sophia came dashing down to greet them. "You're here! Finally!" she shouted, throwing her arms around both their necks.

James smiled and descended the steps. "Madam," he said, bowing over Beatrice's plump, gloved hand and gazing with amusement at the absurdity of her purple hat. "A pleasure, as always. And Adele, how good of you to come. Sophia has spoken of nothing else these past few days."

Adele smiled, while Beatrice blushed and giggled. "Oh, James, you are too charming for words."

He smiled again, and gestured to Martin and

Lily on the stairs. "Do you remember my brother and sister?"

"Of course!" Beatrice replied. She gathered her purple skirts in both hands and hurried up to meet them halfway. She threw her arms around Lily's shoulders and hugged her tightly. "My darling girl, it's so nice to see you again! You look beautiful! Beautiful! And you, Martin, getting handsomer every day."

Adele watched her sister grin flirtatiously up at her husband, who smiled back at her. There was heat and love between them. It was as clear as day.

Adele wanted desperately—*desperately*—to share such a close bond with her own future husband. That was what would save her. That was what a real marriage was all about.

She knew that tomorrow, Harold was coming to London with Eustacia and Violet, and they would be spending time together at a few balls for which they had already received invitations.

Adele looked into her sister's joyful eyes— the eyes of a happily married woman and the proud, loving mother of two beautiful boys— and decided firmly that she, too, wanted a close, happy marriage. She did not want to spoil her chances for that by losing sight of the secure future that was within her reach.

Perhaps, she thought at last, it was time to flirt with her fiancé, and try a little harder to fall in love with him.

Chapter 18

"**I** believe there must be two hundred and fifty people here," Harold said, resting his hand on Adele's waist to step into a waltz, and glancing around the brightly lit ballroom. "You know I have a knack for estimating amounts of things? Go ahead, Adele. Start counting the people. I'll wager an error of no more than ten."

Adele glanced around also, realizing it had not even occurred to her to estimate the number of people here, nor did she feel like counting them. She was more interested in admiring the sheer glory of the room—the sound of the music and the magnificent movement of some of the more skillful dancers. There were also the musicians to watch. They were exceedingly talented, especially the violinists, who controlled their bows with such precision.

"I'm sure you're right," she replied, determined to avoid the chore of actually *counting* them. "Two hundred and fifty to be sure."

Harold smiled. "Yes, two hundred and fifty. I wonder how many hors d'oeuvres they have? They would need at least five per person."

He proceeded to calculate the total.

"You're a magnificent dancer, Harold," Adele said, politely interrupting and gazing up at him with what she hoped was a suggestive grin. "I like being close to you like this."

His eyebrows lifted. "Really? Even when it's so warm? Rather unpleasant, don't you think? All these people dancing . . . It creates an uncomfortable amount of heat. But the warm air rises. We should be thankful for that." He looked up at the high ceiling. "Imagine how hot it is up there. I wish I could send up a thermometer. I could hoist it up by throwing a wire over that chandelier."

Adele looked up, too, then tried to lure his attention back down to her. "Perhaps after this," she said with a teasing lilt to her voice, "we could go for a walk in the garden. In the moonlight."

"I doubt we'd be able to see the moon through the fog, but it will be cooler out there away from this heat, so, yes, it is indeed a splendid idea. I'll ask my mother to join us."

Adele blinked up at him. "I was hoping . . . perhaps . . . that we could go alone."

Who would have thought flirting would make her feel like such a dunderhead? Was she that inept? Or was Harold simply not the type to enjoy flirting?

"Alone?" he said. "Well, I suppose we could, but Mother looks rather lonely over there. Look."

Adele glanced to where Eustacia stood by a table of tarts. True, she did look as if she were waiting for someone to come and talk to her, but one would think that when a gentleman was propositioned for a private walk in the garden with a lady—his fiancée!—he would somehow arrange for some *other* person to entertain his mother.

The waltz ended, and Harold stopped abruptly, waving for Adele to follow him to the tart table.

"Come, my dear!" he said cheerfully. "Those are raspberry tarts, and Mother is about to finish them off."

Adele followed him off the floor. It appeared that flirting with her fiancé was going to prove to be more difficult than she had imagined.

Later in the evening, Adele and her mother joined Eustacia and Violet near the entrance to the ballroom, where they met Sophia and Lily.

"What a delightful ball this is!" Beatrice said. "But you haven't been dancing near enough, Lily. Why aren't you out on the floor? You're young and full of energy. Unlike Eustacia and I."

The two older women laughed and exchanged complaints about their sore feet, while Adele noticed Lily smiling uncomfortably. The fact was, she had danced very little. She could not have enjoyed having it pointed out.

Just then, Lord Whitby approached, looking strikingly handsome in his black formal attire. "Ladies," he said with a bow. "You all look radiant this evening."

Violet raised her arched eyebrow, and smirked. "As do you, Lord Whitby—charming all the women as usual."

His appealing, blue-eyed gaze drifted languidly to Violet's face, dropped appreciatively to her low neckline, then lifted again to her eyes. He smiled. "Only those who are of a nature to be charmed, Lady Violet."

The corner of her mouth curled up, and they stared at each other for a few heated seconds.

Adele wondered why *she* couldn't manage to achieve that sort of exchange with Harold. Everyone else seemed capable of it. What was she doing wrong?

"May I inquire about your card, Lady Violet?" he asked, his smoldering gaze never veering from hers.

"You may," she replied, tilting her head enticingly.

The next thing Adele knew, Eustacia was penciling in his name for later in the evening, and he was walking away, leaving the entire group of them flicking open their fans to cool themselves.

Adele looked around at everyone uncertainly. She had much to learn. Or maybe it was Harold who had something to learn. Perhaps *he*

needed to be awakened—as Lord Whitby undoubtedly was. He was clearly very confident
and experienced with women.

Adele glanced at Lily, who was staring after
Lord Whitby. He had not inquired about *her*
dance card. In fact, he had not even noticed her.
He had been too busy responding to Violet.
Adele glanced discreetly down at Lily's card.
There were no names written in for any more
dances tonight. Lily's shoulders rose and fell
with a sigh, and she consulted her timepiece.

Adele was dressing for Sophia's At Home—
the one day during the week when she was always available to receive callers—when a knock
sounded at her door. "Come in."

The door opened slowly, and Lily walked in.
Her dark hair was pulled into a loose bun on
top of her head, and she wore a simple gown of
dark gray silk. Adele often thought Lily would
look striking in brighter colors, but for some
reason, she preferred not to stand out.

For a long moment, Adele admired Lily's
beautiful blue eyes, so very striking with her
dark lashes and dark hair. Pale skinned, with a
tiny nose and full lips, she was an extraordinar-
ily pretty girl.

Lily stood for a few seconds, glancing around
uncomfortably before she finally met Adele's
gaze. "Can I ask you a question?"

"Of course. Please sit down."

"Thank you." Lily sat on the sofa, and Adele
joined her. "Last night, Lady Osulton men-

tioned her nephew, Lord Alcester. Do you know him very well?"

Adele stiffened, wondering where this was going. "I met him at my fiancé's home when I arrived there. I know him a little."

"The reason I'm asking is because I met him a few nights ago at a ball, and I danced with him. From what I understand, he is looking for a bride this Season."

The room seemed to become very warm all of a sudden. Adele shifted in her seat. "Oh?"

"Yes, and, well . . . I was wondering if you could tell me anything about him."

Adele stared blankly at Lily. "Like what?"

She shrugged. "Are the rumors true? The ones about his mother, and the ones about his former mistress, the actress? They say he used to go to her dressing room after all her performances, and that he was the first man to ever break her famous, unbreakable heart."

"He broke her heart?"

Lily spoke quietly. "Yes, didn't you hear that? Some people are saying that he wishes to redeem himself. He broke off his relationship with Miss Fairbanks two weeks ago, the very day he returned to London after being away at Osulton Manor. Meeting you and your mother, I believe. He told Frances he didn't love her anymore, and she had to cancel her performance the following night because she couldn't stop crying. He hasn't seen her since." Lily lowered her gaze again. "Well, that's what the gossips say, anyway. Who knows how much of it is true?"

The very day he returned to London? That was the day he had kissed Adele in the teahouse. Was that why he had told Frances he didn't love her anymore?

The thought that Damien was no longer making love to his mistress made Adele far, far happier than it should. She had to mentally shake herself, however, and force herself to remember all the reasons that she needed to forget him.

"I . . . I don't know anything about Miss Fairbanks," Adele said. "Regarding the other matter you mentioned—about his mother—I have heard that she led a scandalous life, but obviously, you've heard that, too."

"Yes, but may I ask, do you believe him to be redeemable? Do you think he is seriously looking to settle down and live decently?"

Adele could feel the blood rushing to her head. "Are you in love with him, Lily?"

Lily squeezed her hands together in her lap again. "I don't know him well enough to be in love with him. But he certainly is the most handsome man I've danced with in a very long time. I would like to fall in love with *someone*. But of course that someone has to be respectable and trustworthy."

Adele suddenly envisioned Lily dancing with Damien. Smiling up at him. She loved to ride. She preferred the country over the superficial glitter of the Season. She was very beautiful. She was rich. She was a perfect match for him.

"Would you like me to speak to James or Sophia about him?" Adele asked, secretly hoping that Lily would say no.

Her eyes brightened. "What I was really hoping was that you could tell me what Lord Osulton and his sister, Violet, have said about him."

Remembering the conversation she'd had with Violet in the carriage, Adele strove to remain objective about the information Lily was seeking. "I'm afraid Violet didn't have very good things to say about him. She said he was looking rather desperately for a wealthy bride. But in my family, we believe that each person must make up their own mind about the people they meet, and not judge them by what others say. Perhaps he does want to redeem himself, Lily. My advice would be to get to know him better, and follow your own instincts."

There. That was objective. Well done, Adele.

Lily's expression changed, as if she were disappointed in Adele's response. She gazed out the window behind the sofa. "I'm afraid I don't completely trust my instincts, so I've surrendered to the conclusion that I *must* listen to what others say." She stood up to leave.

Adele wished she knew why Lily was so withdrawn around men, why she didn't trust her instincts. Adele knew that Lily's father had been a cruel man. Perhaps that was the reason . . .

"Don't be discouraged by Violet's opinions," she heard herself saying firmly, with no small amount of surprise. "Lord Alcester might very well wish to change the way he has lived his life. I would recommend that you keep an open mind."

Lily smiled down at Adele, but the smile seemed weighed down with a slight melancholy. "Thank you, Adele. You're very kind, and I daresay very sensible."

Adele hardly felt sensible lately. She couldn't even manage to fall in love with her own fiancé. She set her elbow on the armrest and bit down on her thumbnail. She was beginning to think she should just give up on this whole engagement and return to New York and resign herself to spinsterhood for the rest of her life. Wouldn't that be a relief?

While Lily was sitting in Adele's bedchamber asking questions about Damien, her brother James was asking similar questions on the other side of town.

"Tell me something," James said to Whitby, as they sat in front of the fireplace at his club. "You met Alcester recently when you were at Osulton Manor. What did you make of him?"

Whitby raised his eyebrows and sat forward, intrigued by the question. "Why do you ask?"

"For one thing, Lily danced with him the other night."

Whitby leaned back again and downed the last of his brandy. "That's all? They just danced?"

James inclined his head. "Odd question."

Whitby slowly blinked. "You know she's like a sister to me, James. The fact that you're asking made me wonder."

"Ah. Well, I am indeed wondering a few things myself, mostly because I witnessed some wagering yesterday. Bets are being placed on whether or not Alcester will return to Miss Fairbanks's dressing room after he slips a ring on the finger of a rich wife."

Whitby laughed. "You don't say. Which way did the bets go?"

"Most wager that Alcester will be supporting the arts again very soon."

Whitby nodded, seeming not the least bit surprised. "So you think he's after Lily's dowry."

"It's possible."

Whitby waved a finger at James and smirked playfully. "You brought this on yourself, you know, marrying an heiress and making yourself one of the richest men in England."

"I'm quite aware of that. Fortunately, Lily has a good head on her shoulders."

"Yes." Whitby gazed down into his glass. "She does indeed. What do you want to know?"

James crossed one long leg over the other. "I want to know if you think the man is trustworthy. I won't fault him for looking for money. I was looking for it myself when I married Sophia. But I do need to know if he intends to behave as a gentleman after he gets it."

"I really don't know, James. I spoke to him only a few times."

"But you've been getting to know his cousin Violet. What's *she* like?"

Whitby grinned. "She's enchanting."

James narrowed his gaze knowingly. "She's

rich. At least she will be, once Harold and Adele join hands at St. Georges. Has she ever spoken of Alcester?"

"No."

"Are you going to propose to her?"

Whitby considered the question. "Probably."

With a resigned sigh, James smiled. "And I was so sure you'd come home from America with a Yankee bride on your arm and American dollars in your bank account."

Whitby set his empty glass on the table beside his chair. "In the end, it will still be American dollars. Straight from Adele to Lord Osulton to his sister, Violet. No offense, James."

James regarded his old friend directly. "None taken. It's the way of the world these days. I'll see you at the Wilkshire ball tonight, assuming you're going, of course."

"I am."

"Very good." He stood up to leave. "It should prove to be a lively affair."

Chapter 19

That evening at the Wilkshire ball, all agreed that Adele's gown was the most spectacular—the pinnacle of high fashion. It was a satin, cream-colored gown by Worth, with yellow velvet roses woven into the fabric, and an off-the-shoulder neckline, ornamented with lace and velvet trimming. The form-fitting bodice displayed her tiny waistline to full advantage, and the entire ensemble, studded with pearls and gemstones, complemented her thick, up-swept golden hair.

On any other occasion, she would not have cared a whit about her appearance, but she had wanted to look her best tonight. She had wanted to stand out among the other London beauties, and she could not pretend there was no explanation for it.

She felt like an impostor again, and realized that *still* nothing felt right.

She had not been at the ball long when she spotted Damien on the other side of the room. Earlier that evening, before she had gotten dressed, she had promised herself she would not overreact to the sight of him, but she hadn't seen him for more than two weeks, and now that he was within view, she was quite frankly paralyzed.

He wore a black suit with white waistcoat and white bow tie, and his wild mane of hair was slicked back. He wandered around the perimeter of the room with grace and heaps of charisma, talking and laughing with other gentlemen, attracting the gaze of every woman who looked his way.

It was *impossible* not to look at him, Adele realized miserably. He was breathtaking in every way a man could be—handsome, charming, and most importantly, he was her hero. Her beautiful black knight. He had saved her life. He had been her protector. She had touched him and kissed him and been held by him, and despite the fact that their last conversation had broken her heart, she had spent countless hours conjuring him in her brain. She could not even try to let this opportunity to steal a look at him pass her by.

Just then, he turned, and their gazes locked and held. He started toward her. Adele sucked in a breath. She turned her back on him, and with a sudden tremor of panic, glanced at her mother and the others. Eustacia was laughing and talking. Violet was looking around the room with a hopeful, searching gaze. Lily was listening politely to whatever Eustacia was saying. No one seemed to know that Adele was screaming inside.

She felt him approach behind her. The others glanced at him and smiled, and their circle opened for him. Adele had to force herself to turn and face him and say hello. He inclined his head in return, then he immediately directed his attention to someone else.

"Lady Lily," he said with an appealing, heart-stopping smile, "it's a pleasure to see you again." He made small talk for a moment, then said, "Perhaps I may have the honor of a spot on your card?"

Naturally, the honor was granted, and he bowed politely and went away.

Adele calmly sipped her champagne and nodded at the conversation that had now resumed, while she struggled to come to terms with the fact that she would like to spit. She hated herself for it, of course, because she knew she had no hold over Damien. She was engaged to Harold, and they had both agreed that what happened between them should be forgotten.

Yet she felt jealous. Jealous of Lily, whom she liked very much.

None of her emotions made any *bloody* sense to her, and now she was using foul language in her head. She was evidently not as composed about this as she had thought she could be.

She remembered Clara's advice—that if her feelings didn't go away after a week, there might be a problem. Well, there was most definitely a problem.

At that moment, Harold appeared beside her with a bright smile on his face. "Ladies! What a crush this is! Three hundred people at least! I just counted them, and there are still others coming in!"

Adele, feeling heat in her cheeks and knowing her face was flushed, turned to her fiancé. She needed to talk to him. She could not go on like this. She needed to resolve her future. "Harold, it is indeed a crush. Will you take me outside for a walk on the veranda?"

"Oh." His smile became strained, and he glanced around at the other ladies, looking as if he didn't want to be rude. Adele wished he could have sensed that she needed to be alone with him right now, and had made that his first concern, instead of worrying what the others would think.

Damien would not have given the others a second thought. He would have looked into her eyes, and he would have known.

"All right then," Harold reluctantly agreed, the smile fading further as he offered his arm.

She and Harold walked out to the flagstone veranda and moved to the far end, where a large oak tree stood close to the house and served as a cozy canopy.

"There now," Harold said. "Feel the cool air.

You'll be refreshed and ready to go back inside before you know it."

Adele closed her eyes and turned her face upward toward the dark sky, inhaling deeply and letting it out. "Yes, it is indeed refreshing."

After a few more deep breaths, she began to feel better. She slowly opened her eyes. Harold smiled, then he seemed to take a moment to admire her lips.

"You're a very pretty girl, Adele," he said.

Sudden hope and euphoria coursed through her, because she had been waiting so long for some sign of affection from Harold, and he had finally found it in himself to express it. Grasping at what felt like a last shred of hope for a happy future with him, she turned to see if there were any others on the veranda. There weren't. She and Harold were alone. She gazed at him in the evening light, and took his gloved hand in hers. Then she took a tentative step closer to him, needing to test the waters of her future, and rose slowly up on her tiptoes to touch her lips to his. The breeze whispered gently through the tall oak beside them.

"Adele!" He put his hands on her shoulders and pushed her back down. Her heels clicked on the flagstones. "What are you doing?"

Adele opened her eyes. "I wanted to kiss you," she explained. "We've never really kissed before."

"Yes, we have!"

"Not on the lips." While a part of her felt hu-

miliated and mortified having to explain the
subtle degrees of a kiss, another part of her
wanted to shake Harold. Shake him violently
and tell him to wake up.

"We're in a public place, Adele. It's hardly the
right time."

Staring up at her fiancé in the dim light, she
realized with a sad, sinking feeling, that there
would *never* be a right time. Harold was not in
love with her, nor was she in love with him.

"And perhaps this is acceptable behavior in
America," Harold continued, "but we are *not*
in America, and young ladies do not kiss gentlemen at balls. You're in England now, and
you're going to have to change a number of
things about yourself."

Adele stared blankly at him. There was no
point trying to talk herself into this any longer.
She could not marry him.

"Good heavens, Adele. You need to get some
color into your cheeks. You'll feel better if you
dance." He reached for her dance card and pen-
cil. "I'll write Damien's name in. He's free for
the next few."

She pulled her wrist away. "No, Harold, really, I don't need—"

"Yes, you do, Adele." He grabbed for the card
again. He was not trying to be difficult, she realized. He actually thought he was being helpful.

God! How could he not see that she didn't
want to dance with other men right now, especially his cousin, whom she'd spent three intimate days and nights with?

"You just need a lively dance," Harold said.

"That's not what I need!" she shouted, this time losing her patience completely and yanking her hand away.

He stared at her for a moment, looking perplexed. She was perplexed herself by the total lack of emotional understanding between them, and by her own outburst. She was not doing the proper, polite thing. Nor was she doing what someone else wanted and expected her to do. It was completely out of her realm of normal behavior. It felt surprisingly satisfying.

He straightened his shoulders and smiled again. "Perhaps you just need to rest your feet."

Rest her feet. Adele labored to control her frustration. They really did not know each other at all.

They returned to the ballroom in silence, and he delivered her to her mother and Eustacia. Adele noticed suddenly that Lily was not with them. She turned her gaze toward the people dancing.

There they were. Lily and Damien, waltzing around the room—spinning and swirling. They made a handsome couple with their matching dark hair, both of them immensely attractive in their own right. They appeared to be having a fabulous time with each other.

Adele tried not to stare, but glanced their way discreetly whenever she could. Each time she looked at them, she was sobered by a heavy sadness that hung over her like a cloud. *She* should be the one out there on the floor with Damien, talking and laughing. Wasn't she the one who had shared an intimate bond with him? Or was she the world's worst fool to believe that? Perhaps he made all women feel that way.

The dance ended, and Damien escorted Lily back to Eustacia. Lily's cheeks were flushed, and she was glowing with bright smiles and laughter. Damien stayed for a few minutes, standing beside Adele, talking to Eustacia and Harold.

The intensity of his presence beside her, even though he wasn't touching her or talking to her directly, awakened all her senses. She realized with excitement and a simultaneous measure of sadness that she had not felt so vibrant and alive since he'd left her, more than two weeks ago. She might as well have been asleep all that time.

She shifted her weight and accidentally brushed her arm lightly against Damien's for a mere fraction of a second. The contact was like a drug . . . Intoxicating. Debilitating.

She shifted her weight back again. The conversation sustained its ebb and flow, and Damien did not seem to notice the brief contact. Adele, on the other hand, had to take a moment to recover from it.

She knew at that moment that she was doomed. As much as she had tried to talk herself out of her feelings because of Damien's reputation and the rumors that he was only looking for money, and despite the fact that he was loyal to Harold and claimed he would never betray that loyalty, she *wanted* him. Passionately. With every piece of her soul. And she was hurt by the attentions he paid to Lily, even when Adele knew it made no sense because she had no claim on his affections.

She took in a deep, steadying breath and glanced across at Harold, whose eyes were wide with excitement and interest as he listened to Beatrice talk about American cowboys.

Adele felt sick. Her emotions had defied the sensible plans she had made, and she was going to have to change those plans and disappoint many people. She could not marry Harold. She wanted very much to board a ship and go home.

"Miss Wilson, perhaps I may have the honor of a dance?" Damien asked, turning toward her.

Adele's gaze shot to his face.

"Oh yes, do go and dance!" Eustacia said. "You look bored, Adele!"

"Indeed you do, my dear," Harold agreed. "Damien, take her for two dances, will you?"

Adele felt her heart begin to pound heavily in her chest. She glanced at her mother, who, unlike the others, was *not* smiling.

Damien held out his gloved hand. She met his gaze and realized she couldn't stop herself from taking it if she tried. Here was an opportunity to spend the next few minutes in his strong, capable arms, dancing with him, looking into the depths of his dark eyes. It was an opportunity to satisfy her longings, however briefly that satisfaction would last.

And at this point, what did it matter? She was going to let her family down anyway, and Harold's family, too. Why not steal one last moment of pleasure before she—sensible, dependable Adele Wilson—made the deliberate and conscious choice to leap, for the first time in her life, into the deep chasm of everyone's disappointment?

Damien

Chapter 20

"Are you all right?" Damien asked, sounding genuinely concerned as he led her onto the dance floor.

He held out his hand. Adele stepped into position, and the waltz began. "I'm fine, thank you."

"Did you pull that answer out of your sleeve, Adele? *I'm fine, thank you.* Honestly. I know you're angry with me about what happened that last day at Osulton, and I wish you would just tell me you hate me, or anything. Stop being so polite. So bloody *English*. God, one would never believe you were an American."

"I beg your pardon?" she said. "I'm every inch an American, and just tonight, Harold said I had to *stop* acting so much like one! That's two

conflicting expectations about how I should behave, and quite frankly, Damien, I'm done being what everyone else thinks I should be."

Damien gazed down at her for a moment.
"Well. That was a load off your cart."

Adele's eyebrows pulled together in a frown.
She huffed. Then all her muscles relaxed. He
had done it again. He had lifted the lid on her
boiling emotions and let the steam out. How
did he always know when she needed that?

"Yes, it was a load off," she replied.

He twirled her around the floor, leading her
smoothly and skillfully toward the outer edges
of the room. His voice softened. "Let's start
again, Adele. Please. How have you been?"

She followed him through a sideways turn.
"I've been better."

"I would presume you're torturing yourself
over what happened between us."

It was remarkable how quickly he dove
straight into the heart of a matter. "Of course.
What about you?"

"Naturally. Harold's my cousin. But I've also
been torturing myself over the way I treated you
in the library before I left. You were right to
send me packing. You should have tossed a
glass of water in my face while you were at it. I
deserved it. I am a complete scoundrel, and I
did drag you down with me."

They danced across the width of the room.
"So you no longer believe I am the angelic creature Harold proposed to. Do you still think he is
in danger?"

Damien paused before answering, then he spoke softly and slowly. "Maybe you were never so angelic to begin with."

Adele bristled. She didn't know how to take such a remark. All she knew was that she refused to let him make her feel ashamed. "You *are* a scoundrel, Damien."

He shut his eyes and shook his head. "I didn't mean to insult you. What I meant to say is that you are a woman with passions, Adele, like any other woman, and you should not have been made out to be a saint. That is an impossibly high standard to live up to."

Her heart was racing. She was in pain, heaven help her, and it was because of him, because he touched the depths of her heart, even when she did not want him to. She was so angry with him. Why did he have to do this to her? He should not have asked her to dance. He should have kept his distance.

"But women with passions and desires," she said, "are eventually unfaithful. Isn't that what you think? And because I've shown you those passions, I've fallen from grace in your eyes, haven't I?"

"In a way. But perhaps that was a good thing."

His reply only fueled Adele's antagonism toward him. She wished he did not have the power to hurt her like this, but he did. And the fact that he thought badly of her shouldn't matter. She hated that it did. Hated it. She also hated that she could not keep herself from becoming defensive. She could not let him go on thinking badly of her, because she was not a bad person. She was not.

"I told you before that I will never be an unfaithful wife," she said. "When I speak my marriage vows, I will be true to them."

He made no reply.

"You don't believe me," she said with barely controlled shock and hostility. She shook her head. "This is outrageous. I wish this dance would end."

"I didn't ask you to dance to fight with you," he said.

They waltzed around the room very fast. Adele recalled suddenly how he and Lily had looked when they were dancing together earlier. They had been smiling and laughing. Damien was not laughing now. He was looking over Adele's shoulder, his expression dark and serious.

She tried to push her anger off to the side. "Are you going to propose to Lily?" she asked, when they reached the far corner of the dance floor.

"Probably."

Adele worked hard to keep her composure. "I suppose I shouldn't be surprised."

He considered her statement for a moment, then looked over her shoulder again. "I take it you've heard I have an urgent need for money."

"Everyone has heard it."

The waltz finally did come to an end, and the dance floor began to clear. Damien and Adele remained in the center of the room, however.

"Harold told us to dance twice," he said.

The room hummed with conversation while

the guests found their partners. Then other couples moved onto the floor. Music started up again. Adele found herself unable to do anything but step back into Damien's arms.

They began to dance, and he returned to the subject of Lily and his need for money. "You think that as soon as I get my hands on Lily's dowry, I'll go back to Frances and break Lily's heart."

Adele spoke plainly. "I'm concerned for her."

"Like I was concerned for Harold?"

Adele narrowed her gaze at him. "We keep coming back to that, don't we? It seems we don't respect or trust each other very much. Is it possible we could *ever* get along? We've witnessed each other's disgrace, and when we see each other, we will always be reminded of our own weaknesses. There will always be resentment."

They danced in silence for a few measures. "We're fighting again," Damien said. "Future cousins shouldn't fight."

But they would not be cousins. Adele was going to return to America, just as soon as she tumbled off the pedestal everyone seemed to think she sat upon. Everyone except Damien.

He stopped dancing suddenly and stepped away from her. "You don't think that's why I kissed *you*, do you? Because of your money?"

She considered her answer very carefully while other dancers waltzed by them. "I admit it crossed my mind, considering what the gossips say."

He did not reply right away. Then he took her into his arms again and resumed the dance. "I will be honest with you. The gossip is correct on one point. I do need money. I'm completely broke, and the creditors have been banging at my door for months. I informed my steward that I would do my best to find a wealthy bride before the end of the Season, and I intend to do that. There. That's the ugly truth. But rest assured, I did not kiss *you* because I wanted your father's settlement. I could not even fathom stealing you away from Harold, even that day in the teahouse when I lost all control, and I still cannot. I kissed you because I couldn't resist you. It was as basic and fundamental as that."

"Because you are a scoundrel," she said flatly.

His voice softened. "Yes. Because I am a scoundrel. But I do regret what happened."

"I regret it, too." She hoped that saying it might help her to commit to it.

The music ended, and their dance was over. She stepped out of his arms, but he did not return her to her mother right away.

"I hope," he said quietly, "that we'll be able to move past this. You're going to be Harold's wife soon, and I'm going to be someone's husband. It's my deepest wish that we will forget everything that happened between us, Adele, and go on to have a normal, uncomplicated acquaintance."

She could see in his eyes that he was sincere. He wanted to put this unpleasantness behind them.

For a fleeting moment, she wanted desperately to tell him that she could not marry Harold, that she wished he would get down on his knee right here and now and plead with her to become *his* wife instead. She could take a step toward him and whisper it in his ear . . . *I'm not going to marry Harold*. Then they could join hands and run out of there, as fast as they could, past all the watching eyes, not caring about the gossip, and escape, just the two of them, to his house in the country.

Oh, how a part of her wanted that. If only he knew . . .

But, of course, she could not give in to such a temptation. This man was a self-proclaimed scoundrel who wanted to marry someone— *anyone*—for money, and he had the power to make Adele lose all common sense and reason. He could crush her heart into a thousand tiny pieces when all was said and done, when he returned to his mistress, as she knew he would.

Besides, she owed it to Harold to tell him the truth before she told anyone else. She could not take the coward's way out and run away from that obligation. So she kept her decision to herself. Damien would learn of it soon enough.

Chapter 21

Damien stood alone in the corner of the ballroom reflecting on everything he had just said to Adele, and felt almost dizzy.

It was over. He had apologized. He had told her he intended to move on, which he fully intended to do. He would find a wife, and he would love that woman, whoever she would be. He would not give in to temptation again.

Reaching for a glass of champagne on a silver tray held by a footman, Damien turned when Lord Whitby appeared beside him. "Alcester, good to see you."

Damien noted that Whitby was not alone. He was accompanied by his friend the Duke of Wentworth—a highly respected and sometimes feared peer of the realm, who also happened to be Adele's brother-in-law, as well as Lily's brother.

Damien cursed to himself. It was turning out to be a hell of a night.

They each came to stand on either side of Damien, surrounding him, as it were.

Whitby raised a glass to the duke. "James, I don't believe you've met Baron Alcester."

There were not many men tall enough to meet Damien's gaze on an equal level. The duke was one of the few who could.

"No, I regret I haven't had the pleasure."

Damien cordially inclined his head. The duke responded in kind.

They, all three of them, stood side by side for a moment or two, watching the floor. Then Whitby said, "Pleasant night for dancing, isn't it?"

"It is indeed," the duke replied.

Another moment of silence ensued. Whitby finished his drink. "I believe I see an old acquaintance," he said. "Will you excuse me?"

He walked off, leaving Damien alone with Wentworth.

Damien's instincts were finely tuned when it came to men who were of a mind to protect sisters or daughters from men like himself. Thus, he knew that Whitby had left them alone intentionally. It was an arranged opportunity for questioning.

He turned toward Wentworth, and said simply, "Well."

The duke took his time studying Damien's

eyes with shrewd diligence. He appeared utterly relaxed. He was in no hurry to reply. Then at last, he spoke. "It seems we share a few acquaintances. Adele Wilson, for one. My wife's sister."

"Ah." Damien was surprised. He had rather been expecting the duke to hone in on Damien's intentions where Lily was concerned. Perhaps that would come next. "Yes. Osulton and I are cousins."

"Lord Osulton, Adele's fiancé. I've met him once or twice over the years. He has a keen interest in science, does he not?"

"He does."

"And *you*. Where do *your* interests lie, Alcester? Not in science, I presume."

Damien could feel the inquisition beginning. "No, not in science. At least not on an experimental level."

"I thought not."

Damien turned toward the dance floor again and took a deep swig of his champagne.

"I suppose," the duke said coolly, "that it's high time I expressed some gratitude to you."

Surprised, Damien turned to him again. "Gratitude?"

"Yes. For your . . . How shall I put it? Your *errand*. My wife, Sophia, was greatly relieved to see her sister again."

Damien stared into Wentworth's cool gaze. "I didn't think anyone outside of Osulton Manor was aware of that particular errand."

There was a small hint of a smile in Wentworth's expression. "My mother-in-law finds it a challenge to keep secrets from her daughters."

Damien nodded, understanding. "I've spent some time with Beatrice. She's an interesting woman. She and my aunt have struck up quite a friendship."

"And I would wager they are like two peas in a pod."

"They talk of nothing but wedding bouquets and bridal sashes."

"Ah, the romance of impending nuptials," the duke said. "Nothing stirs a mother's soup like an offspring's wedding."

Damien smiled, amused and a little surprised that this was not unfolding as he had expected it would.

The dance came to an end, and the room mixed and shifted. Damien and the duke remained where they were, however, until the orchestra began again.

"I understand you have a preference for the outdoors," the duke said. "Your skill as a horseman is quite renowned."

"I enjoy riding."

"As do I. I prefer the country. Fresh air, trees and birds."

Damien merely nodded.

"My sister-in-law also prefers the outdoors. Adele, I mean. She, too, loves to ride. Sophia once told me that when Adele was a girl, she sold her hair to keep her horse. That was, of course, before Mr. Wilson introduced himself to Wall Street."

Damien glanced briefly at Wentworth, and nodded again. Wentworth held no drink. He stood with his hands clasped behind his back, watching Damien's face. "But you know about that," he said with a faint smile.

Damien, somewhat unnerved, faced forward again.

For a long time they stood together, saying nothing, until Damien felt the duke's intense gaze turn to him once more. "You've met my sister, as well. Lily."

"Yes."

"I saw you dancing earlier."

Damien was beginning to feel as if the duke had eyes in the back of his head.

"She's a lovely young woman," Damien said. "You must be proud."

"I am indeed."

Damien felt the duke's probing gaze upon his profile, then at last he looked away. "I must return to my wife. She's expecting me for the next set."

Raising his glass to the duke, Damien said, "It was a pleasure, Wentworth."

"Likewise. Good evening, Alcester." With that, he took his leave.

Damien also turned and walked out. He was more than ready to leave, for he had just been sharply and perceptively evaluated by a man who seemed to know far too much. Damien might as well have spilled his guts onto the floor.

Shortly after the duke had approached Damien, Violet approached Lily.

"Are you having a good time?" she asked, checking inside her sparkling, beaded reticule to see if she had brought a fresh pair of gloves. She had. She snapped it shut and smiled. "I saw you dancing with my cousin."

"Lord Alcester? He's a very good dancer."

Violet grinned mischievously and raised an eyebrow. "A good dancer? That's not what most women would say about Damien."

Lily gazed uneasily up at Violet. "No?"

Violet snickered. "No. Most would use the word 'handsome,' or 'virile.'" She nudged Lily. "Don't tell me you haven't fallen for him. He's the catch of the Season."

Lily merely smiled.

"He likes you," Violet said. "I could tell by the way he was looking at you. But you're so pretty, how could any man not fall in love with you, Lily? What do you think of him?"

"Damien?"

"Yes, of course, Damien!"

Lily swallowed uncomfortably. "I think he's very nice."

"Yes, he is." Violet linked her arm through Lily's. "Oh, darling, how I would love for us to be like sisters. If you married Damien, we would be. Damien knows Whitby. They seem to have become friends lately. What a grand four-

some we would make. We could go places together and—oh, it would be just stupendous."

Lily gazed up at Violet, who was very tall.
"You're going to marry Whitby?"

"Well, nothing's official yet, but it will be soon,
I'm certain. He's magnificent, don't you think?"

Lily gazed across the room to where Whitby
was standing. She knew exactly where he was.
She did not give her opinion.

"He's close to the duke, I understand," Violet
said.

"Yes. He and James have known each other
since they were boys."

Violet took in what looked like an exceptionally fulfilling breath. "Whitby and the Duke of
Wentworth. I will enjoy being welcomed into
your circle, Lily. We will have such fun together."

"Yes, I'm sure we will." Lily gazed across the
room at Whitby again, who was helping the ag-
ing, gray-haired Countess of Greenwood rise
from her chair. Lily rested her hand on her
stomach. She felt slightly ill. But she had always
known this day would come.

She decided at that moment that this would
be her last ball of the Season. She was not enjoying herself. She wanted to go home to Yorkshire, to the country. She would leave London in
the morning.

That night, Adele lay in bed staring at the ceiling and thinking of her future. She could not
marry Harold. That much was obvious. Which
meant she was going to have to break the news to

her sisters and her mother, then she would have to explain her decision to Harold. None of it would be easy, but it had to be done, so she would do it, and she would be brave in the aftermath.

Tomorrow, she decided with firm resolve. She would tell everyone tomorrow.

But what then? She rolled over onto her side and gathered her pillow in her arms. She did not think she could remain in London. She did not want to hear about Damien proposing to Lily. She did not want to think about him kissing her, or touching her the way he had touched Adele in the teahouse. Nor could she bear the possibility that she might learn too late that she had been wrong about him, and then have to watch while he turned out to be a perfect husband.

So she would go home to America. She would start again, careful this time not to put herself in the position of trying to please everyone but herself. She would not make that mistake again. She would carve out a life of her own and think about what *she* wanted. If she was lucky enough to marry, it would be for love, nothing less. She would find a man she could feel passion for, as well as trust and respect.

Or perhaps she would consider a career of some sort. Something to do with horses. What would her father think of that?

Adele closed her eyes and thought about what she would say to everyone tomorrow. She predicted that her mother was going to need some very strong smelling salts.

Chapter 22

$\sim\!\!\infty\!\!\sim$

Adele was sitting with Sophia in the Wentworth House drawing room, when Clara, wearing a dark brown, slim-fitting walking-out dress with a matching hat, was shown in. She pulled off her gloves and took Adele's hands. "What is it, darling? I came the moment I read your note."

"She has something she wishes to discuss with us," Sophia said, moving forward to join them in the center of the room.

"Let's sit down," Adele said. They all took places where they could face one another. "I'm not quite sure how to tell you this, because I know it will come as a shock, but I need to break off my engagement to Harold."

Both her sisters went silent for a few awkward seconds. Then Clara spoke quietly. "Is it because of what we talked about at Osulton?"

"What did you talk about?" Sophia asked.

Clara began to explain. "You remember that Lord Alcester brought Adele home from the kidnapper?"

"Yes."

"Well, she and Lord Alcester spent three days and nights together, and—"

Clara didn't need to finish. Sophia understood. "You care for Lord Alcester, Adele? Why didn't you tell me?"

Adele gazed apologetically at Sophia. "I was going to, but there never seemed to be a right time. But it doesn't matter. I don't want Damien. That's not why I can't marry Harold. I would have made this decision even if I had never met him. At least I hope I would have made it."

Sophia glanced uneasily at Clara. "Good heavens, I've been encouraging Lily to consider Lord Alcester. I wouldn't if I had known."

Adele shook her head. "If he is inclined to propose to Lily, that's fine. It's their business, not mine. I just want to go home."

"But Lily left London this morning," Sophia said. "She didn't say why, but we all know she doesn't enjoy the marriage mart."

Adele was surprised. Lily had said she *wanted* to fall in love with someone.

Clara spoke up. "But if Damien has no hold on your feelings, Adele, why don't you want to marry Harold?"

"Because I don't love him. It's as simple as that."

"But you thought you did at one time," Clara said.

"Yes, but that was before—" She stopped herself.

"Before you met Damien," Clara finished for her.

Adele stood and paced around the room. "Yes, before I met Damien. But that doesn't mean I want to marry him. He just helped me see that I wasn't the person I thought I was." She stopped in front of the window. "Mother is going to think he was a very bad influence."

Sophia blew out a breath. "To be sure."

They were all quiet for a moment, digesting the news, then Clara said, "When will you tell Harold?"

"Today," Adele replied. "I'll hate hurting him of course, but I think this is best dealt with in a decisive manner. Then I will go home as soon as possible. I want to find a purpose in my life or a dream of my own to work toward. I'm tired of drifting in the direction of other people's pointing fingers."

Sophia rose to her feet. "I think that sounds wonderful, Adele."

Adele smiled. "So will you help me explain it to Mother?"

Her sisters pulled wary faces.

"Of course we will," Clara said. "I anticipate you're going to need all the help you can get."

* * *

Two hours later—after no shortage of sobs and arguments, and general, all-around misery from Adele's mother—Adele stood on the front steps of Osulton House with her two sisters, tapping the large brass door knocker and trying to keep her nerves steady.

Harold, may I have a moment alone with you? she rehearsed in her mind. Or perhaps she would need to speak to Eustacia first. *Eustacia, would you be so kind as to give me a moment alone with your son?*

Her whole body churned with dread. She hoped Eustacia would not react the same way her mother had, toppling backward onto the sofa with her mouth open wide. Eustacia and her mother were similar creatures, however . . .

Adele turned to Clara. "Do you have the smelling salts?"

Clara patted her reticule. "Do you even need to ask?"

Just then, the door opened, and the butler appeared with his usual stony expression. He took one look at Sophia and Clara, however, and made a bow. "Your Grace. Lady Rawdon." He then turned his gaze to Adele. "And Miss Wilson. Good afternoon."

Adele squeezed her reticule in her hand. "Is Lord Osulton at home?"

"I'm afraid he's not. The family left for the country not more than an hour ago."

Adele's eyes narrowed questioningly. "Whatever for?"

He inclined his head. "I regret to inform you that Lord Osulton's grandmother is ill."

"Catherine?" Adele tensed. "Is it serious?"

"I believe it is, Miss Wilson."

Adele turned to Clara and Sophia. "This is terrible. Poor Catherine. And poor *Harold*. I must go, too. I am still his fiancée after all. Surely Mother will take me."

Adele started back to the coach with speed and determination in her gait—something Clara and Sophia had never seen in her before.

"Thank you," Sophia said to the butler, before she and Clara had to scramble to keep up with their baby sister on her way down the steps.

BOOK THREE

Wisdom

BOOK THREE

Wisdom

Chapter 23

It was past noon the next day when Adele and Beatrice were greeted at the door of Osulton Manor and invited inside. The house was somber. Adele and Beatrice were shown into the drawing room. Eustacia was standing alone at the window.

"Oh, my dears," she said, turning to welcome them. "How good of you to come. We left in such a hurry, we had to leave it to Hendersley to explain where we had gone."

Beatrice embraced her. "We came as soon as we heard."

"Is she any better?" Adele asked.

Eustacia held a handkerchief up to her nose. "The physician doesn't think so. He said it wouldn't be more than a few days. A week at most." She shuddered with a sob, and hugged Beatrice again. "Oh, my dear, dear mother. What will I do without her?"

Beatrice led Eustacia to the sofa. Eustacia lifted her puffy, watery gaze. "Adele, go and see Catherine now. Harold is with her. It will mean so much to him that you came."

Adele leaned forward to squeeze Eustacia's hand, and met her mother's concerned gaze. Beatrice had made no secret of the fact that she had hoped this visit would change Adele's mind about Harold.

Adele did not know what would transpire. Maybe it would change her mind. Maybe it would not. She wished only for clarity and an absolute certainty in her decision, whatever it turned out to be.

She made her way through the house to the east wing where Catherine's rooms were located, and knocked upon the door. No one answered, so she quietly entered the sitting room.

Catherine's space looked the same as always. It was cluttered with old pillows and interesting knickknacks—evidence of a lifetime of collecting special treasures. She passed through the sitting room to the double doors on the other side that led to Catherine's bedchamber, and stopped to prepare herself. Harold was surely going to be distraught. She would do her best to comfort him.

The doors were slightly ajar, so she peered through the narrow opening before she entered, but she could see only the foot of the bed. She heard a quiet weeping.

Oh, Harold.

Adele closed her eyes and bowed her head. She gently pushed the door open, but it was not Harold she saw. The person sitting next to the bed, with his head resting on Catherine's hand, was Damien.

Adele's heart squeezed painfully. She pressed her hand to her chest.

He must have sensed her presence, because he turned and looked at her. His eyes were colored by a dark, despairing anguish, along with a measure of shock from seeing her when he had not expected it.

Adele swallowed over a lump that formed in her throat. Damien—the black knight who could raise his sword and conquer any enemy, and the scoundrel who could, at his whim, seduce any woman . . . He had been weeping.

Damien rose from his chair and crossed the room toward her. He stood for a moment, staring into her eyes, then he pulled her gently, tenderly into his arms. Adele shuddered with surprise at the contact, not realizing how desperately she had wanted to touch him, despite all her reasons not to.

He held her tightly for a long while, then he pressed his lips to her neck. She allowed it, because she could not forget all the times he had helped and comforted *her*. But when he laid a trail of kisses across her cheek and took her face in his hands and gazed down at her lips, Adele realized she was not allowing this to comfort *him*. It was an excuse to take from him what *she* wanted. Pleasure. Closeness. Intimacy.

Elated to be in his arms, jubilant simply to *see* him, she ignored the little voice in her brain that reminded her that anyone could walk in and find them this way, gazing into each other's eyes like lovers. Or that Catherine could open her eyes and see what sin they were committing, what betrayal, when Adele was still engaged to Harold.

But in all honesty, to Adele's utter shame and bewilderment, none of that mattered. Not at this moment when Damien was holding her and telling her with his body that he wanted her, too.

Damien closed his eyes. "God, I'm sorry for touching you like this."

She shook her head. "Please, don't apologize."

He said nothing for a few seconds, his voice a mere whisper when he spoke. "What are you doing here?"

"I heard about Catherine." They glanced with concern at his grandmother. "How is she?" Adele asked softly.

"Not good. All her life, she's had a sparkle in her eye. But not today."

"What did the doctor say?"

Damien explained the prognosis—that at Catherine's age, this illness would take everything she had, and leave her with nothing. Her breathing was already shallow and erratic, which implied the worst.

"Has she been conscious?" Adele asked.

"Not this afternoon. I've been sitting here, talking to her for over an hour, trying to get her to wake up, but—"

Adele reached for his hand and clasped it warmly in hers.

"We were able to talk earlier this morning," Damien said. "She had a great deal to say—and most of it came as a surprise." He pinched the bridge of his nose.

Adele waited patiently for him to say more.

For the longest time he simply stared at the rug, then he glanced uncertainly at her. She sensed he wanted to talk, and she wanted very much to be the person he talked to. "You can tell me if you want to," she said gently.

"I do want to."

"Then I'm listening."

He glanced back at the bed again.

"She told me something I didn't know," he said. "That my father kept a secret from me and the rest of the world." He lowered his head, shaking it, then he lifted his gaze. "There is something I never told you about myself and the way my parents died."

Adele remembered what Violet had told her. . . .

"Damien, you don't have to hide it. I know. Violet told me something after you left for London. She said your father killed himself."

His eyes gleamed with dampness; his brow furrowed with surprise. "You knew that?"

She nodded. "Yes, but I don't know how it

happened. I only know what would be considered gossip."

He swallowed hard. "Well, I don't think anyone knows how much of it I consider my fault."

Adele took a step closer to him. "Oh, Damien, I didn't know *that*. What happened?"

He sent a glance her way—a glance that told her he appreciated her sympathy and understanding. She wanted very much to touch him again.

"I was only nine when I found out my mother was having an affair," he said quietly. "I was furious with her, and I didn't have the sense or experience with life to handle it tactfully, so I told my father. He was devastated, and he went after my mother with a gun."

"Good gracious, Damien."

"I took my horse and followed him through London. He went to the house where my mother's lover lived, but I didn't get there in time. He had found her with her lover. He meant to shoot them both, I believe."

Adele braced herself for the worst. "Did he murder her, Damien?"

He shook his head. "No. He found them together, but he ran out. My mother tried to go after him, and that's when I came along. She took my horse so she could go after my father, but she fell along the way, galloping across the park, and that's how she died. I was the one who found her when I was running after her."

Feeling a deep, excruciating ache in her chest,

Adele spoke in a hushed tone. "I'm so sorry." She squeezed his hand.

"I ran home to tell my father, and that was even worse than what I had told him before. Then, the day they buried my mother, he went into Whitechapel and got himself stabbed. Purposefully, it's believed. I blamed myself, of course, for causing the explosion, which is what it was."

Adele swallowed hard at the shock of hearing this. "But you were just a boy, Damien. It wasn't your fault. You were only the messenger."

"Not a very tactful one."

Adele put her arms around his neck and hugged him. He squeezed her tightly in return.

"But this morning," he said, "my grandmother told me that my father suffered from what she called an unsteady constitution."

"Unsteady constitution? What does that mean?"

"Sometimes he was as happy and energetic as a child, and other times he withstood a deep melancholy that would often last for weeks."

"You knew nothing of it?"

He walked to the foot of the bed. "I remember that he would go away sometimes and I wouldn't see him, then he would come back with gifts and he would want to celebrate. We would stay up all night dancing and playing games. I don't remember any melancholy."

"Perhaps he tried to keep it from you to protect you."

"Yes." He turned around to face Adele again.

"Grandmama also told me that he tried to take his own life more than once. Even before he met and married my mother."

Adele crossed to Damien, and reached up to lay her hand on his cheek. He covered it with his own.

"For years she's been trying to convince me that what happened that day wasn't my fault," Damien said, "but I never believed it."

They both gazed at Catherine for a moment. "Do you believe it now?" Adele asked.

He considered it. "I believe I need to forgive the nine-year-old boy who didn't know any better. But I don't believe I will ever be able to let go of the guilt. I will always feel remorse when I remember the way I told my father. I did not try to spare his feelings. I didn't even think of that. I was only angry at my mother, and wanted to see her punished."

Adele digested all this with a deep, soulful understanding. "You were only nine, Damien. You didn't have the maturity or information to understand what your mother was going through. It's only natural that you would have been angry. And you're right. You do need to forgive the nine-year-old boy you were then. Your regrets are the regrets of a man who knows how he would handle the situation today. And you *would* handle it differently today. I know you would. I've seen the way you've handled everything that had happened with us."

Damien kissed Adele's hand. "You are so kind," he said.

Adele swallowed over the lump in her throat and fought to keep tears from spilling out of her eyes.

"Let's not talk about that anymore," he said. "It's good to see you."

Adele watched his face, so beautiful in the gray light pouring in through the windows. His dark eyes were closed; he looked calm as he kissed the inside of her wrist, sending gooseflesh up her spine. His mouth traced a path up her arm.

"Don't tell me to stop yet, Adele," he whispered. "Please. It's been a trying day. Just give me this moment." He returned his attention to her hand, and kissed it again and again.

Adele trembled. She couldn't have told him to stop if she'd wanted to. All she could do was close her own eyes and revel in the feel of his warm, moist lips upon her skin.

"I'm not going to stop you," she whispered, wanting to be selfish and greedy for once in her life, and barely recognizing the husky thickness of her voice. "I'm tired of fighting it."

He stopped and lifted his gaze. Though his eyes were brimming with desire, he was apparently surprised by her surrender, and he looked to be waiting for an explanation.

She didn't know if she should tell him her decision not to marry Harold or not. She was afraid of what Damien's response would be. He'd accused her of some terrible things recently. Would he see this as another careless, thoughtless act from an inconstant woman who could not be faithful? Or would he be pleased?

Pleased that she was finally following her heart?

She continued to watch his waiting face, then felt her own eyes grow heavy with yearning. She adored this man. She couldn't deny it, and the truth was flailing inside her, kicking and screaming to get out . . .

"I'm not going to marry Harold," she said at last, and the weight of the whole world lifted from her shoulders. There. It was out. Damien knew. "I'm going to tell him as soon as I can."

Shock glimmered in his eyes. Adele waited anxiously for his response. "May I ask why?"

"Because I don't love him, and it wouldn't be fair to either one of us." A hot quivering began in Adele's belly, and she glanced at the bed, wondering fleetingly if Catherine was awake, if she could hear them.

Just then, the outer door of the sitting room opened. Both she and Damien stepped apart in time to see Eustacia and Beatrice push through the double doors to the bedchamber.

Eustacia stopped when she saw them. "Damien. I didn't realize you were here."

Adele glanced at her mother, who looked at her with disapproval.

Eustacia crossed to the bed and took Catherine's hand. "Hello, Mother," she said softly, but Catherine did not stir.

Damien turned his back on all of them and walked to the window. He gazed out at the gray sky. Adele's body was still trembling with unease because of what she'd just told Damien.

She didn't know what consequences would arise from her confession. Her mother was not happy with her decision. That much she knew. What would Eustacia think? And Harold? And what would Damien want after all was said and done? She couldn't deny that she was still dreaming of a happy ending with her handsome black knight. Even now, her body was warm with desire and anticipation after what had just occurred between them. She wanted more of him—more conversation, more touching. She hoped her cheeks were not flushed.

Beatrice moved to stand on the other side of the bed. She turned her gaze to Adele. "I wonder where Harold is?"

Adele heard the reprimand in her mother's voice, for she had always considered Damien a threat, even though Adele had never openly revealed her feelings.

Quite unexpectedly, Catherine stirred. "Did someone mention Harold?"

Eustacia leaned over the bed. "Yes, Mother. Adele is here."

"Adele? The American gel?"

"Yes, that's right. She's engaged to Harold. Remember?"

Adele's heart broke a little at Catherine's confusion and lost memory, for she had spent many enjoyable hours with Catherine over the past few weeks. They had talked and laughed together and shared many stories. Catherine's mind was clearly deteriorating quickly. Adele shared a glance with Damien and knew he was concerned and thinking the same thing she was. Adele could see it in his eyes.

"Oh yes," Catherine said sleepily. "Harold was here earlier, but he went to the teahouse on the lake."

The teahouse. As soon as the words passed Catherine's lips, Damien looked at Adele again. The teahouse was their place together—hers and Damien's—and Harold had gone there.

"Perhaps I'll take a walk down to see him," she said.

"Yes, you should," her mother replied, as if she sensed urgency in the situation.

"He would like that, Adele," Eustacia said. "He is quite worried about his grandmother. He'll be pleased to see your lovely face."

Adele nodded, and walked out.

After Beatrice and Eustacia left the room, Damien sat down beside the bed. "Harold is not in the teahouse, Grandmama. You know he never goes there. Why did you tell Adele that?"

Her white hair splayed out all around her, Catherine slowly, weakly turned her head on the pillow. "Because I thought you needed to be alone with her. You should go down there."

"You heard our conversation?"

"Of course," she said, her voice shaky and lacking any vigor. "And I saw your red-hot lack of discretion, too, holding her in your arms like the scoundrel you are. Perhaps that's why I'm feeling better all of a sudden." She tried to sit up. "I think I might be able to take some soup."

Amused as he so often was with his grand-mother—and more than a little relieved to see a fighting spirit back in her bones—Damien gently pushed her back down. "Don't try to get up, Grandmama. You're ill."

He tucked the covers around her.

"It was a surprise," she said, her speech slightly slurred, "when she said she didn't want to marry Harold. I nearly swallowed my tongue."

"So did I."

"What are you going to do about it?"

Damien rested his elbows on his knees and lowered his head. "I don't know. Harold will be devastated."

"Devastated is not the word. He will be disappointed, without doubt, but that doesn't mean you have to suffer with him."

"But it is almost certainly my fault that Adele is changing her mind. I kissed her. I talked to her about things that were entirely too personal. I corrupted her."

His grandmother took a moment to gather her strength before she answered, managing somehow to smile. "You corrupted her with your charm, you devil. Awakened her to pleasure and joy. You could hardly help it, Damien."

"I will never forgive myself."

She turned her head on the pillow again. "Now that is something I cannot bear to hear. You have tortured yourself long enough over other events that were not your doing, and I will not go to my grave believing that you intend to continue torturing yourself about something new."

She began to cough suddenly, and Damien helped her sit up for a moment.

"But there is something," she said, when he laid her back down, "that I must tell you, Damien. I am deeply ashamed of myself, and I cannot go to my grave if—"

"You're not going to your grave, Grandmama."

"Yes, I am. If not today, it will be another day, because that is life. Everything that lives, dies eventually."

Damien kissed her frail hand. "Have you not told me enough today?"

She shook her head. "No, not nearly enough. There's something you need to know about your mother."

Damien felt all his muscles tense in his body. "What is it?"

She coughed again, then managed to say, "Your mother didn't marry your father for his title to satisfy her own ambitions. She had been most cruelly forced into it by her father."

Damien narrowed his gaze at his grand-mother. "But after she died, everyone said—"

"I know what everyone said, and that is what I am most ashamed of. I could have dispelled those rumors if I had wished to, but I remained silent."

"Why?"

A tear drained from the outside of her eye, down onto the pillow. "Because I was so angry with her for what she'd done with that other man. I was so heartbroken over the death of my only son that I needed to blame someone."

" 'That other man,' you say. There was only one?"

"Only one, and I believe she loved him deeply. He knew your father, you see, and he understood what she suffered. They commiserated together at first, and then—" She stopped and rested for a moment. "She tried to love your father. For many years she tried. But it was not a good match. He didn't really love her, Damien."

"Why are you telling me this now?"

"Partly to ease my own conscience. I should have told you before and I should have been more understanding with your mother. I should have felt compassion. All she ever wanted was love. Instead, I nursed my anger for too many years."

Damien held his grandmother's hand. "But she committed adultery."

"Yes, but she suffered for it, and then she died for it. I don't want you to suffer, Damien. Learn from your parents' mistakes, and marry for love. That is where you will find the honor that has eluded you all your life. You need and seek intimacy, Damien, but you've been settling for temporary intimacy with the wrong kinds of women, because you have always feared heartbreak from a more permanent relationship such as a marriage. But not all marriages end in heartbreak. Not if there is love."

Damien shook himself inwardly. He had been through a great deal today.

"Adele is doing the right thing," Catherine said. "A loveless marriage brings disaster for everyone. She should not marry Harold if she doesn't love him."

He nodded.

"Do *you* love her, Damien?"

"I might," he whispered.

"Liar. There is no 'might' about it. I saw you holding her just now. And aside from being an object of your desire, Adele is intelligent and kind. She has honor and she loves what *you* love—the outdoors and everything equestrian. Any fool could see you are meant for each other. I'm surprised Harold didn't see it and bring her home for you instead of himself. But that is Harold, isn't it? Never really seeing what is outside a beaker. He's got his head in a glass box, that boy. If you want to help him, pull him out and spit in his face. Wake him up. We've all been protecting him long enough, because he is so much like your father and we've all been scared to death he will turn out the same. And you . . . You've been trying to make amends for what happened to your father. *That* is why you've hovered over Harold all your life, and you know it is. But he is a grown man, and his happiness is not your responsibility. To protect him now, and to let Adele slip away, would only force the past to repeat itself. Marry for *love*, Damien. No matter what the cost."

Damien listened to his grandmother with surprise and confusion. She was telling him to betray Harold.

But Damien was not even sure Adele could ever love him back, even if he did do what his grandmother was suggesting. Especially if he did. Adele was unshakably honorable, and she would have reservations about dashing into the arms of her fiancé's cousin, so soon after she'd jilted him.

On top of that, Damien knew she did not respect him. She knew about his search for a rich wife, and about Frances and the other women before her, and she did not believe he could ever be a faithful husband. She'd even said they didn't trust or respect each other, and they reminded each other of their weaknesses. He wasn't sure she could ever let go of those impressions, even if he did everything he could to convince her otherwise.

Yet his grandmother was right. Anyone with eyes could see they were made for each other. They shared the same interests, and Adele was at least attracted to him in the physical sense. She had proven it in bed with him that night and in the teahouse, and again today when she'd admitted she was tired of fighting her passions.

He wondered if he should go down to the lake and talk to her. Perhaps he could try to feel her out, and determine what was possible after she ended her engagement to Harold. Damien smiled at his grandmother and kissed her hand, then he rose from his chair, and left to fetch his horse.

Chapter 24

Adele reached the little round teahouse on the lake and stepped gingerly past the overgrown grasses that lined the path to the door. There was no horse tethered anywhere nearby. Harold must have walked.

Yes, of course he had walked, she thought. He didn't like to ride.

She approached the door and knocked. No one answered, so she circled around to a window, cupped her hands to the cool glass, and peered inside. The teahouse was empty.

She turned and listened for the sounds of another human being. All she heard were the soothing noises of the woods—oak leaves whispering in the soft breeze, English sparrows chirping, and the gentle cooing of wood pigeons. Harold must have come and gone.

Adele closed her eyes and breathed in the fresh scent of the lake. The forest beckoned to her in its usual way, so she decided to take advantage of the solitude. She wandered along the mossy bank of the lake and found a fallen tree to sit upon.

She had been there about ten minutes when she heard a horse nicker, heard the soft tapping of hooves over the grass, and knew someone was approaching. Before she even turned, however, she sensed who it was.

She rose to her feet. Horse and rider appeared from around a bend in the path. It was as she had expected. It was Damien.

She swallowed nervously. What a sight he was—darkly handsome and striking on his black horse. She imagined him as a medieval knight in an enchanted forest.

"I couldn't find Harold," she explained ridiculously.

He walked his horse closer, came to a stop, and dismounted. He stood a few feet away, his expression serious. "I didn't think you would."

Bewildered, she sat down again.

Damien led his horse to a tree and tethered him. "I doubt Harold was here at all today. He hasn't thought of this place in years."

"But your grandmother said—"

"My grandmother is a notorious busybody," he informed her, walking toward her with a smile, bending under a low-hanging branch. Twigs snapped under his footfalls. "And I'm sure it gave her great pleasure to manipulate the goings-on in the household this morning. I think it even made her feel better. She asked for soup."

"That's wonderful news."

Damien joined Adele on the fallen log. He plucked a long piece of green grass and wrapped it around his finger.

"But are you telling me that she saw us?" Adele asked with a sinking feeling in her belly. "I had thought she was asleep."

"She was feigning sleep, because of something I said to her last night that incited her to misbehave."

Adele peered at him, waiting for an explanation.

He gazed into her eyes. "I told her I was ashamed of myself, because I had unhealthy desires for my cousin's fiancée." He tossed the rolled-up blade of grass into the water.

Adele felt strangely numb with apprehension, a simmering fear that events would unfold too quickly, in a way she could not control. "You told her that? What did she say?"

"She said, 'Thou shalt not covet.' Then she fell asleep."

They sat in easy silence for a moment.

"Did Catherine hear me say that I wasn't going to marry Harold?" Adele asked.

"Yes."

She covered her face with her hands. "Oh, I didn't want anyone to know about that yet, not when she is so ill. The last thing I wanted was to come here and upset everyone."

"Grandmother wasn't upset," he said. "She has become forgiving in her old age, I've just discovered, and she can certainly keep a secret."

They sat, saying nothing for a while, and when he spoke, he spoke matter-of-factly. "What will you do, Adele, after you tell Harold the truth?"

"I'll go home to America," she replied without hesitation. "I want to start over again, and take time to think about what *I* want from life, not what my parents want for me, or anyone else. I want to be free."

His voice was calm and serene like the lake. "You would not consider staying here and starting your new life in England?"

"No," she said quickly, because she was afraid to have hope for things she was not sure of, for the happy ending she had dreamed of so many times. "It's not my home."

"But you were willing to make it your home with Harold."

"That was the old me," she said. "The new me knows that I could never marry a man I don't love, nor do I want to live like this." She gestured in the direction of the house.

"In a palace with strict rules and clipped gardens, you mean."

"Yes. I have always felt that I had to be perfect—clipped and manicured—and perhaps that's why I am uncomfortable in a setting like this. I want to go back to the way it was when I was a child, before we had money and became concerned with manners and appearances. As strange as it sounds, I long for natural chaos."

"But what if the home you could live in was a much smaller country manor? A house covered in ivy that no one has been able to control for years. A house with an overgrown garden and a collection of dusty books that is hideously disorganized? What if that house had an impressive stable with horses, and fields and meadows with fences to jump when you go riding? And what if the servants were simple country people, who had always been encouraged to laugh with their master?"

Adele's stomach began to whirl with consternation. "What are you asking, Damien?"

"In my own roundabout way," he explained, "I suppose I'm asking about possibilities, and I want to know if the reason you changed your mind about marrying Harold is because of me."

She turned her face away from him and stared across the still water. "I will confess. My decision has everything to do with you. I would never have known what I was missing if I hadn't met you. You introduced me to my passions, and you taught me that I have a soul of my own, and that I can use my heart and mind to change the path of my life."

"I'm glad. I would hate to think of you like a bird in a cage—a bird who never knew what it felt like to spread her wings and fly."

Adele lifted her head to look up at the clouds overhead. "I'm still not quite sure I do know what it feels like, but I'm going to find out."

He kept his gaze on her profile. "I have come

to admire you very much, Adele, for your spirit and your goodness."

Her heart began to pound heavily in her chest. She could not look at him. "My *goodness*? I thought you believed I was not as good as everyone thought."

"You are as good as anyone can possibly be, because no one is perfect. Perfection is not real, and you, Adele, are real." They were quiet for a moment while they watched a duck land on the still water with a gliding *swish*.

"Adele, would you consider marrying *me*?" he asked.

Nothing could have prepared Adele for the shock of actually hearing the question she had longed so desperately to hear, or for her body's shuddering response. But even while joy and happiness shot gloriously into her heart, she continued to struggle to hold on to her good sense. Though she had decided to be more free, she would never completely let go of "sensible Adele." She would not make any rash decisions.

"I promise I would never put you in a cage," he added.

Adele managed somehow to locate her voice. "Damien, I admit that we have certain things in common, and you know I am attracted to you, but that doesn't mean we should marry. Think of how we have argued."

"But what if I've decided that you are the only one for me? Is there no chance I could win you?"

Adele stared out at the lake. She had to consider that question very carefully. "A few days ago, Lily was the one you wanted. Not long before that, you were making love to Frances Fairbanks."

"I was with Frances before I met you, not after. That's over now. And I was only considering Lily because I believed you were going to marry Harold."

She sighed. "I know you are in need of money, Damien. You told me so yourself, so you must understand my reservations and my need for caution. How could I be sure you weren't simply seizing an opportunity that has presented itself because your cousin is no longer in the picture?"

"That is not the case, Adele."

"But how can I be sure? You've had nothing but casual mistresses in your life, and the whole world seems to think you will return to that life as soon as you find a wealthy bride. You have never been inclined to settle down until now, when you are forced to because of your financial problems. I admit we have much in common, but marriage is more than a sharing of similar interests. It is a sharing of *values*, and that is where we differ."

An intensity filled his voice. "Perhaps we don't differ as much as you think. All my life I have grieved over my parents' failure as a married couple, and I have vowed I would never let that happen to me. I want a real marriage to a woman with honor—a woman I can love and trust."

She could not believe this was happening. Whether his motives were pure or tainted, he was fighting for her—fighting for her!—like the conquering hero that she'd always imagined him to be.

Adele squeezed her hands together on her lap, searching for control. Though she loved that fairy tale quality about him, she could not let herself be blinded by it. She could not close her eyes to the qualities she did *not* like—the qualities that had importance in the real world.

"But you don't trust me," she said. "You have questioned my integrity on numerous occasions, and if I were to run off with you, I would be doing the very thing you believe all women do—betray their husbands. Or fiancé, in this case."

His eyes brimmed with gentle understanding. "I feel differently about that now. I believe I am beginning to forgive my mother for what she did. Just now, when I was riding down here, I was remembering certain things about her—the way she smiled and the way she used to gently kiss the top of my head when I was small—and I didn't feel the ache in my gut that I have always felt whenever I've thought of her. I only felt her tenderness, and for the first time, it felt good, Adele. I felt hopeful. I know now that what my mother did was more complicated than it appeared on the surface, as is everything in life, I suppose."

Adele gazed down at the mossy ground. "I'm glad to hear that, Damien. Truly I am. But what about Harold? I thought you were forever loyal to him. He does not even know that I wish to end our engagement, but here you are, ready to swoop down like a vulture and steal me away before it is even done." Her voice had gained fervor on the last few words.

"I am not indifferent about that," he said. "I will have a difficult time explaining myself to him."

"I should think so. I can't imagine my own dilemma if I wanted a man my sister loved and planned to marry." She stopped what she was saying and gazed out at the lake. Her voice grew calmer. "But to be fair, I don't think Harold truly loves me."

"He believes he does, because he has not experienced much of life. He spends all his time in a room with glass walls, looking out, but never venturing out. He makes choices based on duty and intellect, rather than emotion. Intellectually, you were a good choice."

"Because I'm wealthy," Adele said harshly.

Damien touched her cheek with the backs of his fingers. "Not just that, Adele. You are charming and lovely and decent. He recognized those qualities in you, as I have, and he admired them. So he will be disappointed, even if it is not a passionate love he expresses."

Adele shifted uncomfortably on the rough log. "But I know your propensity for guilt. Would you be able to live with yourself if you hurt Harold, when the strongest dynamic of your relationship has been your need to protect him?"

He spoke with conviction. "Today my grandmother suggested that I have spent my life trying to protect Harold because he is so much like my father, and I've been trying to make up for

what happened. She insisted that I recognize
that Harold is a grown man, and that it is not
my responsibility to ensure he is always happy.
She even suggested it might do him good to suffer a little, because we have all treated him like
something breakable, fearing he would turn out
like my father. She was guilty of it herself, she
said, and I'm sure you've noticed Eustacia always doting, telling him he can do no wrong."

Adele pulled her eyebrows together and
stood up. "So you wish to be cruel to him, do
you? In order to help him escape his sheltered
life? What a convenient time to change your
perspective, when there is an heiress to be had."

She walked away from him and stopped at a
huge oak tree, resting her hand on the rough
bark. She heard Damien rise and follow to
where she stood, but she kept her back to him.

"No," he said firmly. "I will not allow you to
say that, or even think it. I am in love with
you, Adele, and your wealth has nothing to do
with it. I would marry you with or without
your settlement."

Adele stiffened. Her heart had not stopped
pounding this entire time. She struggled for a
clear comprehension of her thoughts and feelings. A part of her reveled in hearing him say he
was in love with her. *In love with her!* And he
would marry her without her settlement?

Though she had her back to him, she could
feel him behind her. How she longed to turn
around and touch him, but another part of her

could not ignore all the reasons that she should be careful.

When she did not respond, he did not retreat. He strengthened his persuasion. "Whether I am making excuses for my lack of loyalty to Harold or not," he said, "I don't know, and I don't care. In the end it doesn't matter. The fact is, I want you, Adele, and my desire for you has eclipsed my loyalty to my cousin. If I must choose, I will be disloyal to him, and I will choose you. There, I've said it."

I will choose you.

Adele was breathing hard now. His words had hit a mark. Her defenses began to collapse and surrender. At long last, she turned.

Damien—tall and dark and massive before her—gazed down with the look of a warrior who was exhausted after battle, but was still every inch the conqueror.

She did not know what to do. She adored him, she knew she did. She had felt connected to him from the first day they met, and she had been denying it all this time because she did not feel he could be faithful to one woman for the rest of his life.

But he had tried to convince her that he *could* be faithful. She had seen him weeping over his grandmother's bed. He had fought this attraction from the very first day, and fought it hard, because he had not wanted to hurt or betray a member of his family.

Perhaps there was more to him than what she

had let herself see. Perhaps she had seen the wrong thing.

"It's been an enlightening day," he said.

"Yes, it has."

He took a step forward and gently covered her cheek with his hand. "Don't say no, Adele."

Chapter 25

An almost tangible, tension-filled need settled in the air between them, as Adele gazed up at Damien's lips. She wanted him—certainly, her body wanted him—and there was no point denying it.

He cupped her chin in his hand, his brilliant gaze holding her captive, then he lowered his mouth to hers. The kiss was tentative at first, as if he were testing the waters of her consent. When she parted her lips for him and slid her arms up around his neck, weaving her fingers into the thick hair at his nape, he deepened the kiss.

The sensual pull of his allure was unstoppable, and an aggression Adele had not known she possessed emerged from somewhere deep within her. She took control, pulling his head down closer and sweeping her tongue into his mouth.

His response was immediate. He gathered her up against him, embracing her with his whole body and backing her up against the tree. He kissed all over her face and down her neck, quickly unbuttoning the top of her high-necked collar and laying openmouth kisses down the front of her throat.

Gooseflesh erupted everywhere as she was overcome by the inconceivable heat of her desires. "Damien," she whispered.

Before she could contemplate what was happening, she felt herself being swept up into his strong arms, as if she weighed no more than a leaf on a breeze. She clung to his neck as he carried her along the mossy bank of the lake, farther away from the rotunda and into the greenery. He carried her while she kissed him, through a grove of poplars, then bent low to enter the private, quiet shelter of a weeping willow, whose graceful branches touched the ground.

He knelt on one knee and laid her on the soft grass, then came down to lie upon her. Again, she slid her hands around his neck and pulled him closer for what felt like a deep, soul-reaching kiss.

Her body began to burn, and any lingering resistance toward this forbidden pleasure crumbled, for she was no longer bound by her sense of commitment to Harold. She wanted Damien selfishly and wantonly, and she wanted out of the cage.

His lips moved across her cheeks and down

her neck again, and she arched her back on the grass. She slid her hands under his jacket collar and over his shoulders, squirming as she tried to push the jacket off. She wanted to feel his skin.

Responding instantly, he sat back on his heels and ripped the garment off, tossing it to the ground beside them, then he came down upon her again. This time, she welcomed him fully with her body, wrapping her arms and legs around him.

Soon, her skirts and petticoats were up around her waist, and only her drawers and his trousers remained between them. Damien positioned himself between her legs, leaning up on both arms and looking down into her eyes while he thrust his hips against her. The feel of his rock-hard erection through the thick fabric of his trousers inflamed her senses in a way she had never imagined possible.

"Tell me to stop at any time, Adele, and I will. All you have to do is say it."

She nodded, though she had no intention of stopping him, at least not yet. At the same time, she was glad he had given her the option. She trusted him, at least in this regard. She knew he would not force her to do anything she did not wish to do.

She reached up again and cupped the back of his head, pulling him down for another kiss. Eyes closed and leaning to the side on one elbow, he began to unbutton her bodice. Seconds later he was pressing it open and rubbing his hand over the top of her stiff corset.

"I want to take this off you," he said, his voice husky with desire. "May I?"

"Please."

She sat up and scrambled out of her bodice, while he unhooked it in the front. The corset came loose, the cool air touched her skin, hot and damp beneath her light, cotton chemise. She closed her eyes and inhaled deeply, marveling with wonder at the liberating sensation of being outdoors and able to really breathe.

Damien reached for the bottom of her chemise, and the next thing she knew, she was lifting her arms, while he was pulling it off over her head. Suddenly, she was nude from the waist up. She shivered with an erotic sense of awe. She was nude. Outdoors.

The shocking realization had barely had a chance to set in, when he eased her back down on the grass and hungrily took her breast in his mouth.

Adele's eyes fell shut and her emotions closed in around the astonishing stimulation of his tongue and teeth, and the deep sound of his labored breathing. She ran her fingers through his thick mane of hair, sighing as he brought a searching hand up the inside of her leg and let it come to rest on the moist, throbbing center between her thighs, on top of her drawers. He applied a pressure with his palm, making tiny little circles. She gasped with a yearning pleasure.

"That feels wonderful," she whispered breathlessly.

Slowly, he let his hand wander upward, and

with eyes still closed while he kissed her, he untied the ribbon on her drawers with expert fingers. He broke the kiss to whisper hotly in her ear, "May I remove these also?"

"Yes."

Perhaps she should have been more inquisitive about what, exactly, he planned to do once he had taken them off, but her passions were thinking for her, and she was lost in the moment, drowning in her desires, and she cared nothing for consequences. She wanted only *this*—the pleasure he offered. The pleasure his body promised.

He sat back on his heels again and tugged gently on her drawers. She raised her hips off the ground to assist. A second later, he tossed the drawers aside, then lowered himself upon her again, stroking the outside of her thigh with his warm, tantalizing hand.

His thumb drifted gently over the scar where the bullet had grazed her, and he stopped kissing her briefly to whisper, "I remember this."

"I remember, too. I remember everything about that day."

"The pain is gone now?" he asked.

"Yes."

He nodded and kissed her again, sliding his warm hand up under her bare behind, massaging her cool flesh, then his hand came around to the front and moved through the soft curls, into her open womanhood. Her body responded with a reverberating echo of trembling delight.

"Damien, this is wicked," she whispered, as he massaged the sensitive bud of her desire.

"Tell me to stop, Adele. I will if you wish it."

She shook her head. "No, not yet."

He held her close, stroking the soft folds of flesh, knowing exactly how to touch her, to ease the stress of her yearnings. Soon, her whole body began to relax under the skill of his hand, and she felt wondrously free and wanton, rotating her hips in circles to match his endless caress, feeling as if she were turning to liquid. Nothing could keep her from enjoying this bliss.

Finally, the last of her inhibitions floated away on the tides of her pleasure, and she slid a hand down into his trousers.

"I want to feel you, too," she said, letting all her repressed emotions and desires come flooding out. She reached into his pants and touched the soft, silky tip of his arousal with a finger, then dove in deeper to wrap her whole hand around him. Shocked by the size and heat of him, she stroked him as he stroked her, with a rhythm she had come to understand as the foundation of all things sexual.

"This is getting out of hand," he said into her mouth, between kisses. "I've never wanted any woman like I want you now, Adele. You have captured me completely. I want to make love to you. Please, let me. Let me show you more than this."

It was not like her to act without careful consideration, but she was no longer the old Adele. She now knew the meaning of rashness, of fevered, out-of-control acts of passion. She nodded frantically.

It was all he had been waiting for. She was

dimly aware of his hand quickly working the buttons of his trousers, and the lifting of his hips while he slid them off. Then he was *there*. Between her legs. Pausing. Waiting. As if to make sure she was not going to change her mind.

A breeze blew the willow branches all around them, and the leaves made a hissing sound. Adele opened her eyes to look up at him in the dim, afternoon light. He was staring down at her, almost fearful. Apprehensive. She had never seen him look like that before.

Then he pushed.

The pressure caused some discomfort, but it also caused a need. She pushed back in return, thrusting her hips upward despite the pain of the invasion. A groan escaped her.

He went still, and whispered, "Are you all right?"

She nodded again, reaching around—almost involuntarily—to put her hands on his firm buttocks and pull him in tighter. She thrust upward with all the strength she possessed in her hips and legs, and felt the rupture of her maidenhead. Pain shot through her, but it eased almost instantly as she comprehended his physical presence within her.

He was inside her. *Inside.* He filled her deeply and completely, and she clutched on to the sturdy anchor of his shoulders, biting down on her lower lip as he withdrew and drove in again.

She was slick down there, which eased the pain somewhat and enhanced the pleasure, she realized, coming to understand what this was about.

Within seconds, the pain was gone entirely, and she was able to lie back and enjoy the feel of him plunging heedlessly in and out of her—over and over until almost without warning, a surge of both desire and fulfillment coursed through her veins, like an electric current through her entire being. Her body pulsed and throbbed, and not understanding what was happening, she arched her back and cried out Damien's name.

What had just happened? she wondered madly, still arching her back and thinking that lightning had just struck the tree above them, and had sizzled through the ground beneath her.

The pleasure continued to crackle through her body on rapid, repeating waves, until all her energy was sapped, and she collapsed flat on her back. She opened her eyes and realized that Damien had continued his thrusting through all of it, and had only now slowed his pace as she relaxed. He had not stopped to make sure she was still alive, so what just happened must have been normal.

Yes, it must have been, because he looked pleased. "You're glorious," he said, then he pushed a few more times, deeper than before, more violently than before, and tossed his head back and cried out, just as she had cried out only seconds before.

His huge, hard body went weak and limp, and he collapsed onto his elbows, then he lowered all his weight on top of her. She touched his forehead, warm with perspiration, and could feel the tremendous heat of his body emanating from beneath his shirt and wool waistcoat.

"I'm sorry that I still have my clothes on," he said, his chest heaving, for he was out of breath. "I would like to be naked with you, to feel your skin against my stomach."

"Oh yes. That sounds wonderful." She began to unbutton his waistcoat.

He leaned up and smiled, though he was still inside her. "Now, Adele?"

"Yes, now. Take this off."

He withdrew. She pulled the waistcoat off his shoulders, and he removed his shirt. Adele's skirts were still bunched up around her waist, so she took them off, too, and they both faced each other on their knees, clad only in their boots.

"We better leave these on," he said with a lift of his eyebrow, "in case we have to jump up and run."

She laughed, and took his face in her hands. "Lie on top of me."

His dark eyes flashed, and he smiled. It was a wolfish smile—the embodiment of sexual, teasing seduction. "With pleasure."

He eased her onto her back again and covered her body with his own. His flat, hard stomach—hot and slick with sweat—touched hers. Adele marveled at the sensation of skin against skin. She wrapped her legs around his. She could feel his genitals touching hers, and instinctively she rotated her hips in little circles.

"If you want to do it again," he said with a

teasing lilt to his voice, "I might need just a minute or two."

"I'm sorry, I can't help it. My body needs to do this for some reason."

"It's instinct."

Then he lowered his mouth to hers and kissed her deeply, sending heat rippling under her skin.

Adele held nothing back. She wrapped her whole body around him and stroked him everywhere. He kissed her neck and she tossed her head back, looking up at the canopy of willow leaves all around them, listening to the chirping of birds and the breezes through the trees.

She had longed for a sense of freedom in her soul, and this was it. This was it. This was what it felt like to soar.

He grew stiff and hard again, and entered her with natural ease this time. He made love to her slowly and gently, for a long time on the soft ground. They changed positions so that she was on top, then they rolled to their sides, facing each other, making love quietly. He turned her over onto her stomach, and made love to her while he lay on top of her back. She tingled at the feel of his hot kisses and his breath at her nape, and when he kissed behind her ears. When they climaxed they were facing each other. He was on top again, gazing down at her while she pulsed and quickened and heaved in the grass. It was the most intense physical experience she'd ever known.

A few minutes later, Damien propped himself up on both elbows and gazed down at her face.

"Adele," he said, sounding serious all of a sudden. "When will we tell Harold?"

She stared at him, her mind blank. *No* . . . She had not wanted to think about that just yet. She was enjoying this freedom too much. She wanted to exist only in the moment, without concern for the future or difficult decisions. The plain reminder of her reality sent her soul crashing down from the sky.

"When will *we* tell him?" Her mood was touched by a hint of apprehension. "That must be my decision, Damien, and mine alone. I do not want to be guided, yet again, by what others tell me I should or must do."

He paused and wet his lips. "I don't mean to tell you what to do, Adele. I only want you to know that I am here for you and with you, not to lead you, but to stand beside you."

Adele's heart gloried in the bliss of his words, yet at the same time, it seemed almost too perfect. She was having some trouble believing it could be real. It was too good to be true. And she supposed there was a small part of her that felt some shame for what they had just done, out of wedlock.

"Damien," she said, "I have just betrayed my fiancé. I have given in to my passions and given myself to a man who is not my husband, under a tree. Doesn't that bother you? There have been so many issues of distrust between us. I worry that—"

He touched his forehead to hers. "No. You gave yourself to *me*, not *any* man. To the day I die, I will believe that I am your only."

Oh, how was it possible that he always knew just the right things to say? Sometimes he filled her with such bliss, she could barely believe she wasn't dreaming . . . "But I will always worry that one day, you will look for a reason to use this against me."

"I won't."

She realized suddenly that she was asking these questions because she was afraid. She had acted recklessly, which was entirely out of her realm of experience, and what they had just done could not be undone. She was searching desperately for assurance . . .

"What about Harold? I can't bear the thought of destroying your relationship with him," she said. "He's like a brother to you. You care deeply for him, as he cares deeply for you."

"I am hoping Harold will care enough to understand, and to want me to be happy, the way I have always wanted him to be happy."

"Perhaps he will forgive you, but he will likely hate me."

Damien stroked her cheek. "It wouldn't matter. What I said before still stands. If I must choose, I will choose you, no matter what the cost. You are my future. I hope you will choose me over all else, too. Please, no more excuses, Adele. No more reasons to stop this from happening."

She smiled lovingly at him, though she was still in turmoil over all of it. She was not yet sure she should leap so quickly from one man to another. A few days ago, when she had decided to end her engagement to Harold, she had imagined herself living on her own, even embarking on a career of some sort. But now, was she being too quick to throw that aside? To rush into a marriage with a man whose integrity she had always doubted?

She knew she adored him; that wasn't the problem. She only wished to do what was wise. Unfortunately, at the moment, she wasn't sure what the wisest course was. She was afraid she was being carried away by the intensity of her passions.

Just then, a twig snapped and there was a rustling in the woods. They both went silent and turned toward the sound.

"What was that?" Adele whispered, reaching for her drawers.

"I don't know. Get dressed," he whispered, rising to his feet.

He reached for his pants, pulled them on, then put on his shirt. He was still buttoning it when he pushed through the curtain of willow leaves and disappeared.

Chapter 26

⟡

Adele could see Damien vaguely through the branches, as he moved about the woods in silence, like a panther searching for prey.

She frantically pulled on her chemise and drawers, picked up her corset, and stood, hugging it to her chest. The willow leaves separated again, and Damien reappeared.

"Well?" she asked.

"I didn't see anyone. It could have been an animal."

"Your horse, maybe?"

"Perhaps." He gazed over his shoulder. "Though it seemed to come from the other direction."

He bent to pick up his waistcoat and pulled it

on. "We should head back to the house."

They helped each other dress, then left the shelter of the willow tree and walked along the path, hand in hand. When they reached the tea-house, Adele said, "I should go and find Harold now."

He nodded. "I'll wait here for a while, so we don't arrive at the same time. We don't want to arouse any suspicions before you've had a chance to talk to him."

She rose up on her toes and kissed him tenderly on the cheek. "I'll come and find you when it's done. We still have a lot to talk about, Damien. I fear this may be happening too fast."

"I have never been more sure of anything, Adele. I want to spend my life with you."

She hesitated, then she nodded and started walking.

Damien called out to her. "Adele!"

She stopped and turned. He was standing beside a rose bush. His hair was a wild mess, his clothes looked ragged and worn. She looked down at his feet. There was mud on his boots.

He took a step forward. "I don't recall if I said it to you or not . . ."

"Said what?" she asked.

He paused, and when he spoke, his voice was soft and velvety. "That I love you."

A leaf drifted down through the air, and landed on Adele's head. She felt only a gentle breeze through her hair, and a simple, joyful contentment inside herself. "I love you, too."

Then, feeling both buoyant and terrified, yet full of cautious hope, she made off for the house.

Adele went straight to the conservatory—or rather the laboratory—to search for Harold. She did not find him there.

Next, she went to Catherine's room, and was pleased to discover she was sitting up with Eustacia, drinking soup. Adele stayed for a short time to talk, but since it was Harold she wanted to see, she said she was tired, and went to knock on his bedchamber door.

No one answered at first, then he called from inside. "Enter!"

She pushed the door open. He was sitting on his bed—had he been staring at the wall?—and turned to see who it was. When he saw that it was Adele, he rose quickly and straightened his neck cloth, as if flustered. "Good gracious, what are you doing here?"

She was slightly confused by the question. "Did no one tell you that my mother and I arrived this morning? To see Catherine?"

"Well, yes," he said awkwardly. "Mother told me, of course. I meant, what are you doing knocking on my bedchamber door? It's hardly proper, Adele."

She forced a smile, remembering how uncomfortable Harold could be about anything the slightest degree outside the rules. He was probably embarrassed that she had now seen his bed.

"I apologize," she said, "but I need to speak

with you privately. Will you meet me in the library?"

"Yes, of course." He pasted on his customary, cheerful smile. "I'll be there momentarily."

She hesitated a moment, because she had thought he might simply accompany her, but it seemed she would have to go and wait for him.

Before she turned to walk out, however, she stole a quick glance at the furnishings, realizing it was probably the only time she would ever see this room.

After Adele closed the door to Harold's bedchamber, he let out a breath of relief and sat back down on his bed.

Violet got up off the floor and smoothed out her skirt. "Good gracious, I'm getting tired of this."

"I beg your pardon?" Harold said.

"Oh, nothing," she said irritably. "It's just that this is not the first time I've had to duck down in a room when that woman enters it."

He simply accepted what she said. He did not question it.

"Will you be all right?" Violet asked her brother, gazing down at him with genuine sympathy, for he was truly no match for Damien. Not in a woman's eyes.

Harold nodded. "Yes. I don't care anymore. I don't care if he hates me. There was a time when we were close, but now . . . I don't think I can ever forgive him for this."

Violet touched his shoulder. "He doesn't deserve your forgiveness, Harold. He knew how much you loved her. He should have to grovel for your forgiveness for the rest of his life."

"I *did* love her, and he *should* have to grovel for my forgiveness. But it wouldn't do any good." He gazed up at Violet with a dark gleam in his eye. "Because we are finished, he and I."

Harold kept Adele waiting for at least ten minutes before he entered the library, looking uncharacteristically serious. "I'm sorry," he said, closing the door behind him with a gentle click. "I wasn't quite ready to come down. I had something to attend to."

Adele rose abruptly from the chair she had been sitting on, while biting her thumbnail down to the quick. She watched Harold cross the room toward her. He stopped in front of another chair opposite and gestured for her to sit down again. She smoothed her skirt in the back and seated herself.

They sat and looked at each other for an awkward few seconds. There had been many awkward seconds between them, but she would try to explain her change-of-heart as kindly and gently as possible, no matter how difficult it was.

She leaned forward, laced her fingers together on her lap, and said, "Harold, I—"

He held up a hand. "No, wait, Adele. I know what you're going to say."

"You do?"

"Yes." He wet his lips, and a few blotches of red stained his cheeks. Adele sat back slightly.

"I saw you today," he said.

Adele went instantly numb. She sat in stunned silence, staring at him, then a wave of horror crashed over her. She covered her mouth with a hand. "*Harold* . . ."

"I saw you under the tree. I know what happened."

Her voice shook when she spoke. "What . . . what were you doing there?"

"Mother told me you had gone looking for me. I went to find you."

She shifted agonizingly in the chair. "Harold, I'm so sorry. I wanted to tell you. That's why I went down there in the first place."

"But Damien got there before I did."

She paused. "Yes."

He stood and paced to the window. "Adele, you cannot know how shocked and devastated I was to hear—" He stopped himself.

Adele was mortified. He had listened to the things they'd said, the sounds they'd made . . .

"Damien . . ." Harold said with grim loathing. "My own cousin. We were the best of friends, ever since we were boys. He was like a brother to me."

"He still is," Adele said, hoping to prevent a complete dissolution of their friendship. She could not bear to think it would be severed because of her.

"No," he replied.

Adele stood and went to him. "He tried to fight it, Harold. He tried very hard, and so did I. It just happened, that's all. Neither of us ever wanted to hurt you."

She touched his shoulder, but he shook her

hand away. "You had already decided you didn't want to marry me?" he asked. "That's why you went looking for me?"

"Yes."

"Because you wanted to marry Damien instead?"

She hesitated before she answered. "No. I was just going to go home to America on my own. I didn't know what I wanted."

He glared down at her. It was the first time she'd ever seen anger and pain in his eyes. He was always so cheerful and happy. "Did he propose to you?"

She breathed deeply. "Yes."

He bowed his head and shook it. "*Damien*," he said, through a jaw that was clenched tight with fury. "He had no right!"

"Harold . . ."

He turned from the window and paced angrily around the room. "And you . . . How could you let him seduce you like that? What were you thinking?"

"I can't really explain it."

"No, I would think not. But you must realize how foolish you were. He has forced himself upon you, Adele."

"No, it wasn't like that. He never forced me."

"I mean he forced the situation to go as he wanted it. He wants your money, and he did what he does best in order to get it."

She shook her head.

"You don't believe that? You think he's in love with you?" Harold continued to pace, looking down at the floor. "I suppose I should not be surprised. He knows what women like to hear."

Adele bristled at that.

"Do you have any idea what's been going on in his life lately?" Harold asked. "Do you know about the creditors? About Frances Fairbanks?"

"Everyone knows about her."

"But they don't know she's pregnant."

An instantaneous jolt caused all thoughts and responses to wedge in Adele's brain. She stared at Harold, not quite able to accept what he was saying.

"She wants Damien to marry her, of course, but she has no money, so he is not inclined to propose. He does, however, possess some miniscule fragment of integrity in his own misdirected way, because he is determined to support her and the child. Hence, the urgency for a quick alliance with an heiress."

Adele swallowed hard, biting back the hurt she felt. *He was going to have a baby with Frances?* He had never said anything. He had led her to believe their relationship was over.

"Do you know this for certain?" Adele asked. "Or is it just drawing room gossip?"

"Damien told me himself, and ridiculously, I was the one who convinced him that he should find himself a fiancée as soon possible. How's that for a stab in the back? He set his gaze on *you.*"

Adele felt sick. She had to sit down.

"Do you believe me now, that he is not to be trusted? Do you understand why I am so furious with him, for acting in such a devious, underhanded manner, and taking advantage of you so deplorably? My own cousin!"

"I don't know what I believe at the moment," she said.

He stopped pacing and met her gaze. "I will still marry you, Adele, if you wish it. It is Damien I am most angry with, and I hold myself partly responsible for this. I . . . I should have taken better care." He approached and took her chin in his slender hand, and looked down at her with a sympathetic expression. "I am of the opinion that you were taken in, Adele, but only because you are so good, and you do not see the bad in other people."

Her dander perked up its head. "That's not true, Harold. Everyone thinks I am perfect, but I am not, and I was not 'taken in.'"

He dropped his hand to his side. "If what happened between you and Damien results in a child, I will accept that child. He would be my second cousin, after all. I would only hope that it would be a girl."

Adele squeezed her eyes shut. "Harold, please don't speak of this sort of thing. I'm sorry, but I simply cannot marry you, and I would feel the same if I had never met Damien. You and I, we don't love each other." She made a fist and held it over her heart. "We do not connect with each other. We have nothing in common."

"You respect me, do you not? Violet told me you said I was the most decent man you knew."

"That is true."

"Well, that's something to build on."

"It is, but . . . I don't want to build on it. I don't want to marry you, Harold, and nothing will change my mind."

"Will you marry Damien? Despite what I've told you?"

"I already said I don't know." She held a hand on her stomach to try and stop the churning.

"If you do," Harold said callously, "I assure you, you will regret it."

She moved toward the door, but stopped and turned before she opened it. "I need time to think about all this. I'll be leaving the house today, just as soon as I can collect my things. I will ask you to say good-bye to Catherine and your mother for me. Please tell them that I'm sorry, that I had come to care for them very much, and I never wanted to hurt any of you. It just can't happen between us, Harold. Again, I'm very sorry."

With that, she walked out.

Harold sank into a chair, covered his face with both hands, and ground out a string of expletives.

Three hours later, Damien stormed into the conservatory, where Harold was setting up for an experiment.

Damien stopped on the opposite side of the table and slammed a letter down with a smack. The table jumped, and a carefully arranged collection of glass bottles wobbled—noisily clanking into each other. Harold bent forward and grabbed for them, hugging them together to prevent them from falling.

Damien leaned forward on his fists. "What in God's name did you say to her?"

Chapter 27

$\sim\!\infty\!\sim$

Harold's face pulled into a frown and he straightened, making sure, however, that the bottles were steady before he let them go. His voice dripped with anger and abhorrence. "You have a lot of nerve coming in here and demanding answers from *me*."

Damien straightened also. They were eye-to-eye on opposite sides of the table. Pent-up rage—from each of them—crackled in the air between them.

"I asked you a question," Damien said.

Harold glanced down at the letter. He picked it up and read it. Damien watched his cousin and recited the letter in his own mind, for he had read it so many times, he'd memorized it:

337

Dear Damien,

I am leaving Osulton Manor today, and please do not try to follow me. I was carried away by my passions today, and I do not believe it would be wise for us to marry. I must protect my own heart in this matter.

   I must also inform you that I spoke to Harold, and ended our engagement. He did not take it well, as he had been the noise in the woods.

                              Adele

"What did she mean," Damien said, "that she must protect her own heart? What did you tell her?"

"What do you think I told her? The truth, of course. Despite the sudden intimacy of your *relationship*, she did not deserve to be kept in the dark about your urgent need for a rich wife, or about your creditors or Frances. I would not allow her to be taken advantage of in that way."

"She knew about all that. I never lied to her."

"This is outrageous!" Harold said. "I should not be the one explaining myself. You should be!" Harold walked around the table. "You seduced and ruined my fiancée!"

Damien stared into his cousin's furious eyes and managed to collect himself. He fought off the shock and anguish over Adele's hasty departure and her decision that she would never marry him, and realized that Harold had his own reasons to be angry. And he was right. Damien had indeed done the unthinkable.

"Perhaps we should go outside," he said, knowing there was much to be worked out, and this room constructed of glass was not the place.

Harold ripped off his apron and threw it on the floor. "Damn right we should." In a most uncharacteristic manner, he forcefully led the way out.

Violet took the news that Adele had left Osulton Manor with neither grace nor understanding. She glared hotly at her mother in the drawing room and balled her hands into fists.

"My brother is an incompetent cretin! If she is gone, it is *his* fault for not knowing how to treat a woman! He is hopeless! Hopeless! No one will *ever* marry him!"

She collapsed into a fit of tears on the sofa, not the least bit comforted by her mother stroking her back.

"Now we shall be beggars!" Violet sobbed. "Harold spends all our money on his silly experiments, and I will have to marry beneath me, because all the best men in London want those rich American girls with their big dowries!" She dropped her head into her hands. "And Whitby! *Oh, Whitby!*"

"There, there, Violet, it's not so bad. You have your beauty."

She peered up at her mother as if she had

grown horns, and wiped the flood of tears from her cheeks. "She's *gone*, Mother! *Gone!* She left Harold, and we will not get her settlement!"

She dropped her head into her arms again, and sobbed, "Oh, why does everything always have to happen to *me!*"

Damien followed Harold out onto the large veranda at the back of the house. They both walked quickly with long strides to the stairs that led down to the rectangular pond. The wind had picked up. The green hedges of the maze were blowing, and low-hanging clouds were racing and changing shape across the gray and white sky. The pond was dancing with shadowy ripples.

Damien descended the stairs. Harold was waiting for him at the bottom, on the clipped, green grass. They faced each other squarely.

"All our lives," Harold said, "you have been the favorite. You were the strong one—fighting off bullies for me at school. You were the generous one—teaching me to play sports, even going so far as to stay behind in a race to run beside me and encourage me. I remember all those things, Damien, and I always believed it was because you were my friend. That is why I trusted you to go and bring Adele home to me."

"Harold, I—"

"I'm not done. You did not help me. All you ever did was make me feel like I wasn't strong enough to do anything on my own, and if it weren't for you—watching over me all the time like I was a weakling—maybe I would have gone to get Adele myself."

Damien stared at his cousin. "I *was* your friend, Harold."

"No, you weren't. You just wanted to show off to everyone, and pound your chest."

Damien shook his head. "Wait. You make it sound like I was the one with all the blessings. Dammit, Harold, no one ever thought I was the better man. *You* were the one who could do no wrong. You've always had everything—parents who loved each other and loved you, a perfect palace to live in with a mother who still takes care of everything. You don't have money problems. You are happy all the time because you have nothing to worry about except the results of your experiments. I was orphaned at the age of nine with the burden of guilt for my parents' death, left with debts you could not even fathom . . . So forgive me for learning how to be tough."

Harold's red eyebrows lifted. "You're suggesting that you resent *me?* I've never heard anything so ridiculous in all my life! No one can resist your charm. Grandmother has always favored you, and don't pretend not to know it. You flatter her and flirt with her like she was a debutante, and she would do anything for you. You have her wrapped around your devious little finger."

"For what *devious* purpose, may I ask?" Damien replied, trying to grasp his cousin's logic. "She has nothing to leave any of us in her will. It all went to my father's debts. She has only the pleasure of her last days, and I will not apologize for caring about her enough to simply enjoy making her feel good."

"Like you made *Adele* feel good?" His tone suggested the worst.

Damien labored to control his anger. "You'll forgive me for saying that that is something you, as her fiancé, failed to do. You were too busy mixing potions."

"That is low, Damien. I loved her."

Damien laughed. "Did you now? Tell me another one!"

"I did! You don't know what I feel!"

"I know you had no time for her. I know you didn't care enough to worry that she had been ravaged by her kidnapper. You didn't even want to hear what happened to her, because it was not pleasant for *you*. I also know that you wanted her for her father's interest in your chemical inventions. You were hoping to make the history books."

Damien and Harold stood motionless, staring at each other like two wolves, each waiting for the other to attack.

"Let's see who's the strong one today!" Harold grunted as he lunged and slammed his shoulder into Damien's gut.

Damien staggered back. "I won't fight you, Harold!"

"You damn well better, or I'll knock you off your feet! And it's about bloody time I did!"

They fell over onto the grass. Damien went down on his back, and Harold straddled him.

He threw a punch, catching Damien in the jaw. Pain shot through his whole head. He tried to grab Harold's arms, but Harold was thrashing— slapping uncontrollably at him.

"I won't fight you, Harold!" he said a second time, finally wrapping his own large hands around his cousin's slender wrists to restrain him. He had to use all his strength. Harold was still trying to slap at him.

Damien's voice was low and grinding when he spoke. "I could flatten you in a second, cousin. I suggest you stop now, before I'm forced to defend myself."

Harold slowly, eventually gave up the fight. He bowed his head in defeat and rolled off Damien. They both lay on their backs in the grass, looking up at the sky.

"Damn you," Harold said. "I hope you go to hell."

"You're not the first person to say that."

Harold turned his head toward Damien. His voice was cold and unfeeling. "Every one of your mistresses, I presume."

"Every damn one."

Harold looked back up at the sky. "Well, if I can't have Adele, I'm glad she's gone. You would have made her miserable."

It was Damien's turn to look at Harold. "How can you say that? Did you ever stop to think that I might have really loved her? Surely you must have. You *know* me, Harold. You must have known I would not steal a woman from you—my cousin, my friend—without a very good reason. I would not hurt you for a temporary flirtation. Or for money."

Harold was not moved by Damien's pronouncement. "She told me you proposed."

"Yes, I did. I wanted her, Harold, with every piece of the man that I am. It *killed* me to think of her marrying you, but I weathered it. For a long time I weathered it, because I couldn't bear to hurt you. But eventually I couldn't do it anymore. The love I felt for her chipped away at my strength and resolve, and eventually I had to choose between her and you. I just couldn't let her go. I loved her too much. It killed me inside, but it was a risk I had to take."

"Even though you would betray me in the process."

Damien sighed. "I had hoped you would understand."

He sat up and gazed toward the pond. Harold sat up, too. For a long while, they sat in silence while the wind blew all around them, until Damien turned to his cousin.

"I'm sorry for making you feel weak when we were children," he said quietly, looking him in the eye. "That was never my intention. I *was* overly protective of you, but only because I blamed myself for my parents' deaths, and I felt happier when I could help *you*. I didn't want you to end up like my father. I wanted to make sure you were always content. You were all I had."

Harold simply stared at Damien.

"And I still cling to the hope," Damien said,

"that you will understand what happened between me and Adele, and forgive me, because she is gone now, and I am . . . devastated." His voice trembled on the last word.

Harold went pale. "You're devastated?"

"I loved her, Harold. So much so, I betrayed my family."

Harold's eyes narrowed. "But . . . I thought you wanted her money."

Damien dropped his hand. "Did *Adele* say that?"

"No, but considering the circumstances . . ."

Damien leaned on one arm. "What *circumstances*, Harold? I must be stupid today, because I am missing things."

Harold shifted to sit on his heels. "I know about Frances."

"What, exactly, do you know?"

Harold paused, then he whispered, even though there was no one within earshot to hear them. "I know about the baby."

Damien felt his forehead crease. "*What* baby?"

"*Your* baby. I know you want to provide for the child."

The child. Damien's head began to spin. "I beg your pardon? A baby with Frances? This is bloody news to me."

"You didn't know?"

Damien almost laughed. "You say it like I'm the *last* to know. It's not true, Harold. I know it's not."

"How do you know?"

"If you want me to be blunt, I know because

the last time I made love to her, she started her courses that very night."

Harold's mouth dropped open. The wind was blowing even harder now. "You're sure?"

"Yes, I'm sure. I always kept very careful track of these things. Who said otherwise?"

After a few seconds, Harold faced the other direction. He seemed to be considering something very carefully. "Violet."

Damien rose irritably to his feet. "Violet said that?"

"Yes," Harold said, rising also. "But there's something else you should know. I . . . I told Adele that *you* told me about Frances and the baby. I lied about that because Violet suggested it would be better if it wasn't just drawing room gossip. I'm sorry, Damien. I believed there really was a baby. Violet said it was true, and I was so angry with you."

Damien rested his hands on his hips and bowed his head.

"And Damien," Harold said, "I wasn't the one who saw you in the woods today. Violet was." He dropped his head into his hands. "I guess I'm not such a decent fellow after all, am I? I'm a bit of a liar, in fact. And not only that, I'm about the worst fool in the world. I was manipulated by my spoiled brat of a sister."

Violet was still sobbing uncontrollably when Damien and Harold burst into the drawing room. Eustacia looked up—shocked by the sudden, rather passionate intrusion. "What in heaven's name is going on?" she asked, putting her arm protectively around Violet.

Eyes red and puffy, cheeks stained with tears, Violet sat up. She wiped the back of her hand across her cheek and frowned at Damien. "You bastard."

"Violet! Your language!" Eustacia shouted.

Violet did not take her eyes off Damien. Her lips pursed into a thin line. "Why couldn't you leave her alone? Why *her*? You could have any woman you wanted, and you had to go and spoil Harold's chances for happiness!"

Damien approached her. His eyes were dark and hooded, his voice quiet and dangerous. "You have some explaining to do, cousin."

She shuddered with a weepy intake of breath. "What are you talking about?"

"You told Harold that Frances Fairbanks was having my child."

Eustacia gasped and put a hand over her mouth. "God in heaven!"

Violet shifted nervously on the sofa. "I did not."

Harold stepped forward. "Yes, you did."

"No, I didn't!"

"Yes, you did!"

"No, I—"

Damien held up a hand. "You lied, Violet, and Adele has made decisions with erroneous information. You will fix the problem."

"But I didn't have anything to do with it!"

Harold stepped up. "It is just like you, Violet, to blame someone else. Remember when you broke the blue vase in the gallery, and you said you didn't know who did it? I saw you do it, you selfish brat, and I saw you deny it. That was last year! You were old enough to know better." He turned to Eustacia, pointing his finger. "Mother, *she* did it. She was practicing tossing her shawl over her shoulder."

Harold turned to Damien. He gazed at him for a long, drawn-out minute. His voice grew calmer; his shoulders relaxed. "If she won't tell Adele the truth, Damien, *I* will tell her."

"Harold . . ." Damien said, interrupting.

"No, let me finish. I . . . I'm sorry, Damien. I should have been able to see that you and Adele were better suited to each other, and that you cared for each other. I should have been more aware of what was going on around me."

"Harold, I'm so sorry."

"No, you don't need to be. You're my friend, Damien. I should have known you would never seduce Adele just for her money. I will tell Adele that I was wrong to doubt you. I will tell her that I am sorry for not loving her the way she deserved to be loved, and I will tell her that *you* love her, and that I know it's true because you told me, and you are the most decent man I know."

Damien gazed with disbelief at his cousin. "I would be obliged," he said.

Harold smiled in return. "She'll be at her sister's place soon. Perhaps we should go now."

Damien and Harold left the drawing room and headed to their respective rooms to get their things.

Just before they separated at the end of the hall in the east wing, Harold stopped. "Do you think Whitby will still propose to Violet, if she doesn't have money from Adele's settlement?"

Damien inclined his head. "That remains to be seen." Then he went quickly to fetch his belongings.

Chapter 28

⌒◯◯⌒

Wentworth House
London

That night, Sophia quietly pushed open the door of her husband's study and peered inside. "Are you busy?"

He leaned back in his chair and smiled at her. "Not at all. Come here." He held out his arm.

Sophia went to him and sat down on his lap. "I wanted to tell you that Adele and Mother have arrived."

"Is Adele all right?" James asked.

"I don't think so. She told me about what she said to Harold when she broke the news to him, and he didn't take it well. But she is more upset over what happened with Damien. Oh, James, I believe she is desperately in love with him. She hasn't told me everything, I don't think, but she did tell me that he proposed."

"Did he now?"

"You're not surprised?"

He shook his head. "I recognized a certain look in his eye when I spoke to him about Adele at a ball one night."

Sophia rested her head on his shoulder. "Well, she refused him, and she is determined not to change her mind. She just wants to go home."

James's dark brows drew together. "Why? It is my opinion that Alcester has been misunderstood by many people who think—"

"Frances Fairbanks is pregnant," Sophia told him. "It's Damien's. He admits it, but he refuses to marry her because she has no money. It appears that the relationship is not over."

James lifted Sophia off his lap, and stood. "Where in the world did Adele hear that?"

Sophia shrugged. "I don't know."

He shook his head. "If it's true, I'll eat my valet's boot."

"What do you know, James?"

"I know that the manager of the theater where she appears is a great supporter of hers, giving her all the best parts, and it's a well-known fact that two gentlemen of substantial means have been providing for her rather extravagant means of living, and I assure you, they all collect their rewards. So there is no way she could ever prove the child was Alcester's, if there even *is* a child."

"Oh, James, that is positively sordid."

"Yes. Alcester was wise to break it off with her. Besides that, I've made it my business to learn everything there is to know about Damien Renshaw, and by all accounts, he is a good man."

"Why didn't you say anything?"

"I assumed it would all work itself out, that Adele would see the light. But this lie that is circulating is unfair. Would you like me to look into it?"

"Oh yes, James. Yes."

He touched her cheek with the back of his hand, and kissed her tenderly on the lips. "If it will ease your mind, Sophia, I will go straight to the source. I will speak to Miss Fairbanks myself."

Chapter 29

The next morning, the butler entered the drawing room and announced Lord Osulton and Lord Alcester. Sophia, Beatrice, and Adele all stood up. Adele put a hand on her stomach to quell the sudden nervous butterflies.

The two men entered, and everyone stood in awkward silence for a second or two until Sophia composed herself, smothered her surprise, and gestured for her guests to sit down. "Would you like some tea, gentlemen?" she offered.

"That would be lovely," Harold said, sitting down.

Damien sat, too, though he never took his eyes off Adele.

Sophia stood up and walked to the velvet bellpull, but Damien stood before she had a chance to put her hand on it. "If you don't mind, Duchess, may I request a moment alone with your sister?" He bowed down at Beatrice. "A moment with your daughter, Mrs. Wilson?"

Adele stiffened with apprehension.

Beatrice rolled her shoulders. "I should think not."

Sophia winced. "Mother . . ."

Damien glanced at Sophia. "It's quite all right." He turned toward Beatrice again. "I know you have not always approved of me, Mrs. Wilson, but I assure you, my intentions toward your daughter are honorable. A moment is all I ask."

Beatrice gazed pleadingly at Harold. "Lord Osulton?"

He stood also, and bowed. "His intentions are indeed honorable, Mrs. Wilson. I will vouch for him."

Beatrice stammered with bewilderment. More than a little surprised herself, Adele met Harold's gaze. What had happened between them? What had changed Harold's opinion of Damien? The last time she'd spoken to him, he had considered his cousin a scoundrel and a fortune hunter. Had he learned what James had told her?

Sophia crossed the room and stopped before her mother, who was still sitting. "Come, Mother. We'll wait right outside the door."

Beatrice rose reluctantly. Harold went with them and held the door for the ladies. Just before he walked out, he gave Adele an encouraging smile. They closed the door behind them.

She looked at Damien, and swallowed nervously.

"In your letter," he said, "you asked me not to follow you, but I couldn't let you go on believing something about me that is simply not true. I have not fathered another woman's child, Adele. I am positively certain of it."

Her heart pounded, as it often did when Damien was nearby. Slowly, she made her way around the table in the center of the room, to cross toward him. "I know."

He tilted his head to the side. "You *know*?"

"Yes."

"How?"

She sighed. "James seems to have a high opinion of you. He has been making inquiries, you see. Evidently, most of the information he received has been irrefutably positive. Except for the item regarding a baby with Frances. That, I'm pleased to say, was negative. He spoke to Frances himself last night. She knew nothing of a baby, and was surprised such a thing was even suggested."

Damien's broad shoulders heaved on a long exhale.

Adele stopped before him, close enough to put her hands on his chest if she wanted to. She *did* want to, but for the time being she resisted the urge. "What happened?" she asked. "Why did Harold lie to me about Frances? And why is he here this afternoon, vouching for your honor in front of my mother?"

Damien turned his hat over in his hands. "He

didn't know he was lying. Violet made up the story about Frances, and encouraged him to tell you that I had admitted to being the father of the child. Violet wanted you to marry Harold, so that she herself would have a large dowry to settle upon the man of her choice."

"Lord Whitby?"

"Most likely."

"She admitted to it?"

He tilted his head to the side. "Not really, but she's always had a problem admitting to her misdemeanors. Harold is going to work on that when he gets home."

Adele felt her eyebrows lift in surprise. "Harold is going to work on it? I am glad to hear that."

"Adele . . ." Damien took a small step forward, even closer. His voice was strangely hushed. "I came here to tell you something else. Something you must hear from my own lips. Something I hope you will believe." He stood before her, his dark eyes gleaming, his chest rising and falling with shallow breaths. "I know you have many reservations about me, and after all that has happened, for good reason. But I vow by all that is holy that when I become a husband, I will never be unfaithful to my wife."

She eyed him with scrutiny. Despite her foray into her own wild passions, she had come this far never *completely* letting go of her prudent nature. She would not simply tumble into Damien's arms now after one small promise of fidelity. Nor would she base her decision on the opinion of her brother-in-law—that Damien was not what people thought he was. She was going to use her own mind and form her own opinion.

In that light, she needed more from Damien. If she had learned anything from her experiences over the past month, it was to think of what *she* wanted in life, and to ask for it, to settle for nothing less. She knew she wanted Damien, but she would be absolutely certain of him first, before she gave him her whole heart.

"People have been placing bets," she said, "that you'll go back to Frances, or someone like her, after you've married an heiress for her money. Did you know that?"

He pressed his lips together with disdain. "People should mind their own business. I gave you my word that I am not after your money. I don't care about it and I *will* prove it. We can make do without it, Adele."

She sighed. "Damien, you enjoy women. You have never been able to commit to just one."

"But have you ever stopped to consider why I have formed temporary relationships with women like Frances?"

She glanced at the door, hoping no one was about to barge back in, because she wanted desperately to hear what he was going to say.

"Because contrary to what some people think of me," he said, "I take marriage very seriously. I admit that I have not been a monk. All my life, I have craved some form of intimacy with women—perhaps because of what I missed in my life, having no mother—but I was careful to choose women who were open and honest about wanting relationships without commitment, because I never wanted to risk being forced to marry a woman I did not love. I did not wish to be miserable like my parents and destroy a family because of it—especially if there were children involved. I always intended to be in love with the woman I married and confident in my decision to marry her. And it would help if she loved me, too."

"But you had concerns about me, Damien. You said it yourself—I was not faithful to my fiancé. As I became more open and aware of my passions, you became more threatened by memories of your parents. You *did* think I was like your mother, and it broke my heart that you believed I was dishonorable, even though it was true in certain ways. The fact is, I couldn't go through life feeling as if my husband did not trust or respect me completely."

"I didn't know the truth about my mother, Adele, and I was self-righteous. I was angry with her because she was not perfect, but she had a difficult burden to bear. I know that now. I have to forgive her for her weakness, like I have to forgive myself. And you . . ." He took a step closer to her and laid a hand on her cheek. "You are not perfect, Adele. I know that. At first I thought you were, which is why I was enamored with you in the beginning. But then I saw the passion in you, and yes, I mourned the loss of my perfect, pure Adele, and I felt guilty for being the cause of that, but I needed you to break out of that perfect shell in order for us to be together, and you *did*. So now, I cannot idolize you anymore. You have flaws. You made a commitment to my cousin, and you fell in love with another man and broke that commitment. But that man was *me*, and hurting Harold was the right thing to do. So when I look at you now, I know that you are as close to perfect as any real person can be. I *do* trust you, Adele. Completely."

Adele stared, speechless, stunned by his bluntness, his vehemence, his honesty. She remembered suddenly the morning she had awakened next to him at the inn, the final day of their travels. She had felt so happy and content next to him. Everything had felt right. There was no other word for it.

All at once, she wanted more than anything to wake up beside him again and feel that same sense of contentment—that all was right with the world—every day for the rest of her life. It was where her heart was meant to be. With him. In his home. At Essence House.

It was time to admit the truth to herself. She *loved* him. She loved Damien Renshaw, with every inch of her soul, and she believed in him. Wholly and absolutely. It was time to trust her heart. To follow it, and to go after what she wanted.

"From the first moment I met you," she said

shakily, "I was drawn to you, and it brings me some reprieve to finally know that I was not so wrong after all to care for you the way I did. I believe my heart had seen better than my eyes."

She watched the strain in his face fade away. He wet his lips, looking hopeful and joyful, though still tentative.

"There was more to you," she continued, "than what could be seen or heard about through other people's misguided opinions. What I have learned about you this morning—that in your own strange way, you have always wanted love and fidelity—I like very much."

He gripped both her hands in his. She had never seen him look so vulnerable or anxious before. Her knight. Her black lion, who feared nothing.

"Is that all, Adele? You *like* what you have heard? Can there ever be more? Because I must have more."

"There is already more," she replied, feeling an overwhelming urge to laugh out loud with outlandish, bubbling joy. "Much more. I love you quite hopelessly, Damien Renshaw, and I have loved you for what seems like forever."

His lips fell upon hers suddenly, without reservation or composure. He swept her up into his arms until her tiny feet lifted clear off the ground, and Adele shook with bursts of laughter. Or were they sobs of joy?

He kissed her deeply as if the intimacy could erase all the agony and frustration of the past month—when they had both been certain they could never have each other.

Well, they *would* have each other. Utterly and completely for the rest of their lives.

Damien pulled back and dropped to one knee. He held one of her hands in his and kissed it tenderly before he lifted his gaze to look up at her face, into her eyes.

"Adele, I love you. I want to be with you forever. I want to have children and grandchildren with you, I want to laugh with you, go for long walks in the woods with you, make love to you, and I want to make you the happiest woman on earth if I can. You are the only woman in the world for me, and I cannot imagine living without you. Will you marry me, Adele?"

She squeezed both his hands and pulled him up to his feet. "Yes, Damien. Yes to everything."

He pressed his lips to hers again, with passion and love and the promise of forever. Then he rested his forehead upon hers and smiled down at her. "You have made me so happy. I've never been this happy before. Not once in my life."

"There is more to come," she promised. "I will make you happy again, every day if I can. I am a better person for knowing you. I am happier with myself. When I look in the mirror, I no longer see a stranger. I know the things I want. I know I want a simple life with you in your messy, unpretentious house." She grinned.

"Then messy and unpretentious is what you

shall have. I am most pleased to be marrying a woman who will not make me get my hair cut."

Her eyes widened in horror. "Cut it? I should think not!"

He smiled. "It's a fright in the mornings."

"It's beautiful."

Damien pulled her into his arms again, and kissed her hand. "What's this?" he asked, taking a closer look at her hand.

"It's my thumb."

"I'm quite aware of that, but half your nail is gone."

"Yes, it's been a stressful few weeks."

He kissed it. "We'll just have to relieve you of your stresses, then, won't we? Perhaps this will help."

He reached into his pocket and pulled out a red candy stick. Adele's lips parted in surprise as she took hold of it.

"Damien . . ."

"I've been wanting to give you this and so much more ever since that first night you told me about wanting something you didn't think you could have. So here it is. You can have what you want, Adele. I will devote my life to making sure you know it."

Adele took his face in her hands, and kissed him passionately on the mouth. "Will Harold be all right with this?" she asked. "Will Eustacia and Catherine ever forgive us?"

"I believe they all will," he replied, "because Harold is a true friend. We will move past this, and he will be fine."

She smiled. "He will be my friend, too, Damien. He always was."

"There will only be one problem," Damien said, glancing off to the side.

She cringed with a pang of apprehension. "What is that?"

"We will all have to continue to put up with Violet. God give us strength."

Adele laughed, and pulled him down for another kiss.

Epilogue

Wentworth Castle, Yorkshire
Two months later

It was just beginning to rain when Lily walked quickly back from the stables following her early morning gallop over the fields. She wore a black riding habit with a top hat, but her shiny new boots—crunching over the white rocks in the courtyard—were pinching her feet. She was looking forward to getting out of them and finding her old ones before someone gave them away.

She entered the house and was pulling off her gloves, when a footman approached with a letter on a silver salver. "For you, my lady," he said.

She picked up the letter and glanced at it. It was from Sophia. She stuffed her gloves into her

pockets and tore at the seal. Lily slowly climbed
the stairs while she read it . . .

My dearest Lily,

*The Season is finally over, and James and I and
the boys will be coming home soon. Martin
will follow a day or two later.*

*I can hardly wait to see you and Marion,
and the boys are looking forward to returning
to the country where they can run about and
play with the ponies. They have especially been
missing the little gray one.*

*You will be pleased to hear that Adele is very
happy in her new home at Essence House. It
was exactly as she had imagined it would be,
and she told me she felt she was born to live
there. I'm so happy for her. She sends her love.*

*(In case you're wondering, my father in-
sisted on giving them a very generous wedding
gift, even though they protested it strongly.
But you know my father. When he wants to do
something, he does it. Adele has grown to be
very much like him, I daresay.)*

*Please tell Marion that I found a lovely hat
for her yesterday, and I believe it will go well
with her blue day dress with the navy velvet
trim. I'll bring it when I come.*

*I hope all is well at home, and I will see you
in a few days.*

Love,
Sophia

P.S. Whitby left London early this Season, and returned to his country house three weeks ago. James said he was trying to avoid Miss Violet Scott, who evidently was making rather a spectacle of herself, following him everywhere. What a shame. She was very pretty. Though I don't think she was quite Whitby's type.

See you soon,
S.

Lily stopped at the top of the stairs and read the postscript again. A single tear ran down her cheek. It was not sadness, but rather relief that she felt—a most delightful, invigorating wave of relief.

Author's Note

The heroine of this book, Adele Wilson, is
the youngest of three fictional sisters who
leave old New York to go husband hunting in
London in the late-Victorian period. While
these sisters are entirely fictional, I based each
of them on a number of real life American
heiresses, as well as some fictional characters
from the works of some nineteenth- and
twentieth-century novelists.

The most obvious models for this trilogy are
the Jerome sisters—Jennie, Clara, and Leonie,
who according to the book *To Marry an English
Lord*, by Gail MacColl and Carol McD. Wal-
lace, came to be known as "the Beautiful, the
Good, and the Witty." My own three fictional
sisters I would similarly describe as "the Beau-

tiful, the Adventurous, and the Good."

Jennie Jerome married Lord Randolph Churchill, second son of the seventh Duke of Marlborough, and they became parents to a baby boy who would later lead the nation—Winston Churchill. You can read about Jennie and Randolph in the book, *Jennie: The Life of Lady Randolph Churchill*, by Ralph Martin. Jennie's two sisters also married Englishmen.

Another real-life American heiress was Consuelo Vanderbilt, who married the ninth Duke of Marlborough in 1895. She is perhaps the most prominent example of an American heiress abroad, partly because she wrote a book about her life—*The Glitter and the Gold*. In it, she describes the hardships and heartbreaks she faced as a young woman who was expected to do her duty to her family by marrying into the British aristocracy. Sophia, the oldest Wilson sister, in my book *To Marry the Duke*, is the closest to Consuelo, as she also marries a duke and experiences much loneliness as an outsider.

In this series, Adele's mother, Beatrice Wilson, is loosely based on Consuelo's mother, Alva Vanderbilt, who aggressively fought the social divisions between the old New Yorkers and the nouveaux riches. In March 1883, Alva held a costume ball in honor of her friend Lady Mandeville, a fellow American who had married an English lord in 1876. Alva invited a thousand guests, and all were anxious to see the extravagant mansion Alva and her husband had just built on Fifth Avenue. She neglected to invite the old New York matriarch, Mrs. Astor, however, because according to protocol, Mrs Astor—being the social superior, who had not acknowledged the Vanderbilts previously—had to call on Alva first. Mrs. Astor finally did have a card delivered to Alva, and was subsequently invited to the Vanderbilt ball.

My fictional heroine Adele describes the Knickerbockers in New York when she's in the cottage with Damien. If you're interested in reading about Old New York, try *The Age of Innocence*, by Edith Wharton. Wharton was born into an old New York family, but spent much of her life abroad in Europe. In addition to *The Age of Innocence*, she wrote about American heiresses in London in another of her novels, *The Buccaneers*, which is one of my favorite books of all time and inspired me to write this series.

Edith Wharton became good friends with Henry James, who was also born in New York and chose to live much of his life abroad. He, too, wrote a number of great books about Americans mixing with Europeans. My favorite of his novels is *Washington Square*, set in old New York. This—and the society Edith Wharton writes about in *The Age of Innocence*—is the socially exacting world Adele is so anxious to leave behind.

I hope you enjoyed this trilogy about the Wilson sisters. Lily's story is coming soon in 2005.